the atonement series

RESTORED

BOOK TWO

STELLA JACKSON

Syncterface Media
London
www.syncterfacemedia.com

RESTORED
ISBN: 978-0-9933860-6-0
Copyright © October 2018
Stella Jackson
All Rights Reserved

Published in the United Kingdom by

Syncterface Media
London
www.syncterfacemedia.com
info@syncterfacemedia.com

Cover Design:
Syncterface Media, London

This book is printed on acid-free paper

*To Gemma
with love and
all of God's blessing
from Stella*

*To the emotionally, physically,
mentally and sexually abused
without a voice*

Foreword

As with 'Broken Vessel', from the first paragraph of 'Restored', I was gripped. Totally gripped!! I found myself drawn into Josie's world, albeit on an emotional roller coaster. I went from excited to hurt to curious to concerned to angry. I was anxious, I was livid, I was sad and then I was happy; I laughed, I cried and I held my breath. I was totally in there. Quite a journey in the pages of a book! Stella's writing draws you in and makes you feel like you are a part of the story; I was in every scene and felt every emotion.

'Restored' is a story of hope, a clear example of how all things work together for good and how nothing happens by coincidence. A spellbinding book with fascinating characters and a thrilling story line. I cannot wait for the next book in the series.

~ *Tinuke Akinbulumo* ~
Writer, Blogger and Editor

Prologue

The Qantas Airline flight from Melbourne slowly taxied through the cold, thick fog and finally came to a standstill in its designated slot at London Heathrow's Terminal Four. It had been a long flight but thanks to Jennifer, Sir Ian and Lady Donna Doland were met by two airport porters with wheelchairs as they alighted from the plane. The porters helped the couple with their luggage and gently wheeled them through Customs.

As Jennifer ran towards them, a tear rolled down her cheek. She had mixed feelings about this reunion with her parents, especially after everything that had happened, but as she wrapped her arms around them, she actually felt happy.

Aware of the bitterly cold weather she politely asked the porters to wait with her parents while she brought her car round to the exit doors. Finally, with the old couple seated comfortably in the back seat, Jennifer started the journey to her parents' place in Whitley.

Fortunately, even though Donna was against it, Ian had decided to keep the house after they relocated to New Zealand, and Jennifer and Winnie made sure that the house was well looked after by hiring a caretaker.

"So, how was the flight?" Jennifer asked excitedly as they drove down the motorway.
"Actually, it was rather pleasant. Your mum and I slept for most of the journey," Ian smiled. "Also, thank you so much for making such thoughtful arrangements with the airline, and for taking time out of your busy schedule to pick us up. We really do..."

"Good old England!" Donna exclaimed. "Just look at the weather; horrible and miserable as usual." Trying to catch her daughter's gaze in the mirror, she shouted, "Jennifer, don't you think you're driving a bit too fast? Are you sure you can see through this fog?"

Jennifer was a bit irritated and surprised. It was pretty obvious that no one on the motorway could speed because of the weather.

"Don't worry mum; I am driving carefully. As you can see, it's almost impossible to speed in these conditions anyway."

Remembering how Donna and Jennifer hardly ever agreed on anything, Ian wisely stepped in.

"It's alright dear; your mum has gotten used to the leisurely way we do things down under; no one is ever in a hurry over there."

As they approached Wiltshire, Jennifer called her husband and Winnie, her sister, to let them know that she had picked mum and dad. She also spoke to the caretaker and told her they would be home shortly.

The fog had all but lifted by the time Jennifer pulled into the Doland's driveway. One could just about see the bright rays of sunlight, but it had no effect on the temperature. It was freezing!

1

Aunt Jacqui

The train journey to Aberdeen was a very lonely one. As the train pulled out of Kings Cross Station, it dawned on Josie that this was the first time she was actually travelling alone; prior to this, it was either a school trip or a family holiday.

Since there were only a few passengers on the train, Josie chose to sit towards the back of the carriage. She dropped her rucksack on one of the seats and slumped in the other. She stared emptily into space and wept silently as once again the events of the last few months came rushing back to her; how her innocence had been snatched away, and how her parents had betrayed her.

Josie wiped her tears away and pulled a novel out of her bag as the train passed through Peterborough. "Maybe this will help take my mind off things", she thought. Surprisingly, it worked because while she was reading she fell asleep, and by the time she woke up, the train had just stopped at Edinburgh Market Station.

Josie was beginning to feel the hunger pangs, but unfortunately, all she had on her was a small pack of skittles and a bottle of orange juice which she had bought before boarding the train at Kings Cross. She hurriedly emptied the skittles into her mouth, almost choking, and downed the orange juice to alleviate the sudden dryness in her mouth.

As the train pulled out of the station, the sun rays strewed into the carriage where Josie sat. Interestingly, she was beginning to enjoy the Scottish scenery; the rocky beaches, the waves and the long coastal lines dotted along the North Sea bed. By the time she got to Montrose, her mind was made up; she would be staying here for quite some time.

Josie had told her mum's sister, whom she fondly called aunt Jacqui, about the trip and asked if she could stay with them for a while. She had made her auntie promise not to tell her parents, and even though aunt Jacqui had agreed, Josie had sensed the reluctance in her aunt's voice. So, as the train finally arrived at Aberdeen Station, Josie found herself hoping that her auntie had not backtracked on her promise.

Josie jumped off the train, and as she walked through the ticket barrier, towards the exit, she saw her auntie, Mrs Jacqueline Murray, smiling and waving frantically. Josie ran towards her and flew into her arms. She didn't know why but as she hugged her auntie tears flowed endlessly from her eyes.

"Wow, what's with all the tears young lady?" her auntie asked as she held her close to her bosom.

Josie didn't say a word. She just hugged her tight and continued sobbing and sniffing. Finally, Josie loosened her grip.

Jacqueline looked straight into her niece's eyes wondering what the matter was as they quietly walked into a cafe in the station's mall and sat down.

"Josie, what would you like to eat?"
"Anything. I don't really mind."
"Are you sure?"
"Yes, auntie," Josie nodded.

Jacqueline ordered a drink and sandwich for Josie and watched as her niece wolfed down the meal. She needed to know what was going on before facing the rest of her family, but she didn't know how to broach the topic. She was also reluctant to ask because she was afraid of what Josie might tell her. "What if she was pregnant?"

Jacqueline pondered.

After eating, Josie magically came to life.

"Okay aunt Jacqui, let's go." Josie flashed a broad, bright smile.

Jacqueline knew that she had to find out what was happening but she had decided to wait until the time was right. So, they got up and walked towards the station's exit.

As Josie and Jacqueline approached the car park, Rebecca and Lovette, Josie's cousins, flew out of the car and jumped on her. They looked so excited to see her. Before she knew it, Rebecca had whisked her rucksack off her back, and Lovette hooked her arm around hers. Finally, they all piled into the car.

As they drove through the city towards the countryside, Josie found it hard to take her eyes off her cousins. Rebecca and Lovette were twins, and only two years younger than her, but you would never have known. Not only were they unidentical in looks, but also in character and poise.

By the time Jacqueline drove into the little village of Bridge of Don, the girls had regaled Josie with the latest trends in Scotland. They told her about their school and how they were both looking forward to next September when they would be going to different Colleges to study for their A-levels.

While they all laughed and joked, Rebecca noticed that Josie hardly had any luggage.

"Where is the rest of your stuff?" she asked. "Mum told us that you would be staying with us for a while."
"Girls, after the long trip I'm sure you know your cousin

is tired. So, let us leave the questions till later." Jacqueline caught her niece's gaze in the mirror and smiled. She could see the relief in Josie's eyes.

Finally, they pulled into the driveway and parked in front of the garage. As the girls stepped out of the car, the family spaniel appeared from nowhere wagging its tail. It was massive and almost pushed Lovette to the ground as it jumped on her. As Josie stooped down to stroke the spaniel it turned and started licking Josie all over.

"I guess we are now friends then," Josie laughed wiping her face.

Once inside, Jacqueline showed Josie her room.

"It's a bit on the small side, but I hope you like it," she said looking at her niece.
"Thank you so much aunt Jacqui. I really do appreciate everything you have done for me, especially at such short notice." Josie gave her auntie another hug as she tried to hold back the tears.
"Josie, you are like a daughter to me, and I will do all I can to help you through this rough patch." Jacqueline gently raised her niece's chin and looked straight into her eyes. "If there is anything you need, anything whatsoever, just let me know."
"Thank you, auntie," Josie whispered.

Jacqueline smiled, and as she was about to walk through the door, she said, "Dinner will be ready in about an hour, so get some rest and don't worry about the girls, I will get them to help out in the kitchen."

2
Missing

The Kimberley household was in disarray. Where was Josie?

Bruce was the first to realise that his sister was missing when he went to check up on her with a cup of coffee. He knocked, called her name, and when there was no response, he opened the door. At first, Bruce thought Josie was in the bathroom, but she wasn't. Then sensing that something was amiss, he ran and burst into his parent's bedroom.

"Mum, Dad. I can't find Josie!" Bruce shouted.

Angela and John jumped out of bed, startled and confused. Then Lois and Daphne ran into the room.

"What's the matter?" they asked.

Bruce first hesitated, but he knew they would have to tell them sooner or later.

"It's Josie; we can't find her."

They searched everywhere; the garden shed, the loft, the garage, anywhere and everywhere they could think of, but Josie was nowhere to be found. It soon became apparent that Josie was not at home.

Lois and Daphne started crying, Bruce was confused, and Angela and John had a bewildered look on their faces. "Where could she be?" they wondered.

Bruce ran to the kitchen, picked up the landline and dialled Lily Ann, Josie's friend, hoping that she might know something about his sister's whereabouts.

"Hello, who is this?" asked the voice on the other end.
"Hi Lily, it's me, Bruce. Sorry to call you so early but, you wouldn't know where Josie is would you? She's not at home, and no one seems to know where she is. I was hoping that you might be able to help. Do you know where she is?"
"Not really. What made you think that I would know?"
"I just thought that if anyone knew it would be you. When was the last time you spoke to..." Suddenly, the line went dead.

Lily Ann was in two minds. She had promised Josie that she wouldn't say a word but, what about her relationship with Bruce? Lily Ann just couldn't bring herself to lie to him, and even though it was rude and felt odd, dropping the phone felt like the only logical thing to do.

She wanted so much to tell him what Josie had told her, and where she had gone but, what would that say about her friendship with Josie. There was no way she was going to break the promise she had made to her best friend. However, deep down Lily Ann knew the secret would not hold for long, especially as her brother Drake was bound to talk to Josie's sisters sooner or later. "I should warn that little rat to keep his mouth shut," she thought.

Something wasn't right. Lily Ann dropping the phone had left Bruce bemused and a little curious. Had he offended her by asking about his sister's whereabouts? The more he thought about it, the more suspicious he became. Lily Ann was a naturally calm person, so what just happened was totally out of character. Was she hiding something?

Back in his sister's room, Bruce checked to see if he had missed anything; maybe Josie had left a note. There was nothing! He looked in her wardrobe and from what he could see the only thing missing was her favourite holdall. "She couldn't have packed much in that small bag of hers, so she is bound to come back soon," he thought. How he wished she would walk through the front door after an early morning jog, but somehow, she wouldn't.

Bruce had noticed that broken look in his sister's eyes the night before and remembered thinking to himself that she was a fighter and somehow, she would find a way through her pain. They had always been the best of friends and hardly held anything back from each other, so usually she would have confided in him, but the events of that fateful night had put a strain on their relationship.

Bruce still hadn't forgiven himself for not being there to protect her, and now this was happening. "Lord, wherever my sister is, please look after her and keep her safe," he muttered as he closed the door to Josie's room.

As Bruce walked into the lounge he saw Daphne, Lois, Mum and Dad silently huddled up on the couch; the gloomy expression on their faces said it all. Angela finally broke the silence.

"Bruce, did your sister leave a note or anything?"

Bruce looked at his parents; he felt so sorry for them, but at the same time he couldn't help but think that they were partly to blame for what was happening.
"No, I didn't find anything, mum," he said as he slumped into a chair. "Maybe I should call Lily Ann again," he thought.

Then suddenly it dawned on him. In the midst of all the confusion, no one had actually tried to call Josie on her mobile phone. Bruce jumped up, startling the rest of the family, ran for the landline and dialled her number. It went straight to her voicemail.

The Kimberleys had sat quietly together for about an hour when the phone rang. Daphne picked it up.

"Hello... hello." The line went dead.

"Drake, what do you think you're doing?" Lily Ann snatched the phone from her brother and dropped it.

The look in Drake's eyes gave him away, but he still tried to put on a brave front.

"Hey, what did you do that for?" he said glaring at his sister. "You think I don't know that you were trying to call the Kimberleys?" Lily Ann responded.
"And? If I want to talk to Lois and Daphne, who, by the way, happen to be my friends, is that any of your business? After all, you don't pay the phone bills around here."
"Now, you listen to me, Drake Burton..." Lily Ann lowered her voice so as not to rouse their parents, but her anger was evident.
"Don't lecture me," Drake interrupted. "I can, and will, call anyone I want, whenever I want."
"Well, for the records, it is my business when you do not mind your own business. Whatever you want to gossip about can wait, and I mean that, kid brother."

With that note of warning, Lily Ann turned and left the room.

Drake stood there contemplating his next move. It felt as if he was being bullied and there was nothing he could do about it. Drake knew his sister had the tendency to make good on her threat, and dared not call her bluff, but at least this bust-up had confirmed his suspicions. He wondered if the Kimberleys would check their caller display and if, on seeing the number, they would call back. Drake could hear his sister singing in the bathroom. So, he waited, eyes fixed on the phone, praying that it would ring.

Fifteen long minutes went by, but the phone didn't ring. Drake had all but given up and was silently hoping that it wouldn't ring now that his mum was in the kitchen making breakfast and being the only meal that the Burtons ate together, the kitchen was bound to get busy very soon.

Drake strolled into the kitchen, greeted his mum and plumped himself down beside the phone. "At least, if it rings I'll be here to pick it up," he thought.

"Drake, can you please tell your father and Lily that breakfast will soon be ready. Thank you."
"But mum, why can't we just call them on their extensions; I mean that is the reason why everyone has one in their room, right?"

Drake's mother threw a stern look at her son and he quickly apologised for his rude behaviour.

"Sorry mum, I don't know what came over me."
"It's alright dear, and by the way, the extension in your sister's room is faulty."

As soon as Drake left the kitchen, the phone rang. He tried to sprint back and pick it but, it was too late. Drake stood there; he wanted to ask if it was either Lois or Daphne but, it soon became clear that it wasn't.

"Hello Angela, how are you?"

Drake noticed the puzzled look on his mum's face as she turned and handed him the phone.

"Give the phone to your sister. Mrs Kimberley would like to talk to her."

Drake ran to his sister's room and knocked on her door. Lily Ann, still wrapped in her towel, peeped out.

"It is Mrs Kimberley. She would like to talk to you."

Lily Ann snatched the phone from her brother and promptly closed the door behind her. Drake was tempted to do something mischievous, then decided against it.

"Hello, Mrs Kimberley." She could hear voices on the other end, and before she knew it, there was a man's voice on the phone. It was Josie's father.

"Hello, Lily Ann. I was just wondering, when was the last time you heard from Josie?"
"That was a few days ago sir. Why? I hope she is okay?" Lily Ann asked innocently. Her palms were sweating. She didn't want to lie to Josie's family; in fact, she hated it but what choice did she have? What else could she do?
"Well, we woke up this morning to find that Josie had left home with a few of her belongings. Her passport is also missing." John replied. "Anyway, if you do happen to hear from her, please let her know that we really miss her, and can she please get in touch with us as soon as possible."
"I'm so sorry to hear that but I know Josie; she will not do anything foolish. Anyway, if she calls me, I will give her your message."

Lily Ann hung up and sat on her bed. She needed to talk to Josie urgently. She got dressed, sneaked out of the house, avoiding the prying eyes of her little brother and took out her phone. The call went straight to Josie's voicemail. Lily Ann decided to send Josie a text message instead. It read: "Josie, call me as soon as you can. It's urgent!"

Confronted

woken by the pleasant sound of birds chirping in the tree
outside her bedroom window, Josie felt refreshed after
yesterday's journey. The atmosphere was so peaceful and quiet that
it made her want to stay and snuggle under the duvet. The thought
of staying in bed all day crossed her mind for a split second, but
Josie knew that was a dream that wouldn't come true. While she
lazed in bed, she heard her phone vibrate.

Josie had resisted the urge to even look at her phone from the
moment she stepped onto the train to Edinburgh, but for some
reason, she also decided not to switch it off. As much as she wanted
to talk to Bruce and Lily Ann, she knew, for obvious reasons, that
until she had a proper plan in place, she had no choice but to
keep quiet. Then there was the awkward, yet unavoidable, issue
of having to talk to her aunt Jacqui. She had gotten her auntie
involved in this embarrassing mess and even if she didn't ask, she
owed her an explanation.

There was a knock on the door. It was tentative; loud enough for
Josie to hear if she was awake, and quiet enough not to wake her
up if she was still asleep. The thought of pretending that she was
still sleeping crossed her mind, but after a few brief seconds, she
decided against it.

"Come in," Josie said, in a little above a whisper.

The door opened, and aunt Jacqui walked in, a soothing smile on
her face, carrying a tray with tea and toast.

"Good morning, auntie. Thank you so much, but you didn't

have to. I was going to come down for breakfast anyway," Josie looked embarrassed.

Jacqueline seemed to ignore her niece's words and gently placed the tray on the bedside stool.

"How would you like your tea, darling?"

Josie hesitated but realised from her aunt's gaze that she was going to be served breakfast in bed whether she liked it or not.

"Lots of milk and two sugars, please. Thank you, auntie. I really appreciate your being here for me in my time of need," she stuttered.

Mrs Murray was taken aback by Josie's words and was almost moved to tears. As she finished making Josie's tea, she sat on the bed and pulled her niece to her bosom. There Jacqueline held Josie for what seemed like a pleasant eternity until she felt the wetness of Josie's tears through her blouse.

Holding Josie at arm's length, Jacqueline wiped away her niece's tears.

"Now then, are you going to tell me what is going on? Why did you run away from home?"

There was an uncomfortable silence.
"Your mother called this morning to tell me that they did not know where you were and wondered if I had heard from you. I told her that the food in the oven was burning and that I would call her back later. I had to lie to my own sister!" Jacqueline exclaimed sadly.

Josie got up, walked to the bathroom and looked at herself in the mirror. What was she supposed to say? How could she make her auntie understand the reason why she had done what she did? Josie wiped her face, walked back into the room and sat on the bed beside her aunt.

She couldn't bring herself to look her auntie in the eye as she spoke.

"Aunt Jacqui, I know I owe you an explanation. I apologise for getting you involved in this unpleasant situation, but all I can say for now is that mum and dad betrayed my trust and staying under the same roof with them had just become unbearable."

Jacqueline was at a crossroads and didn't quite know what to say. Apart from being sisters, she and Angela were like best friends and keeping secrets from each other just felt so uncomfortable, but at the same time, she knew that she needed to be there for her hurting niece.

"Josie, your secret is safe with me. However, I'm going to need to know what went wrong between you and your parents."
"Auntie, I promise I will tell you everything at the right time. I promise." The tears began to stream uncontrollably down Josie's face.
"It's okay Josie; it's okay. Take your time but trust me, a burden shared is a burden halved."

Jacqueline sighed, stood up and as she walked towards the door said, "Try and eat your breakfast before it gets cold, and feel free to come downstairs whenever you want to."

As her aunt closed the door, Josie pounced on the toast and tea. At first, she didn't know why she was so hungry, but one look at the wall clock and it all made sense. "Wow! It's almost noon. How come aunt Jacqui didn't say anything about church? That's strange," she thought.

Josie later found out that the Murrays attended the Sunday evening service, and this was mainly because of Mr Murray's job.

Glen Murray was a firefighter and unfortunately in the city of Aberdeen, Saturday nights were every fireman's worst nightmare. Like clockwork, Glen would stumble tiredly through the front door no earlier than six o'clock on Sunday morning, have a bite to eat, then sleep till around three in the afternoon. It was the unspoken rule in the Murray household that nobody disturbed him while he slept.

Jacqueline had hardly entered the kitchen when Rebecca and Lovette burst in.

"Good morning mum. What's for breakfast this lovely Sunday morning?" they asked.
"By the way, where is Josie?" Rebecca asked.
"Is she awake? Can we go up and see her?" Lovette echoed.
"No, do not disturb your cousin. I am sure she will come down soon," Jacqueline replied with a stern voice. "Why don't you both sit down and have some breakfast."

The girls dragged their chairs out and slumped down disappointedly, but they soon pepped up when they realised they were having pancakes for breakfast. In fact, they were enjoying the pancakes so much that they didn't notice Josie walk into the kitchen.

"Hello Rebecca, hi Lovette," Josie startled her cousins.
"Hi Josie," Lovette smiled.
"You're just in time for mum's famous pancakes. Mum makes the best pancakes on this side of Scotland," Rebecca enthused.
"Well, I've had some toast already, but who can resist Aunt Jacqui's pancakes? I still remember your mum making them whenever she visited us in London. Simply delicious!" Josie

salivated.

Lovette watched Josie curiously as she took a seat on the table. "How come she looks so skinny, and her eyes; they seem to have lost that lovely, happy twinkle," she thought to herself.

For one so young, Lovette had always been a deep thinker with a broad perspective, often noticing what others didn't. In character, she was a carbon copy of her father. There and then, Lovette made up her mind that she was going to get to the bottom of what was going on with her cousin, and just as she was about to ask, the phone rang. Her mum picked it up and cradled it between her ear and shoulder.

"Hi Angela, do you mind if I call you back in five minutes? I still have my hands full here in the kitchen."

The girls looked at each other, then at their mum, but she refused to look at them. Their mum enjoyed chatting with her sister no matter how busy she was, and she always gave them a chance to speak to their auntie. So, what was going on? They turned their gaze to Josie, but their cousin was looking straight down at her plate so they could not see the agony on her face.

"Mum..." Rebecca broke the silence.
"Not now, Becky. You can see that I am busy. I need to get lunch ready before your father wakes up." Jacqueline rambled. "Lovette, have you finished your breakfast? Remember to show Josie the garden, especially the flowers you planted last month. Becky, you and I will do the washing up."

Immediately, Lovette and Josie left the kitchen while Rebecca turned an accusing eye to her mother.

"Mum, what is going on? It is unlike you not to want to speak to auntie Angela. As far as I can remember, you have never done that before."

"I did say I would call her back later, didn't I? I think you're reading too much into this, young lady."

"But mum...," Rebecca tried to protest.

"Becky, do not interrupt me when I'm speaking, and by the way, this is none of your business," her mother snapped.

Jacqueline hung her apron and stormed out of the kitchen. She walked into the study, closed the door, and called her sister. The phone rang through to their voicemail message. "They must have left for church," Jacqueline thought. She tried Angela's mobile number, and that also went through to her voice mail. So, Jacqueline left a message.

"Hi Angela, it's me, Jacqui. When you get this message, please call me back. Thanks."

Jacqueline dropped the phone and heaved a huge sigh of relief. She still didn't know what to say to her sister. "God, please help me," she whispered.

Found

*L*ater on, that afternoon, after the church service, Angela looked at her phone, saw her sister's missed call and called her back immediately.

"Hi Jacqui, do you know where my daughter is? Have you heard from her? Is she with you? "
"Angela, slow down. What is going on? What has happened to Josie? Is she in trouble?"
"Jacqui, Josie has run away. She didn't leave a note or tell anyone anything. We have tried calling her, but her phone just goes straight to her voicemail. We have called her friends, but no one has heard from her. We have no idea where she is. I'm trying not to think about it, but what if she has been kidnapped?"

Angela was close to tears; there was a desperation in her voice, the emotion was tangible; Jacqueline couldn't take it any longer.

"Angela listen. Josie is here with me."

The line went silent for a few seconds, then Jacqueline continued.

"She arrived here yesterday, but she hasn't told me why she ran away."
"Thank God!" Angela heaved a huge sigh of relief. "I guess I should come over to yours as soon as possible, maybe tomorrow."
"No, please don't. Josie is in a delicate place. No one seems to know what is going through her mind at the moment, and the truth is I am not too sure how she will react if she

sees you. We need her to confide in someone, and if I can get her to trust me, then that someone just might be me."

"Well, at least she is in safe hands," Angela hesitated. "I'll let everyone know, especially Bruce. He hasn't stopped beating himself up over what happened to Josie two years ago, and now this."

"Poor boy," Jacqueline sighed. "Even my girls are asking questions. I'm not sure what to tell them just yet, but I don't want their minds running riot if you know what I mean. I just pray this whole saga will be resolved very soon. Anyway, give my regards to John and the children."

Jacqueline had taken the call in her bathroom to keep the conversation away from Josie and the prying ears of her daughters. However, she had assumed that Glen was still fast asleep, but he wasn't! As she quietly opened the door to the en-suite bathroom and stepped out, she froze in shock. Glen was looking straight at her, and from the look in his eyes, she knew he had heard everything.

"Don't you think you should have spoken to Josie first before telling Angela that she's here? She came here because she trusted you and now you have betrayed that trust. At times you women don't know when to stop!" Glen shook his head.

"So, what was I supposed to do?" Jacqueline replied. "Was I meant to go ahead and lie to my own sister? Angela is Josie's mother, and she has a right to know that her daughter is alive and well. And by the way, you didn't hear what she sounded like on the phone; the least I could do was put her mind at rest."

Glen couldn't hide his disapproval.

"I just think you could have handled the conversation a bit better."

"Glen, I do not appreciate your tone," Jacqueline parried. "At least I diffused the tension and made sure that Angela didn't catch the next train to Aberdeen."

"Well, true. All I am saying is that you could have told your sister that Josie had rung you from the station and said no more. Anyway, please try and keep me out of this Kimberley feud."

With that, Glen stomped past Jacqueline into the bathroom and slammed the door behind him.

Jacqueline was almost in tears. She didn't like the way her husband had accused her of interfering in something that he thought was none of her business. After all, it's not as if she planned to get herself into this situation; Josie had gotten her involved and whether Glen liked it or not, she had to do what she believed was right.

Angela stood motionless, looking down at her phone.

"Mum, what's the matter?"

Bruce was standing in the doorway, and it looked like he had been there for some time. "Had he overheard her conversation with Jacqui?" she wondered.

"Mum, what did aunt Jacqui say? Is she there? Is Josie with them?"

"Yes Bruce, Josie is in Scotland with your auntie and her family. She arrived there yesterday."

"So, what are we waiting for?" Bruce tried to contain his excitement.

"When are we going to Scotland? She needs to know how much we love and miss her and how sorry we are for everything that has happened."

"Well, Jacqui advised against it. She said that, from what she can see, if we don't tread carefully we might push Josie further away. So, for now, my dear son, we wait and pray that your sister will come to her senses and stop this silly, childish behaviour."

Bruce didn't agree. He couldn't speak on behalf of anyone else, but he was determined to go to Aberdeen whether his parents approved of it or not. He hurried back to his room, closed the door and called his University roomie, Peter Rowe who lived with his parents in Edinburgh.

"Hi Peter, it's me, Bruce. How's it going over there?"
"Good. What's up?"
"Peter, I'm thinking of coming up north next Tuesday, and I was wondering if you wouldn't mind picking me up from the station?"
"Why, sure. So, what are you up to, because since I have known you, you've never expressed a desire to visit Scotland?" Peter laughed.
"Don't you worry about that. I just need you to pick me up. I'll send my itinerary over once my trip is confirmed."

Bruce was determined that nothing was going to stop him, not just from seeing Josie but from bringing her back. He always believed that his sister was jeopardising her future when she decided not to go back to school and he intended to do all he could to make her see reason and hopefully continue her education irrespective of what had happened. Also, though it wouldn't be easy, Bruce hoped they could all forgive, forget and move on.

"How did it all come down to this?" Bruce thought. His once fun-loving family was now under a cloud of darkness all because of a certain Michael Doland. Josie would have been happily on her way to university if not for that rapist.

Bruce was still struggling to forgive Michael and had all but concluded that he never would. Whenever he thought about Michael a rage, almost uncontrollable, rose up inside him.

According to Bruce, the Doland boy was pure evil and the fact that his parents refused to press charges in spite of all the evidence had only made this mess worse.

If there was one thing that Bruce wanted, it was revenge, and over the last few months, he had decided that he would rectify the mistake that his parents made. As far as he was concerned, the so-called agreement that his parents had with Michael's parents was not binding and therefore null and void. He was not and never would be a party to that shenanigan, and he planned to engage the services of an uncompromised legal expert to advise him on how to bring Michael to justice.

To ensure that he could progress unhindered, Bruce also decided not to let his parents in on what he planned to do. He was now Josie's self-appointed protector. No one was going to stop him from accomplishing his goal; not his parents, not Michael, and certainly not Sir Doland and that wife of his.

Bruce remembered something he read recently in one of the daily newspapers. A rape survivor who had been abused continually between the ages of seven and eleven said, "Aristocrats feel entitled to abuse people." This is precisely what's wrong with our society, mused Bruce. The elite think they can commit a crime and get away with it; they expect to be sheltered from jail and protected by the justice system because of their wealth and riches. Well, not this time. Bruce was determined not to rest until Michael Doland was behind bars, facing the consequences of his actions.

5
Bosede

For obvious reasons, Josie needed some clothes and a few other items, something which incidentally had been on Jacqueline's mind. So, when Josie asked her she was more than happy to help.

"Yes, of course. We can go shopping tomorrow, and you can pick what you need. Is that ok with you?"
"Yes auntie, that would be great. Thank you so much."

Rebecca and Lovette were very excited when their mother told them they were going shopping because they knew that they would eventually end up in Jimmy's restaurant, right beside Central Aberdeen Station. They were also looking forward to spending some quality time with their cousin, hopefully without any restraints.

Though their parents hadn't said much, the girls knew that something really bad must have happened between Josie and her family for her to come up north to stay with them. They didn't know what it was, but they were determined to make their cousin happy and help her through this rough patch.

The following morning Mrs Murray and the girls all drove down to Aberdeen and after about half an hour they pulled into the Shopping Mall car park. After picking a parking slot Jacqueline gave Rebecca some money to pay for parking at the meter and when she returned with the ticket they all jumped out of the car and embarked on their shopping spree.

Before leaving home, it had crossed Jacqueline's mind that her highly independent niece just might insist on paying for the things she wanted to buy. So, she devised a plan, just in case Josie tried to protest.

The first shop they popped into was Marks and Spencer. While Josie picked out underwear and tried on some skirts and dresses, Jacqueline selected a few items for herself and her daughters. When they were all happy with their selections, they made their way over to the till. As they approached the cashier, Jacqueline noticed Josie trying to line up on another queue.

"Excuse me young lady, what do you think you're doing?"

After imposing herself on her aunt and her family, Josie didn't want to burden her aunt with any extras.

"Auntie, I can..."
"Josie," Jacqueline smiled and shook her head, "you can pay another day. Today's shopping is on me."
"But, auntie..."
"Josie, I insist."

And that effectively ended Josie's resistance.

From Marks and Spencer, they went to Nine West. This was more for Jacqueline than the girls. Her friend's daughter was getting married in two weeks' time, and she needed purple shoes and a bag to match. She tried on several pairs but was in a quandary as to whether to go for high heels or not, and when Jacqueline finally made up her mind she was told that the matching handbag was currently not available. So, they swiftly walked over to Dune.

Immediately they entered, Jacqueline saw the shoes she liked along with the matching handbag. Josie and her cousins also tried on several pairs of shoes. There was a specific pair that caught Josie's fancy; there was a glow in her eyes as she slipped them on. Then realising that if aunt Jacqui knew she was interested in them she might want to buy them for her, she quickly took the shoes off and placed them back on the rack. "There is no way I am going to let her pay for these," Josie thought to herself. Little did she know that her auntie was watching her all along.

"Has everyone found what they like?" Jacqueline asked.

The girls shook their heads implying that they hadn't.

"Well, I guess it's only me then."

So, Jacqueline paid for her shoes and handbag, and they left the shop.

Next, they all popped into John Lewis to do some school uniform shopping. As Rebecca and Lovette slowly scanned through the uniform racks, Jacqueline asked Josie to keep an eye on them while she popped back to Dune to pick up an item she had forgotten to buy.

Jacqueline walked straight to the aisle where the shoes that Josie had looked at so longingly were and asked the attendant for a pair in Josie's size. After buying the shoes, she hid them inside one of the Dune bags she was already carrying so as not to arouse any suspicion and made her way back to John Lewis where the girls were waiting for her.

Rebecca and Lovette had placed their uniforms along with the other items of clothing they needed for school in the shopping basket. They showed their mum the contents of the basket, and after she had given the nod of approval, they made their way to the till and watched as their mum paid the cashier.

As they walked out of John Lewis, Jacqueline noticed that the girls were rather quiet. She knew what that meant.

"Is anyone hungry?"
"Yes, yes," Rebecca and Lovette's faces suddenly lit up.
Lovette turned to Josie. "Do you like Chinese food?"
"I sure do," Josie replied.
"Well, we've got the place for you," smiled Rebecca.

This was their opportunity to tell their cousin about the fantastic restaurant near the station called Jimmy's. Rebecca and Lovette gave Josie a full low down on the restaurant. How popular it was, the different ethnic cuisines, the famous buffet and how they had concluded that this was one of the few restaurants that catered for almost every taste, hence making it a personal favourite each time they were in the city.

Rebecca and Lovette clearly loved Jimmy's, and by the time they approached the entrance, it was obvious that they weren't the only ones. The place was jam-packed as lunchtime revellers melted into early dinner diners.

Jacqueline and the girls took their place on the long queue. Luckily the weather was pleasant, so time seemed to fly by, and after about fifteen minutes, a waiter approached them and led them over to a table for four near a window and quite a distance from the kitchen hub, opposite the bar. They ordered their drinks; Jacqueline had a glass of fresh carrot juice, Josie a coke and Rebecca and Lovette had their usual orange juice.

The twins hardly ate much but when it came to Jimmy's they always seemed to develop a huge appetite. Today was no different. Since they were in for the afternoon buffet, the girls dashed over to the serving points to get their starter leaving their mum and Josie at the table. By the time Josie and her auntie finally got to the table with their first course, the girls were on their way back for more.

"Wow! I didn't know they were that hungry," Josie watched the girls in astonishment.

"It doesn't surprise me any longer. That's what happens every time we come here," Jacqueline smiled.

Jacqueline wasn't too bothered anyway because she had dished all she intended to eat. She had never been a heavy eater, which explained her size twelve silhouette figure, and even when she ate it was more of veggies and fruits rather than carbohydrates. She also loved eating fish, her favourite being salmon which, living in Scotland, was the best as far as she was concerned.

Both Rebecca and Lovette had their mum's envious figure, but unlike their mum, they ate whatever, whenever and luckily, they seemed to get away with it.

The girls had just come back from their third encounter with the buffet dishes when Mrs Murray turned to Josie.

"Josie, don't tell me that's all you are going to eat."

Josie was a bit overwhelmed; there was just too much to choose from.

"To be honest auntie, I think I need some help with what to choose," Josie smiled, a shy glint in her eyes.

The girls were lost in their own little world of food, so Jacqueline offered Josie a helping hand. Josie took her auntie's advice and filled her plate with seafood, steamed vegetables and chips.

As she made her way back to the table a young lady, who herself was on her way back to her seat, bumped into Josie. The girl turned immediately looking embarrassed and sorry, and just as she was about to apologise, she laughed in amazement.

"Josie, it's you! Wow, long time. How are you?

"BA! I'm fine," Josie beamed, "How are you?"

By now aunt Jacqui, Rebecca and Lovette as well as those on the other girl's table were staring at both of them.

"I'm good. It's so nice to see you, Josie. Do you live in Aberdeen now?"

"No, I'm just visiting my mum's sister and her family. What about you? You're the last person I expected to see up here. The last time we spoke, you said you were moving back to Nigeria. Did you change your mind?"

"No, I'm still in the process of relocating," Bose shrugged her shoulders and smiled. "My parents want me to continue my university education back home, and the last time I checked they hadn't changed their minds. I only came to Aberdeen to see my big sister and some friends. I should be leaving finally in about a month's time."

Bose spotted her sister looking at her suspiciously from her table.

"You know what, I need to get back to my table; my sister and her fiancé are giving me that curious look. I'll come over before I leave so we can exchange details. I hope that's okay?"

"Of course," Josie replied.

They both walked back to their tables.

As Josie sat down, she braced herself for the barrage of questions she knew would come from her cousins and maybe even her aunt, who sat silently with a querying glint in her eyes. It didn't take long for Lovette to jump in.

"Fancy meeting someone you know up here in Aberdeen of all places. It goes to show that you can run but you can't hide. Like they say, 'The world is a global village.'"

"Okay, I'm guessing she's your friend, right? Where did you guys meet?" Rebecca asked.

"Alright girls," Jacqueline came to Josie's rescue, "let Josie finish her food now. I am sure she will tell us everything in due time."

Josie sat back and smiled at her cousins as they stared at her, curiosity written all over their faces. It was a pretty amusing sight, and it wasn't long before she burst into laughter.

"Okay, okay, I'll tell you," Josie giggled. "Bose and I were classmates at St Magdalene's College. Her full name is actually Bosede Archibong, but we nicknamed her 'BA' because of her bubbly nature and the way she walked; like she was about to take off. Coincidentally those were her initials anyway, so it went down a treat."

"She's really beautiful. I thought she was a model!" said Lovette.

Josie laughed and continued.

"BA is one of those girls who has it all together; she's pretty, unassuming, really intelligent, so kind it's unreal, and she comes from an extremely wealthy family back in Nigeria. Her mum is mixed race, and if I remember correctly, her dad is Nigerian. They met while they were studying in the same University here in Aberdeen."

"Well, here she comes," Jacqueline whispered.

"Hi BA, this is my aunt, my mum's younger sister, Mrs Jacqueline Murray. And these are my lovely cousins, Lovette and Rebecca. I have already told them a bit about you. Lovette thought you were a model," Josie laughed.

"Good afternoon ma," Bose shook Mrs Murray's hand with the usual courteous Nigerian bow.

"Hello Bose, nice to meet you," Mrs Murray smiled

Bose turned and flashed a huge smile at the girls.

"Hello Lovette, Hello Rebecca. I've got to say that I'm flattered you thought I was a model but I don't think I have the stomach for that lifestyle."

Bose and Josie exchanged numbers, and Josie promised to get in touch with Bose before she left for Nigeria.

"I'll give you a buzz before you leave. Maybe we can meet up for lunch and catch up on old times."
"Yes, that will be nice. I look forward to hearing from you. Thanks."
"Do say hello to your sister and her fiancé."
"I will," Bose smiled.

She said bye to the Murrays and went back to her table.

Lovette and Rebecca watched in awe at the languid way Bose walked; it was as if she was floating.

As Bose walked back to her table, Jacqueline saw a look on her niece's face that she had not seen since she arrived; a look that said, "If only I could turn back the hand of time, then that could have been me!"

Glasgow

*B*ruce booked a last-minute ticket for Tuesday morning on the East Coast train leaving St Pancras Station for Edinburgh. At first, he wasn't going to tell his parents about the trip because he knew they would do everything within their power to persuade him not to go. He planned to leave a note explaining where he was going and why he had to do it. However, considering the pain the family was currently going through, he decided against it.

So, on Monday night with Daphne and Lois sound asleep, Bruce broke the news of his trip to his parents.

"Mum, Dad, there's something I need to tell you."
"What's the matter, Bruce?" Angela asked, her face painting a vivid picture of concern.

Bruce had thought long and hard about how to break the news, but it seemed there was no easy way to say it. So, he chose the direct approach.

"I'm going to Aberdeen tomorrow. I have to see Josie."

Angela and John were taken aback by the air of finality in their son's voice, making it quite clear that it was not up for discussion.

"But Bruce...," his mum started.

John placed a gentle hand on his wife's arm and shook his head.

"Honey, his mind is made up," John said looking straight into his wife's eyes. Then turning to his son, he asked, "So, what do you intend to achieve with this trip of yours, and when do you plan to come back?"

"Like I said dad, I'm going to see Josie and hopefully persuade her to come back home. To be honest, I'm not too sure when I'll be back, but I've got six weeks before I resume classes. So, hopefully before then."

John placed a hand on Bruce's shoulder and after a brief silence said, "Okay son, we wish you a safe and successful journey. May God be with you all the way."

"Thanks dad, thanks mum."

Bruce stood up and slowly walked to his room.

Angela couldn't quite believe what had just unfolded before her eyes. For some reason she was unable to object; it was as if there was an invisible hand over her mouth. Finally, she found her voice.

"John, I hope we are doing the right thing."

"Well, it's all in God's hands now; all in God's hands," John replied.

It was just after five on Tuesday morning. Bag packed, Bruce was ready for the journey ahead, or was he? As he stared out of his bedroom window a barrage of questions flooded his mind. "Would Josie be happy to see him? Would she open up to him? Would she reconsider and come home?" So many questions and Bruce didn't have an answer to any of them. "Well, here goes a journey into the unknown," Bruce whispered to himself. He picked up his bag and opened the door.

As he approached his parent's bedroom, Bruce stopped. He hesitated for a second then knocked on the door and peeped in.

"Mum, dad, I'm off."

Unsurprisingly, his parents were wide awake, and from the bags under their eyes it was obvious that they were suffering from sleep deprivation.

"Take care of yourself and make sure you tread softly with your sister," said Angela as she gave her son a tight hug.
"Okay mum," Bruce replied
"Do you need a ride to the station?" John asked.
"Not really dad, but thanks a lot."
"Well, all the best then, and please keep us updated."
"I will, dad."

Angela and John escorted their son to the front door and waved goodbye. Then they looked on as Bruce walked down the road towards the bus stop.

Bruce had planned to catch the Metropolitan line underground train from Finchley Road station, which was not too far from home, to Kings Cross St Pancras station where he would board his train to Edinburgh. However, to his dismay, Finchley Road station was closed. He saw a London Underground attendant advising commuters to use alternative transport to get to their destinations, and when asked why, the attendant explained that a young man who jumped on to the track had been run over by an oncoming Metropolitan line train.

Though Bruce wasn't exactly a fan of bus rides, it was the only alternative he could afford. It took a while before the bus to St Pancras arrived, and when it did, it was packed. Bruce assumed this was because of the station closures. Anyway, by the time the bus pulled into the station, he had missed his train.

This trip had not gotten off to a good start, and Bruce was beginning to feel that things were working against him, but there was no way missing his train was going to make him give up on his quest. Bruce made his way over to the Information Desk to find out when the next train to Edinburgh would depart.

"The next train to Edinburgh departs at 14:55 and from what I can see it's already full," said Tom, the man behind the Information Desk.
"You mean there's not one seat left on it?" asked Bruce. "Could you please check again? I need to be in Edinburgh today. It's an emergency!"
"Okay, let me take another look."

Tom took a few minutes, tapping away on his keyboard and checking his monitor while Bruce looked on anxiously.

"Oh, there you go! I have got you a seat young man," he looked at Bruce excitedly, then Tom's expression changed. "Oops, it looks like it will cost you an extra £30.00. Is that okay?"
"Not really," Bruce thought, but he didn't have a choice. "Okay, can you please reserve the seat for me. Thanks a lot, Tom."

Bruce paid the balance, and Tom handed him his ticket. After reserving his seat, Bruce called Peter to tell him about what had happened, and as a result, he would be getting to Edinburgh later than scheduled.

"Not to worry Bruce," Peter said. "I'll be there to pick you up. The only downside is that we will have to spend the night in Edinburgh and make our way up to Aberdeen tomorrow. I hope you are okay with that?"
"Well Peter, I don't think I have much of a choice. Thanks for helping me out. I really appreciate it."

As Josie lay in bed that night, she looked back over the last twelve hours. It had been a long day, but she enjoyed every second of it. The visit to the Shopping Mall was tiring, but it was also lots of fun. Then there was lunch at the famous Jimmy's; the thought of the food still made her taste buds salivate. And imagine running into BA; was that a coincidence? Josie suddenly found herself contemplating what she would do next.

"Maybe I should call BA tomorrow and see when we can meet up for lunch. Who knows, she just might be able to help," Josie mused.

The more Josie thought about meeting up with Bose, the more it all seemed to click. For once Josie felt at peace, and for the first time since arriving at her aunt's place, she slept like a baby, without a care in the world.

When Josie woke up the next morning, she called Bose who told her that even though she was still in Aberdeen, she would be travelling to Glasgow later on in the morning for an appointment at the Nigerian Consulate because she needed to renew her Nigerian passport.

Josie needed to talk to Bose and she was not about to watch this opportunity slip through her fingers.

"BA, is it okay if I come along with you? I mean, I would totally understand if you said no, but I really need to talk to you," she blurted.

Bose thought about it for a brief second; as she was going to Glasgow by coach, she could actually do with the company. So, travelling with Josie wasn't exactly a bad idea.

"Sure Josie, I would love you to come along. In fact, bring your passport with you too, maybe we can travel to Nigeria together," Bose laughed jokingly.

Josie was not sure if her friend actually meant what she just said.

"BA, are you serious or are you messing around?" she asked. "I really would like to go to Glasgow with you, but I'm a bit confused as to why I should bring my passport along."

Bose could hear a whimper of sadness and frustration in Josie's voice, and she immediately regretted her silly joke.

"Oh no Josie, I am really sorry. I did not mean it like that. You are more than welcome to come along, but I was only joking about you bringing your passport. However, if you really want to visit Nigeria, then you can bring it along. I can vouch for you at the Consulate office, and most likely they will process your visa while we're there."

Josie looked at the clock in her room; it was ten o'clock on the dot.

"So what time are you leaving for Glasgow because I am still in bed?"
"Well, I was planning on taking the eleven o'clock coach, but we can catch the one o'clock instead. We can't leave any later though because the Consulate closes at three in the afternoon. Is that okay?
"Yes, that should give me more than enough time to get ready," Josie replied.
"We will be staying with a family friend in Glasgow; the resident Consul to be precise. He and my dad were schoolmates and have been very good friends ever since; he is like family. Is that alright?"
"That's alright BA. Anyway, let me get ready. I'll meet you at the coach station before twelve thirty."

Josie dropped the phone, jumped straight out of bed and headed for the bathroom. After a quick shower, she combed her hair and picked what to wear. As she looked in the mirror, she felt her heart pounding excitedly. Josie felt alive!

While having a shower, she had toyed with the prospect of travelling to Nigeria with Bose. She hadn't planned to take her passport when she was running away from home; it was a last-minute decision, but could this be the reason why? Josie packed all her essentials into her holdall along with her bank card and passport and went downstairs.

Jacqueline was alone in the kitchen having her breakfast.

"Good morning auntie."
"Good morning my dear, I hope you slept well?"
"Yes, I did. Where are Rebecca and Lovette?"
"They went out with some of their friends about half an hour ago for a programme organised by their Sunday school teacher. You look all dressed up, where are you off to?"

Josie smiled at the tone of her aunt's voice and the alarming look in her eyes.

"I am only going to Glasgow."
"What do you mean by you're only going to Glasgow? What for? With who?"
"There's no need to worry aunt Jacqui. It's just that there is something I want to do in Glasgow which is very important for my future. I should only be gone for a day. So, God willing, I'll be back tomorrow. Who knows, maybe I want to be a missionary!" Josie giggled.

Jacqueline didn't exactly see the funny side of Josie's joke but was happy that her niece was in a jovial mood. She looked so mature and grown up all of a sudden; not like the wilted flower she picked up from the station the other day.

"Don't worry aunt Jacqui, I'll be fine. I will call you when I

get there, I promise."
"Are you sure you don't want me to give you a ride there? I can actually wait for you to finish whatever you want to do and bring you back you know?"
"No. That won't be necessary auntie but thank you."
"Okay then, at least let me drop you off at the station."

The last thing Josie wanted was for aunt Jacqui to know that she was meeting up with Bose. She knew that if her auntie got suspicious she might not approve of her trip to Glasgow. While this thought was going through her mind her phone buzzed. It was a text from BA saying they should meet at the Costa Coffee shop by the Central station. Josie felt relief sweep through her. She knew that once aunt Jacqui dropped her off, she wouldn't hang around because cars weren't allowed to wait at the station entrance.

Josie ordered herself a cappuccino while she waited for Bose, who was running late. As soon as she arrived, they made their way to the Coach stand, purchased their tickets and took their seats on the coach that was due to leave for Glasgow at one o'clock that afternoon.

The coach pulled out of the station at exactly five minutes past one. The atmosphere was perfect; the air conditioner was blowing air at just the right temperature, and pleasant melodies were flowing through the overhead speakers. So, unsurprisingly, no sooner had the coach left the city the girls fell asleep.

They were eventually awoken by the announcement from the built-in tannoy speaker system informing the passengers of their arrival at Glasgow Station. Everyone was advised to take all their belongings with them and in the event of losing anything to call the head office.

Before leaving Aberdeen, Bose had called Mr Adewale Dada, the resident Nigerian Consul in Glasgow, to inform him of the time their coach would arrive at Glasgow station. So, as they stepped off the coach, the girls were met by Mr Dada's official driver, Steve Gladstone, a chirpy Scottish man who believed that Scotland should be separate from the rest of the United Kingdom.

Steve easily identified Bose from the description his boss had given him, but he wasn't too sure what to make of the white girl who accompanied her. Anyway, he took their bags and led them to where he had parked the embassy car.

Mr Dada had told Steve to take his guests straight to the house where his wife would be waiting for them. After dropping them off at the official residence, Steve made his way back to the office to pick up Mr Dada.

Mrs Maureen Nkechi Dada, the wife of the Consul, opened the door as soon as she heard Steve pull into the driveway. Bose smiled and curtsied as she greeted auntie Mo, the name she fondly called Mrs Dada.

> "Good Afternoon my dear," Mrs Dada gave Bose a warm hug. "And who have you brought along with you?"
> "Auntie, this is a friend and former classmate of mine, Josephine Kimberley, Josie for short. Josie this is my auntie Mo, Mrs Dada, the Consul's wife."
> "Nice to meet you, ma'am," Josie responded.
> "You are welcome to our home, Josie. Hopefully my husband will be back a bit earlier today. He would have been here to welcome you himself but something urgent came up in the office. In the meantime, let me show you to your room."

Mrs Dada led the girls upstairs and opened the door to a room looking out on to the park. The scenery was lovely, and the girls gushed as they looked out over the balcony. The room had a double bunk bed that was more than suitable for the two girls.

"Thank you so much, auntie Mo," the girls chorused as they blushed with excitement.

"You are welcome girls," Mrs Dada smiled and turned to leave the room. "I will send the housekeeper up to let you know when dinner is ready, but please feel free to come down whenever you want."

7
Bruce

ruce's train finally arrived at Edinburgh Market Station. The journey was a bit longer than he had anticipated but he was glad that he made it, and he sure was happy to see Peter waving to him as he stepped on to the platform.

"Hi Pete, thank you so much. I really appreciate this."
"Man, it's the least I can do. After all, that's what friends are for, right?" Peter smiled and as they walked to the car park he offered to carry Bruce's bag, which was quite light.
"I'm still curious as to why you're here though. From the weight of your knapsack, it's obvious that you're not planning on staying long."

Bruce didn't respond immediately as Pete's words suddenly made him realise that he actually didn't have a plan B should his rescue mission fail.

"Not to worry Pete, I'll tell you why I'm here soon, but first can we catch something to eat? I am starving."
"Sure, I know a nice restaurant down the road, they do a splendid fish and chip dish. I'm guessing you still like your fish and chips, right?"
"I sure do," Bruce laughed.

Peter dropped Bruce's luggage in the back seat, and they drove down to the restaurant which was a five-minute drive from the station. Peter parked the car, and as they made their way to the restaurant entrance, they saw a queue of people. Bruce's heart sank. He was hoping that if they could grab a quick meal, he just might be able to persuade Pete to drive to Aberdeen, but the longer they stood in the queue the more unlikely that option became. By the time it was finally their turn to be served, Bruce was so hungry he could eat a horse.

Both of them took their bulging trays of large fries and crispy cod in batter, along with a half-litre glass of Coke, and sat at a table by the window. Bruce thought now would be a good time to tell his friend why he was here.

"Pete, I guess you still want to know why I actually came to Scotland?"
"Of course, I do," Peter replied.
"Well, it has to do with my sister, Josie."
"What happened to her? Is she alright? What is she doing up here anyway?" Peter looked genuinely worried.

Bruce gave Peter a brief version of all that had happened without saying anything about the rape and the baby. He felt that the less other people knew about that, the better.

"So, she came to Aberdeen and is currently staying with my mum's sister and her family."
"Surely, if she is with your aunt then she is in safe hands. So, what makes this trip of yours so urgent?" Peter looked confused.
"You see, Josie had a misunderstanding with mum and dad and, without telling anyone, she left home."
"Oh, so you're saying Josie ran away?"
"That's right. So, I'm here to try and convince her to come back home."

Bruce couldn't exactly decipher the look on his friend's face. He wasn't sure if Peter believed him or not, but at the end of the day, he felt it wasn't really his friend's business anyway. After all, if the roles were reversed he would lend Pete a helping hand, no questions asked.

By the time they finished their meal, it was well past nine in the evening. Bruce hadn't taken into account where he would sleep if he did not make it to his aunt's place in Aberdeen on the same day. For a split second, he was tempted to try and convince Peter to drive him to Aberdeen, but he knew that would be pushing it.

Just as Bruce was about to ask Pete for the nearest bed and breakfast his friend interrupted his thoughts.

"I hope you don't mind staying at mine tonight? God willing, we can leave for Aberdeen first thing tomorrow morning."
"Oh no, I wouldn't want to impose. I think I have already inconvenienced you enough."
"Nonsense," Peter replied. "That's what friends are for, and besides there's no way you can think rationally without a good night's sleep, on a nice, comfortable bed," Peter smiled and winked at Bruce.

Bruce had met Mr and Mrs Rowe on several occasions when they visited their son in university. Pete was an only child, and though both of his parents were politicians, they were always able to make time for their only son.

Peter's father, Alexander Rowe was the Mayor of Edinburgh while his mother, Edith Rowe was a Scottish National Party (SNP) MEP in Brussels. Bruce liked Peter's parents because they came across as humble people who cared for others. Their prestigious positions in society did not make them despise others and, from what he could see, they were not the proud type.

Mr and Mrs Rowe welcomed Bruce into their home with open arms.

"Hello Bruce, nice to see you again," Mr Rowe said. "How are your parents and your siblings?"

"They are all fine, thank you," Bruce replied.

With the pleasantries out of the way, Peter took Bruce upstairs to the visitor's bedroom, which was next to his. Once Peter left, Bruce washed his face and jumped into bed, clothes and all, and promptly fell asleep.

While Bruce slept, he had a strange dream. He saw his sister but for some reason he couldn't reach her. Then he started calling her name, but she gradually disappeared into the distance making signs at him that implied that he should go back; that she was okay and he shouldn't worry about her. Then she was gone!

Bruce woke up in a pool of sweat. "The dream, what did it mean?" he asked himself. Was this trip in vain? No! Bruce was determined not to let anything deter him. There was no way he was going back without Josie. He was here to take her back home, and that's exactly what he intended to do.

Bruce assured himself that he would accomplish his mission no matter what.

8
Decisions

It was the morning after their arrival in Glasgow and Bose was eager to find out what was on Josie's mind.

"Josie, have you thought about what I told you? I know it started out as a joke, but the truth is you can actually come to Nigeria as my guest if you really want to. After all, it has always been your dream to travel and explore the world. This could be the perfect opportunity, and it just might provide the new beginning you've been searching for."

"BA, I really appreciate the offer, but I can't just get up and go. That won't be fair on my family. I don't want to hurt them any more than I already have."

"I understand Josie," Bose sighed, "but in case you change your mind, my offer still stands."

Josie walked into the bathroom and gently closed the door behind her. She looked at herself in the mirror and tried to hide the tears that threatened to flow from her eyes. Ever since that terrible night, her emotions had been all over the place, and she seemed to cry at the least provocation. "You need to get a grip," she muttered to herself. After all, Bose was only trying to help so why was she crying?

After the girls had showered and gotten dressed, they headed downstairs for breakfast. Mrs Dada had told them the night before that breakfast would be served at eight thirty so that they could all eat together before her husband left for work. It went without saying that Mrs Dada was an excellent cook; breakfast was simply delightful!

After breakfast Josie found herself admiring the pictures on the lounge mantlepiece. She noticed the children in the pictures; "I wonder where they are," Josie thought. While she was admiring the photographs, Mrs Dada walked in. Josie felt as if she had been caught nosing around, but Mrs Dada's almost child-like smile put her at ease.

"Those are our children. We have two sets of twins; two boys and two girls," Mrs Dada explained.
"They look so lovely," said Josie.
"The boys, our first set of twins, are twenty-two years old and they are currently studying in the United States, while the girls are in boarding school back home. They are going to be seventeen this year."

Mrs Dada was about to ask Josie a question when her husband walked into the lounge with Bose. Josie didn't know what she wanted to ask her, but she felt she had just been spared having to talk about her own family. Mr Dada asked Bose and Josie to accompany him to his office so that they could renew Bose's passport.

On the way to the Consulate, Josie started thinking seriously about what Bose had said.

"A penny for your thoughts?" Bose asked seeing that her friend seemed lost in a world of her own.

Josie smiled and was about to respond when her phone rang. For some reason she had forgotten to put it on silent; "How could I have made such a silly mistake," she thought. Josie tried to ignore the call, but it kept ringing. She could feel Mr Dada and Bose's eyes on her. The last thing she wanted to do was draw attention to herself, but what excuse could she give for not answering her phone.

The phone seemed to ring for an eternity until finally Josie summoned the courage to answer it. As she picked the phone out of her coat pocket and looked at the display, she realised it was her brother, Bruce.

Bruce and Peter had driven straight to aunt Jacqui's house, only to find out that Josie had gone to Glasgow. Bruce immediately remembered the dream he had the night before. "What am I supposed to do?" he asked himself. He felt so frustrated and inadequate, but after giving it some thought Bruce decided to call Josie. He was hoping she would pick up and was overjoyed when he heard his sister's voice on the other end.

> "Hi Josie, it's Bruce. How are you? I hope you are okay. I am at aunt Jacqui's, and she told me that you had gone to Glasgow."

The speed at which Bruce blurted out his words was proof he was nervous and desperate. The last thing he wanted was for Josie to drop the phone; he had to try and control himself, or this call would be over before it even started.

Josie had picked up the nerves in her brother's voice.

> "Hello Bruce," she replied in a very low tone lacking any form of excitement. "I'm fine. How are you?"
> "Look, Josie, I came to Aberdeen to take you home. This running has got to stop."

As soon as the words left his lips he knew he had made a massive mistake; a faux pas he might live to regret. Josie was silent. Bruce could hardly hear her breathe. Then Josie took a deep breath.

> "Bruce, I will call you once I have finished what I came to do in Glasgow," and with that, she cut the line.

"What have I done?" Bruce whispered.

Before the call, Josie was in two minds about Bose's proposal, but her brother had just helped make up her mind. There and then Josie decided that she was going to Nigeria. She turned to Bose.

"BA, is your offer still on?" she asked. "If it is, then I am coming with you."

Mr Dada overheard what was going on. He turned to Josie.

"What about your family and school?" he asked. "I am sure you know that you should tell your parents about what you are planning to do. We don't want them thinking that you have been hoodwinked by a friend, do we?"
"Yes, I know and I will tell them," Josie replied, "but first, would it be possible for you to issue my visa? Please, Mr Dada."

Once again Josie's eyes began to well up. Mr Dada looked puzzled, he didn't think he said anything to make her cry. He looked at Bose who also looked confused as she shrugged her shoulders. Giving her a visa was the least of his problems, after all, she was over eighteen years old, but there was something about Josie that he couldn't quite place; something that just didn't sit right. "Why did she suddenly want to follow Bose to Nigeria?" he wondered.

Mr Dada decided that he would discuss the matter with his wife once he got to the office. She was his confidant; a wise, compassionate and discerning woman. He trusted his wife's advice when it came to issues like this.

"Josie, there is really no need to cry," Mr Dada patted her hand and gave her a clean hanky. "I will think about it and hopefully come to a decision. Is that okay?

Josie nodded her head and wiped her tears away.

"I'm really sorry Mr Dada, I don't know what came over me."
"That's alright Josie." Mr Dada smiled.

What was left of the journey to the Consulate was unsurprisingly quiet.

Visa Approved

*H*ead drooped, Bruce cut a forlorn figure.

"So, what are you going to do now?" Peter asked.

"I don't know," Bruce shook his head slowly, "I really don't know."

"Bruce," aunt Jacqui placed her hand on her nephew's shoulder. "For now, we need to give Josie some space. Your sister has never been a problem child, and even though she is young, I believe she has her head screwed on right. We just need to be there for her when she needs a shoulder to cry on."

"Okay, auntie."

Bruce felt like he had failed his sister once again. Here he was, so close yet so far away from her. Going to Glasgow was no longer an option, and now it didn't make sense getting the police involved. The last thing he wanted to do was drive a bigger wedge between Josie and himself. If only he knew how to fix this mess, but he didn't.

In the midst of the many thoughts running through his mind, Bruce suddenly remembered his Christmas holiday job interview lined up for the following day; if he was going to catch that interview he would have to make his way back to London as soon as possible.

As Peter drove him to Aberdeen station, Bruce decided to send his sister a text message:

"Hi Josie, it's me. I just want to say that mum, dad, Daphne,

Lois and I really miss you. We all love you so much and wish you all the best in whatever you decide to do. I will never stop praying for you, and I hope that one day you find it in your heart to forgive mum and dad; I know they never meant to hurt you, even though they did. Remember, if you need anything, anything at all, I am just a phone call away. I love you, sis."

Josie and Bose had been in Glasgow for four days. During this time, Bose had renewed her passport and, even though the process wasn't straightforward, Josie had been granted a Nigerian visa.

To apply for Josie's visa, Bose had written a letter of invitation confirming that her parents would be Josie's sponsors. When Mr Dada ran the visa issue by his wife, she had surprisingly chosen to sit on the fence, giving reasons for and against it. So, though he felt uncomfortable about the whole idea, nevertheless he decided to grant Josie's visa.

As he handed Josie her passport, he advised her to take some time to think things through before making a decision to travel or not. Josie appreciated Mr Dada's kind, genuine concern and promised that she would do as he had advised.

On the last day of their stay in Glasgow, the girls went to the city to do some window shopping. They also took a tourist trip to some of the castles on the old side of the town. On the whole, they had loads of fun.

Bose and Josie had really enjoyed their stay with the Dadas; they had been the perfect hosts, and to put the cherry on the cake, Mr Dada had arranged for his driver to take them back to Aberdeen, so they didn't have to take the coach.

The girls were tired, and as Steve drove them back to Aberdeen, sleep finally caught up with their weary eyes. When Bose and Josie finally woke up, they realised they were about to turn on to Beaufort Street, where Bose's sister lived. However, the plan was to go to Josie's place first. Bose gently tapped Steve on the shoulder.

"Mr Gladstone, I'm really sorry I didn't say this earlier, but can we please drop Josie off first?"
"That's not a problem," Steve replied with a smile. "What is Josie's address?"

As they drove to Bridge of Don Steve caught a glimpse of the girls through his rear-view mirror. They sat quietly in the back seat like well-mannered children, but for some reason, the English girl looked a bit unsettled. "Well, at least she has a friend who is looking out for her," Steve thought. He finally pulled into the Murrays' driveway at about six o'clock in the evening.

Josie gave Bose a tight hug, said a big thank you to Mr Gladstone and got out of the car with her holdall. Josie was tempted to run after the car as it disappeared into the distance, but she just about managed to hold herself together. When she could finally see them no more, Josie turned and walked to the front door. She rang the bell and her auntie opened the door.

"Hello, aunt Jacqui."
"Welcome back, Josie," her auntie sniffed, as if she had been crying.

Something wasn't right, Josie thought. Everywhere was quiet; way too quiet.

"Where is everyone? Where are Rebecca and Lovette?" Josie asked.
"Oh, they went over to their grandmother's place."
"So why does it seem like something is wrong? I can sense

it."

"Well," Jacqueline sighed, "the truth is, Glen and the girls are actually at the hospital. You see, when the girls got to her house, they rang the bell, but no one answered. They knew she was in because they had spoken to her just before they left home. Anyway, after ringing the bell a few times, Rebecca peeped through the letterbox and saw her grandma lying on the floor panting heavily. To cut a long story short, she was taken to hospital in critical condition. If you hadn't called to say you were on your way home, I would have been at the hospital too."

Jacqueline paused and slowly shook her head. She was struggling to hold back the tears.

"The girls were very close to their nan, especially after my mother passed away."
"I am so sorry aunt Jacqui."
"Is uncle Glen her only child?"
"No, your uncle has an older brother and two younger sisters, but we live pretty close to her; her house is just a fifteen-minute walk from here, on the other side of the bridge. Anyway, you must be hungry and tired after your journey. You can help yourself to something to eat in the kitchen. I'm off to the hospital."

After hearing about what had happened, there was no way Josie was staying at home, even if she was tired and hungry.

"Aunt Jacqui, I am coming with you."
"Are you sure?"
"Positive."
"Alright then, let's go."

Jacqueline and Josie made sure that all the windows were closed and everywhere secure before locking the front door and driving to the Teaching Hospital on the outskirts of Aberdeen.

They parked the car and made their way to the Accident and Emergency department where they saw the Murray family huddled together in the waiting area. Josie noticed that uncle Glen was wearing a pair of large dark glasses and immediately concluded that he was hiding his tear ridden eyes, which was understandable. The twins, on the other hand, were crying uncontrollably.

Then she saw someone who looked like a carbon copy of her uncle except he was a bit older and wore a large moustache. He appeared to be in control by the way he was talking to the doctor and nurse who were giving him an update on grandma Murray's condition. Unfortunately, it wasn't good news. Grandma Murray had passed away!

Robert shook his head as he listened to the doctor explain all they had done to try and save his mother's life.

"We appreciate all you and the team have done," Robert said to the doctor. "It is just a shame that mother had to die this way."

After a brief silence, the doctor asked if Robert and the rest of the family would like to see her.

"Yes, yes, we would," Robert replied.

The doctor led everyone to the room where the old woman lay. As he pulled the curtains back they saw her; eyes closed, stone cold, lying on the bed in a hospital gown. No one said a word. The room was quiet, except for the sound of sobs and sniffles.

Then all of a sudden, the curtains were flung wide open, and there stood a lady decked out as if she was off to a party. Her perfume filled the whole room; the scent was so overpowering that Josie couldn't help but wriggle her nose. She had lots of jewellery on, and she wore ridiculously high stiletto heels. If not for what had just happened, it would have been hilarious watching this apparition of a woman, Josie thought.

The lady approached the bed, her eyes fixed on the still body, and before anyone could even move, she lifted her hand, slapped Grandma Murray's dead body and screamed at her.

"Why mother? Why now? Why?" She roared. "I told you last week I was going to get married, and when I told you who he was you said, 'Over my dead body'. And now, just like you said, you're dead."

She started breathing heavily, shut her eyes for a while, then continued.

"Alright mother, so now I can go ahead and do it, and no one can stop me, not you, not my brothers, not my sister, no one. Not now, not ever!"

With those final words, this apparition in human form turned and waltzed away the same way she came.

Josie looked around, the raw pain was evident on every face in the room. She was a bit surprised that no one had said anything, no one had even moved while the lady ranted, but she soon deduced that the lady must have been uncle Glen's youngest sister since she was the only one who wasn't married. She was still thinking about what had just happened when uncle Glen broke the silence.

"The same old selfish Genevieve," you could almost taste the bitterness in his voice. "Always a disgrace to the family. Thank God, mother no longer has to suffer the pain. Mark my words, one day that girl will reap the rewards of everything she has done."

"Please, don't say that," Jacqueline said. "All Genevieve needs is a touch of God's love, and she will get off her high horse. I'm sure that under all the huff and puff is a heart of gold."

They were still inside the room when Robert called the funeral home. After about thirty minutes on the phone, they had agreed to pick up Mrs Murray's body from the hospital later that evening and promised to make the necessary arrangements for her burial in two weeks' time. This would give their other sister, Kathy and her family enough time to return from their holiday in Thailand.

It dawned on Josie that after all that had happened she would have to delay her trip to Nigeria; she couldn't abandon the family that gave her shelter in her time of need. She would have to call Bose and hope that she would understand.

Josie still intended to go to Nigeria though; that hadn't changed. So, if she was to meet up with Bose in Nigeria, she needed an alternative plan.

Most likely she would leave Scotland after the funeral, but how would she break the news to her aunt? After giving it some thought Josie decided that she would just have to cross that bridge when she got there.

The Flight

*T*wo weeks had passed since grandma Murray's funeral, and Josie was becoming restive. She no longer felt comfortable staying in Scotland. "Maybe I should go back to London," she thought, but was that really an option?

One day, Josie and her uncle, Glen Murray got talking. He was curious to know why she had decided to run away from home.

"Josie, I really don't mind you staying here with us, but I hope you realise that there is nothing like family. They most likely will not be perfect but they will always be there for you."

Even though he didn't say so, Josie got the impression that her uncle was not entirely happy with her being in his home. This galvanised her into getting in touch with Bose. From their last conversation, Bose had told Josie to let her know when she's ready so she could make the necessary arrangements. It looked like that time had come.

Josie thought the whole journey through in her head; how she would pack the few possessions she had, use her card to book a domestic flight to London Heathrow and also purchase a return ticket with British Airways to Lagos, Nigeria where she and Bose would eventually meet up.

So early one morning while everyone in the Murray household was still sound asleep, Josie quietly crept down the stairs hoisting her holdall onto her shoulder and left a note addressed to her auntie on the kitchen table. Then she opened the front door and peeped out hoping that the dog wouldn't bark. It didn't!

Josie felt a sense of déjà vu as she closed the door behind her and walked to the bus stop. Uncle Glen's words resonated in her mind. Was he right? Would she, one day, regret running away?

"Now is not the time to think about all that," she told herself. She needed to focus on the task ahead.

Josie had only been at the bus stop for about ten minutes when the airport shuttle bus pulled up.

On the way to the airport, Josie found herself thinking about what she had written in the note to aunt Jacqui; how she had decided to continue her soul-searching journey, and it was something she believed she had to do on her own. She also asked aunt Jacqui to please find it in her heart to forgive her, and that hopefully one day she would be able to explain this complicated situation. Josie knew that leaving a note wasn't ideal, but she didn't know what else to do.

At Aberdeen Airport Josie checked in all the way through to Lagos. Then she made her way through the Security section before finally heading towards the departure gate. As she sat down waiting for her flight, Josie brought out her phone, stared at it for a few seconds, then turned it off. She was determined not to talk to anyone until she arrived in Lagos. Her silent prayer was that she would not run into anyone she knew.

Though Josie had always enjoyed her relationship with God, of late she had refused to let Him into her thoughts, conveniently stilling the guilt that she occasionally felt. Having convinced herself that she was a victim of her family's betrayal, she was now determined to do what she wanted, when she wanted. She was done being the one who was always there for everyone. It was time to take care of number one.

Every now and then Josie remembered how much she missed her two ever so cute and mischievous twin sisters, her mother's caring smile that always made her feel like everything was going to be alright, and her father's wise counsel that had helped her out on numerous occasions.

Interestingly, she also found herself missing the aroma of fresh tobacco from her father's pipe. Smoking a pipe was a habit he had picked up after her mother gave birth to the twins. In between puffs, he would justify his new habit by saying, "This is my only worldly pleasure; God understands."

She remembered how she and Bruce would crack up each time he said it and then in the same breath try and drum the dangers of smoking and drinking into their ears. They called it the KFJ; the Kimberley family joke.

However, each time Josie found herself smiling at these precious family memories she would consciously retreat behind the wall that she had unconsciously built to protect herself from the world around her. In her mind, shutting her family out was the only way she was going to become the independent woman she planned to be.

"The next time we meet they will be proud of who they see," Josie told herself.

Even though she had no idea of how she was going to achieve her goal, deep down inside Josie hoped that when she got to Nigeria, Bose and her family would help set her on the right path.

When Josie's British Airways flight to London Heathrow finally took off from Aberdeen airport, she knew then that there was no going back.

The flight was smooth and turbulence-free, but after an hour and a half in the air, she was eager to start her new life on another continent. Growing up she had been to Disneyland in Florida with her family, and also on student exchange programme trips to France and Germany, but this was different.

Josie was so eager to get going that she had forgotten the need to be careful and extremely alert, and as she made her way to Terminal Five, she ran into their family lawyer, who incidentally had been on the same flight as her.

"Hello Josie, were you also on the British Airways flight from Aberdeen?" Mr Salmon Goldberg asked. "I am actually going to see your father this afternoon. Would you like a lift home?"

Salmon Goldberg and Josie's father had both been students at Cambridge University, where they became very good friends. They also had something specific in common: Their parents had suffered at the hands of the Nazis.

Josie hated lying, even for self-preservation purposes, but right now she needed to think on her feet or else this family friend could wreck everything.

"Thank you, Mr Goldberg," Josie replied, "however I need to catch up with a friend who is arriving on the next flight. I mistakenly got my hand luggage mixed up with hers. Unfortunately, she has a transit between terminals so I need to go to Terminal Five to swap cases. Thank you for the offer though."

Josie made a last-ditch attempt to change the topic.

"How is your family?"

"They are fine. Thank you for asking. Little Ruth is now in boarding school. We hardly see you anymore. In fact, I almost didn't recognise you; you are a far cry from the tiny girl of yesterday," Salmon quipped.

Josie smiled and found herself blushing at the compliment. However, she had to get away from this man as quickly as possible; more importantly, she needed to be in the air before he spoke to her father. Just then, there was an announcement from the loudspeaker system asking a Mr Salmon Goldberg, who had just arrived on the British Airways flight from Aberdeen, to make his way to the Information desk. "Saved by the bell," she thought. Josie said goodbye to the lawyer and briskly made her escape.

Once outside Josie took a taxi to Terminal five. This was simply because she didn't want to risk running into anyone else she knew. In case she didn't know before, her encounter with Mr Goldberg was proof that liberty came at a price: eternal vigilance!

Josie had no luggage to check in, so after going through Security she took a look at the departure screen to confirm the estimated departure time and the gate for her flight to Lagos. Since she had arrived quite early this information was currently unavailable on the screen so she took the opportunity to chill out in the departure lounge.

After sitting for a while Josie got up to use the bathroom. As she came out of the ladies, she stopped suddenly.

"No, it can't be," Josie muttered.

But it was. Right there, looking at the departure screen was Mrs Maureen Dada, the wife of the Nigerian Consul who she had met in Glasgow. She wasn't sure whether to say hello or pretend that she hadn't seen her. But Josie knew that it would be dumb not to greet Mrs Dada especially after all she and her husband had done for her. Apart from that, Josie also suspected that their paths would cross when she eventually got to Nigeria. So, she slowly walked towards her.

"Good morning ma," Josie said, remembering how Bose had greeted her when they were in Glasgow.
"Hello! It is Josie, isn't it; Bose's friend? How are you?" Mrs Dada was obviously very surprised.
"I'm fine, thank you," Josie replied.
"I must say that I was not expecting to see you here. Where are you travelling to?"

There was a brief silence as Mrs Dada looked at Josie curiously. Then her eyes slowly widened with wonder.

"Don't tell me you were actually serious about travelling to Nigeria?"
"Yes, I was, ma. I am just waiting for my flight to Lagos. Bose is expecting me and has promised to show me around when I get there."
"Well, that is interesting. Anyway, if you need my help in any way please do not hesitate to let me know," Mrs Dada smiled then suddenly looked very serious. "I hope your parents know and approve of your trip to Nigeria?"

"Here we go again. Why won't these adults leave me alone and just mind their own business," Josie thought. She wanted to scream and let out the frustration that was building up inside her, but instead, she flashed an ingenuous smile and said, "Yes, they know, and they approve."

What Josie really meant was, 'Josie knows, and Josie approves. After all, it is Josie's life!'

"Well, it's almost ten o'clock, so we still have about an hour to go before boarding, and I am hungry. Would you like some breakfast?"

"Yes please. Thank you so much," Josie replied.

Josie was famished. She hadn't eaten the night before and considering the circumstances under which she left the Murrays house, breakfast wasn't exactly an option. So, Josie and Mrs Dada headed over to one of the restaurants located in London Heathrow's Terminal Five.

While they were waiting for their order, Mrs Dada's phone rang. Whoever she was talking to wanted to know where she was. It turned out that Mrs Dada had planned to meet up with a friend of hers who had just arrived from New York and was transiting to Lagos.

After telling her friend where they were, Mrs Dada placed her phone on the table, dipped her hand into her bag, brought out a small, fancy-looking powder container and touched up her face. Josie couldn't help but wonder why she needed the touch up because from what she could see it simply wasn't necessary. Mrs Dada was a stunningly beautiful lady, and her skin was flawless. It was hard to believe that she was the mother of four because when she walked, she was the epitome of glamour.

Josie caught herself staring intently at Mrs Dada. For some weird reason, which she didn't quite understand herself, Josie thought she could be herself with the older woman.

"So, are you going back to Nigeria for good? I remember Mr Dada saying that his stint at the Consulate in Glasgow was about to come to an end", Josie enquired in a timid voice.

"Yes, I am. My husband left last week, but I had to stay behind to tidy up and ship some of our belongings back to Nigeria."

As the waiter carefully placed the plates on the table, Mrs Dada's friend appeared, waving and smiling as she approached. She gave Mrs Dada a bit of a hug, sat down and ordered a cup of black coffee. Mrs Dada introduced Josie to her friend, Mrs Sola Deinde.

Mrs Deinde was a paediatrician in one of the top hospitals in New York and she had just been posted to head a World Health Organization (WHO) station in Lagos.

Maureen and Sola's friendship went back a long way; all the way back to when they were students at Queens College in Lagos. Unfortunately, Sola hadn't changed one bit; she and another girl called Kathleen Akinjide had been Maureen's only friends back then simply because they all came from the same background of rich parentage. However, while Maureen was brought up to be polite and respectful, Sola, being an only child for almost ten years, was spoilt rotten and had the general impression that she was better than most of her colleagues. Josie noticed this attitude immediately.

Going by the way the lady carried herself, Josie had concluded that she was a very proud person.

"She is nothing like Mrs Dada," Josie thought. She wondered how two individuals with totally different personalities happened to be such good friends.

Mrs Deinde had completely ignored Josie after the introduction and behaved as if she wasn't even there. So, Josie quietly ate her meal and didn't say a word while the two ladies laughed and spoke Nigerian vernacular, a language that Josie obviously did not understand.
Mrs Dada, realising that they had totally neglected Josie, apologised for their bad manners.

"It's alright," Josie smiled, but in reality, she felt like an outcast. Apart from being ignored, Josie thought it was quite inconsiderate of them to speak in a language that she did not understand a word of. She heaped all the blame on Mrs Deinde because left to her, the woman was vain and conceited.

Josie excused herself, pretending to need the ladies. As she walked to the toilet, she actually felt like crying, but somehow managed to hold back the tears.

When Josie finally came out, she noticed that Mrs Dada was sitting alone. She was tempted to walk past and ignore her, after all she had the perfect excuse, but in the end, she decided against it. Instead, she told Mrs Dada that she was off to do some window shopping in the Duty-Free shops and promised to come back soon. However, to Josie's surprise, Mrs Dada jumped up and walked with her.

Maureen knew that Josie wasn't impressed with her friend.

"Josie, I am sorry about what happened at the table, and please don't mind Mrs Deinde. She did not mean to be rude."
"It's alright. I understand."
"Are you sure?"
"To be honest, it did feel a bit odd but I am okay."
"I am really sorry, Josie," Mrs Dada apologised once more. "Is it okay if I buy you something from the duty-free shop? Let us call it a peace offering."
"You really don't have to do that, ma."
"I know, but I would like to."
Josie smiled then asked, "So, what happened to your friend anyway? Where did she go?"
"She had to meet up with her other colleagues. They are all travelling to Nigeria together."

While Mrs Dada and Josie were shopping, their flight was announced over the airport speaker, and the gate number came up on the departure board.

Mrs Dada was travelling First Class while Josie was in the Premium Economy section. So, when the announcement for First Class passengers was made, Mrs Dada told the airline staff that Josie was her guest and they were travelling together. The staff, noticing that Mrs Dada was carrying a diplomatic passport, told her not to worry, that they would take good care of her guest.

Josie did not realise what Mrs Dada had done until she took her seat. As she was making herself comfortable, she saw Mrs Dada walking towards her.

"Hello Josie, I just wanted to make sure that you are okay. By the way, I think there are some empty seats in First Class so after we take off, we'll get you into one of them," Mrs Dada winked.

Josie wasn't really keen on moving to First Class, especially as she knew that Mrs Deinde would most likely be there, but in the end, it didn't really matter. Minutes after the plane took off, Josie fell asleep. She was oblivious to everything around her; she didn't know when Mrs Dada came to check on her and wasn't even aware that food had been served.

She eventually woke up when she felt her seat shaking. Around the same time, a steward came over and politely asked her to adjust her backrest and fasten her seat belt. Josie could see some passengers holding the armrests tightly and praying, fear written all over their faces. To Josie it was a funny sight but she dared not laugh.

The turbulence lasted for about thirty minutes and as soon as it was over, a number of passengers rushed to the toilet. Not too long after the passengers had taken their seats a chirpy, reassuring voice rang out over the sound system. It was the pilot's. He informed everyone that they would soon start the descent to Murtala Muhammed International Airport and advised all the passengers to fasten their seatbelts.

Josie could feel the excitement bubbling inside her. Lagos was just minutes away.

Lagos

*T*he British Airways flight from Heathrow London Airport landed in Lagos at exactly six o'clock in the evening. Once the plane came to a standstill and the fasten seatbelt light went off, all the passengers got up, removed their hand luggage from the overhead locker and disembarked. Josie was one of the first to stand up. She was so excited.

As Josie approached the front exit door, she saw Mrs Dada. As First Class passengers were always the first to alight from the plane, Maureen had waited for Josie. This simply reinforced what Josie thought: Mrs Maureen Dada was a genuinely nice person.

"I hope you enjoyed the flight," she asked.
"Yes, I did, and thank you for waiting for me," Josie replied excitedly.
"You are welcome, Josie."

Josie had already told Mrs Dada that though she had been on a plane before, this was the first time she was travelling all alone. Maureen told Josie not to worry, that the airline crew knew that she was her guest. All Josie needed to do was walk beside her and she would be treated accordingly. So, Josie walked alongside Mrs Dada, and to the young girl's amazement, she received VIP treatment from the airport staff and made it through Customs in record time.

Unknown to Josie, her phone had been on silent vibrate throughout the flight; she had forgotten to switch it off. So, she was shocked to feel it suddenly buzzing around in her coat pocket. In her excitement, thinking it could only be Bose, she quickly took the phone out of her pocket and answered it without looking at the display.

"Hello..., hello..., Josie..." It was aunt Jacqui.

Josie froze. "What am I supposed to say? I can't cut her off, that would just be rude," Josie thought. Then slowly it dawned on her; she was thousands of miles away from the United Kingdom so nobody could touch her, no one could tell her what or what not to do. With newly found confidence Josie answered the call.

"Hello aunt Jacqui, how are you?"
"Josie, where are you? Have you checked your phone? Can you see all the missed calls? And the note you left me, what was that supposed to mean? Please Josie, talk to me."

Suddenly the line went all fuzzy and then she seemed to lose reception. Josie could tell from her aunt's voice that she was worried. The last thing she wanted to do was hurt her family, but right now that seemed inevitable.

As Josie and Mrs Dada walked towards the baggage hall, she thought long and hard about what to tell her auntie; should she tell her where she was or not? Finally, she decided that she would call her back and just tell her the truth. But first she needed to freshen up.

What Josie didn't realise was that her auntie was still on the line. Jacqueline, though faintly, could hear the noise in the background, and when she heard an announcement through what sounded like an overhead speaker system, she began to wonder where her niece was.

"Hello..., Josie, are you still there?"

Josie thought she heard a faint crackle on her phone. She looked at the display and could hardly believe her eyes; her auntie was still connected!

"Hello aunt Jacqui," Josie whispered, trying to confirm if her auntie was still on the other end.
"Yes. Josie, what is going on?"
"Auntie, can I call you back please, I need to...," Josie suddenly realised that she was about to let the cat out of the bag, and quickly cut the call. "I need to get myself a Nigerian SIM card as soon as possible," she thought. At least with that she would be able to kill two birds with one stone; it would make it a bit more difficult for anyone to contact her, and at the same time avoid her racking up a huge telephone bill with her UK provider.

Mrs Dada and Josie finally made their way out of the baggage hall, with the porters wheeling their luggage behind them. Josie felt a bit embarrassed as, unlike Mrs Dada who had four large, heavy cases, she only had a small holdall which she could have conveniently carried herself. However, Mrs Dada had insisted that a porter should assist her.

As they exited the Murtala Muhammed International Airport, they saw Mr Dada, Bose and their drivers, waiting outside.

After exchanging pleasantries, Josie and Bose climbed into the back seat of the Toyota Highlander while the driver placed Josie's bag in the boot. Then they drove out of the airport car park.

"Wow. So, you finally made it," Bose said, with a big, wide smile on her face. "I am so happy to see you, and I pray that you will enjoy every minute of your stay here. Lagos is known as 'The Centre for Excellence', but I can tell you that quite a few things are far from excellent. So, when you see anything that doesn't exactly line up with the nickname, just close your eyes, pretend you didn't see it and have a good laugh."

"Come on BA, it can't be that bad," Josie laughed.

"Trust me, it can," Bose replied. "By the way, your baptism of fire starts right now, on these Lagos roads. The drivers over here are crazy, and most of them don't even have a driving licence, not to talk of car insurance. Then, you see those trucks?" Bose pointed to some large trucks on the other side of the road, "Some of them have worn tyres and brakes that could give way at any time."

Josie covered her eyes with both hands.

"Are you sufficiently scared?" Bose laughed.

"It will take a bit more than that to scare me," Josie laughed. She was already enjoying the adventure.

*"This is what makes Nigeria,
especially this city of excellence, unique.
It might sound strange but,
even with all its imperfections
and the chaos,
I feel more at home and at peace here
than anywhere else in the world."*

12
The Archibongs

The traffic between the airport and Victoria Island, where Bose's parents lived, was better than anticipated and they made it home within an hour and a half.

Bose showed her friend to a spacious, fully furnished en-suite room then looked at Josie.

"What do you think?" Bose asked. "I hope you like it."
"Very much," Josie nodded smiling, a look of pleasant surprise written all over her face.
"Well, try and get some rest. I'll be back later." Bose smiled and closed the door behind her.

Josie stretched and skipped excitedly to the bathroom. She washed her face, opened her holdall, which had been carefully placed beside the wardrobe, and slipped into something light. After living in the cold and rain of the UK all her life, Josie was now experiencing the warm, delightful weather of Lagos.

Flopping onto the soft, queen-sized spring mattress, Josie stared at the ceiling and started daydreaming. She really appreciated everything Bose had done, and more than ever she was determined to make the best of her stay here. With these thoughts on her mind, Josie drifted off to sleep.

Josie was awoken by a knock on the door, and before she could answer, an excited Bose breezed in.

"Hi Josie, I hope you got some rest. Just to let you know that dinner is ready and everyone's waiting for you." Bose winked mischievously, then took Josie's hand, pulled her off the bed and together they walked to the dining room.

Josie's heart was beating faster and faster with each step. She was stepping into the unknown; she didn't know what to expect. Bose noticed the nervous look in her friend's eyes and assured her that everything was going to be okay.

"Don't worry, they won't bite," Bose said, keeping a straight face.
"Very funny," Josie took one look at Bose and they both burst into laughter.

As they walked into the dining room Josie was greeted by a loud, yet soothing voice. It was Bose's dad.

"Hello Josie, it's nice to finally meet you. I hope you like your room?"
"It is so lovely! Thank you so much for taking me in on such short notice. I am very grateful," Josie replied sheepishly.
"You are welcome, love. Please come and sit down," Bose's mum smiled as she patted the chair beside her.

With Josie seated, Bose's mum introduced Josie to the delicious looking dishes laid out on the table.

"Here we have what we call jolloff rice. You may have eaten this before," she continued. "This is fried plantain. It is commonly called 'dodo' over here, and it tastes really nice when eaten with rice. Then, this is what we call 'moin-moin'. It is made from black-eyed or brown beans, and last, but definitely not the least, is the vegetable salad, Nigerian style."

This sent everyone into hilarious laughter because the salad was made up of so many different ingredients, it was actually a meal in itself.

Having not eaten anything during the flight, Josie was extremely hungry. She could hardly wait to tuck in, and tuck in she did. Her eyes lit up, and she threw caution to the wind trying out every dish on the table.

"Take it easy Josie," Bose cautioned, "the food is quite spicy."
"Thank you, but I'll be the judge of that," Josie replied jokingly.

Josie was so engrossed with her meal that she hadn't noticed the look of apprehension on all the faces around her. Bose had been especially worried about the amount of food and the speed at which her friend was eating, so she wasn't exactly surprised when, after everyone had finished eating, she saw a perturbed look in Josie's eyes.

"Are you alright Josie," Bose asked, trying not to be sarcastic.

Josie looked at Bose but didn't say a word; the unsettled look said it all. She was so full that she was struggling to stand up, and when Bose's mum returned from the kitchen with a pot of green tea, Josie couldn't hide her relief.

"Thank you so much, ma."
"You are welcome Josie," Bose's mum flashed a knowing smile.

Finally, after saying "Good night" to everyone, Josie staggered to her room. She opened the door, made a dash for the bathroom sink and threw up.

Bose wasn't surprised to find her friend bent over the sink. She knew that Josie wasn't in a good way and had popped in to see how she was feeling. It was a good thing she did. Bose helped Josie clean up, change and tucked her into bed. Her concern for Josie's health grew as she sat at her bedside.

"Josie, you look really pale. I'm going to get my father."
"Don't worry Bose, I am okay," Josie said assuringly. "I am only feeling sick because I gorged the food too quickly. I should have known better, but I'm sure I'll be fine after resting a little."
"Okay, but call me if you need anything."
"I will," Josie said with a tired smile.

Bose still felt anxious as she left the room but decided to give Josie the benefit of the doubt.

True to her word, the next morning Josie was feeling just fine. She jumped up nice and early, had a shower and got dressed. As she went downstairs, she noticed that the house was rather quiet. Josie found Bose tidying up the sitting room. Bose's mum had already left home for her boutique where she sold all kinds of clothing for ladies and gentlemen. Mrs Archibong worked with the British Council but ran her boutique by the side. Bose's father had also left for his office. So apart from a few other staff who helped around the house and the driver who was ready to take them wherever they needed to go, Bose was the only one at home.

Bose and Josie had breakfast together and caught up on old times. Then they put together a plan for the day.

"Josie," Bose began, "We need to get you a Nigerian sim card so you can start making calls. It's about time you let your parents know where you are; it is the right thing to do. I'm sure they would love to hear from you."
"Yes, you're right. I was actually thinking of calling them sometime today."

So, after breakfast, they jumped into the car and drove to the shopping mall to get Josie's sim card. This was also where Bose's mum's boutique was, and since Josie really wanted to thank her once again for the kind hospitality, they were able to kill two birds with one stone.

After leaving Mrs Archibong's shop, they went to the University of Lagos, the university where Bose had been enrolled. While the girls were there, they remembered something they had discussed in passing back in Glasgow; about Josie pursuing a university degree if she came to Nigeria.

So, they took the chance and asked around about the possibility of Josie being admitted to the same university. They were advised to see the Dean of the faculty for the course that Josie was interested in pursuing, but when they got there his secretary told them that he was away on holiday and would not be back until the following week.

On their way back home, they were held up by traffic around the university. Drivers were banging their horns, swearing and gesturing with their hands; tempers were boiling over.

"Is this normal?" Josie asked looking aghast.
"This is nothing," Bose replied. "Sometimes, you can be stuck in traffic for hours. A journey that normally shouldn't take more than twenty minutes can take up to two hours or more. I did warn you," Bose laughed. "This is what makes Nigeria, especially this city of excellence, unique. It might sound strange but, even with all the imperfections and the chaos, I feel more at home and at peace here than anywhere in the world."

For Josie, as long as the car windows were wound up, and the air conditioning was functioning perfectly, she was okay. She watched as hawkers, both young and old, crossed the roads carrying wares perched on their heads and selling to those sitting inside their vehicles. One of the hawkers, on seeing her supposed interest through the car window, came running towards her pointing to the goods in the basket she was carrying. Josie didn't know what to do so she asked her friend.

"BA, what is in the basket?"
"It is dried, fried plantain," Bose replied, "but I wouldn't advise you to buy anything sold by the roadside; most likely it is unhygienic."

Josie agreed and shook her head at the hawker who was still waiting expectantly.

Not too long afterwards the traffic started moving again and the driver, who knew the roads pretty well, decided to take alternative routes to beat the traffic. Though the roads were not as good as the one they would have taken normally, they were able to get on the third mainland bridge in record time and continue the journey to Victoria Island.

"By the way Josie, we are having the Dada's over for dinner tonight. This morning mum told me that they had not seen Mr Dada since he came back from Glasgow. It sounds like he is planning on leaving the Foreign Office so he can go into politics."
"Coincidentally, I was just thinking that I need to call Mrs Dada to thank her for looking out for me during the flight from London Heathrow. I guess I'll just wait until this evening then."

As they drove home, Bose entertained Josie by showing her different sights like the Ikoyi Bridge, the Dolphin Estate, Kingsway, Queen's Drive and some parts of Banana Island. Unsurprisingly, by the time they got back home, they were both tired.

Bose got them some biscuits and cold soft drinks while they lazed comfortably in the air-conditioned sitting room watching movies on the Africa Magic channel, and before too long they had slept off in front of the telly.

The girls were still fast asleep when Mrs Archibong came back so she decided not to wake them up. However, they were soon roused from their slumber by Bose's younger brother who had just come back from his holiday.

"Hello, what's going on here," he screamed at the top of his voice.

"What does it look like?" Bose replied jokingly. "Tope, meet my friend, Josie. Josie, this is my kid brother, Tope. He's a spoilt little brat."

"Oh, so you're the famous Josie? Pleased to meet you. I hope my sister has not told you any lies about me; I am as cool as a cucumber, no shaking!" And with that, he ran out of the room.

The two girls rolled their eyes, laughed and made their way to the kitchen to help Bose's mum who had already started preparing for the evening ahead.

13

Second Thoughts

*I*t was almost seven in the evening when Josie remembered that she had not called her family. She excused herself and went up to her room where she could have some privacy. First, she called her friend Lily Ann. She felt bad that she had embarked on this rush, hush, last minute trip without telling her.

Lily Ann had always been a good friend, and despite the pressure she faced from Bruce and Josie's parents she had stayed true to her word. So, after everything Josie had put her friend through, the least she could do was update her on the happenings so far. Josie knew that Lily Ann would almost have a fit if she told her she was in Nigeria, but she owed her this call and was ready to face the consequences if any.

Finally, Josie dialled Lily Ann's number. It rang for a while, and just as Josie was about to hang up, she heard Lily Ann's voice.

"Hello."
"Hi, Lily."
"Josie, is that you?"
"Yes, it's me. how are you?"
"I'm fine. I wasn't sure whether to pick the call or not because of the foreign number that came up on my display. Where are you?"
"First of all, I want to apologise for not getting in touch earlier. After everything you've done for me I should have told you how things were going. I'm really sorry about that."
"That's okay Josie. Look, I'm not going to pretend to understand what's going on. To me, your family is wonderful, and from what I have seen over the years, they have always

loved you and been there for you. So, what's really going on?"

"Well, the truth is I just got fed up with everyone telling me what to do and how to live my life, so I have decided to take matters into my own hands."

"Josie, you're beginning to freak me out," Lily Ann was starting to feel uncomfortable with the tone of her friend's voice. "Look, Josie, I am your friend; we have known each other since elementary school. Tell me, where are you?"

"From the phone number, you would have noticed that I am not calling from the United Kingdom," Josie stuttered. "Actually, I'm in Nigeria."

"What! Where did you say you were?" Lily yelled. "Josie, are you out of your mind? What are you doing in Nigeria? Are you crazy?"

Josie knew that Lily Ann would be shocked when she told her where she was, but she wasn't expecting this reaction. For some reason she had expected Lily to support her decision. Josie wanted to scream back at Lily, but instead she decided not to say anything. In fact, she was so quiet that Lily Ann thought she had hung up.

"Josie, are you still there?"

"Lily, you're starting to sound like Bruce and my parents. I have to go," Josie said in a small, cold voice. "I'll call you back later."

"Josie, I am so sorry. I didn't mean to shout. It was just the shock of hearing where you were. So, tell me, how did you get there? How did you get a visa? Who..."

Lily Ann noticed that she couldn't hear anything on the other end.

"Josie... Josie... are you there?"

Lily Ann couldn't believe it. Josie had actually hung up on her.

After dropping the phone, Josie quickly called Bruce. After what had just happened she knew that Lily Ann would most likely try and contact him.

"Hi Bruce, it's me."
"Hi Josie, it's good to hear your voice again," Bruce replied calmly, even though his entire being was screaming to know the whereabouts of his sister and what she was up to. He had been in the middle of writing an article for the local newspaper when Josie called, so he hadn't noticed the odd-looking number on his display.
"Thank you, Bruce. How are mummy and daddy, and the girls; I hope everyone is alright?"
"We're all doing the best we can without you. But, where are you?" Bruce's voice was gradually getting louder. "The last time I called aunt Jacqui she sounded worried as she didn't know where you were, but Mr Goldberg said he saw you at Heathrow. What is going on, Josie?"
"Bruce, please do not shout. Right now, I am trying to find myself in Nigeria and..."
"Where? Nigeria!" Bruce screamed so loud that their mother came running into the room to find out what was going on.
"Josie," Bruce continued his rant, "What are you doing in Nigeria? Have you lost your mind?"

Bruce didn't mean to lash out but the frustrations of the past weeks were now boiling over, and he had thrown caution to the wind.

"Bruce, give me the phone, let me speak to my daughter." Angela grabbed the phone from her son.
"Hello Josie, it's mummy. How are you? I have missed you so much."
"Oh mummy, I have missed you too. I'm so sorry, but this was something I had to do for me, and if it turns out to be a mistake then I will only have myself to blame."

Josie paused for a brief second.

"How are Lois, Daphne and daddy; I hope everyone is alright? Please tell them that I am so sorry about everything. Hopefully, one day you will all be proud of me."

"Josie dear, we have always been and always will be proud of you."

"Thank you, mum," Josie's eyes were beginning to well up. "I promise to be good and do the Kimberley name proud."

"I know you will, my dear. Remember, if you need anything do let us know." Angela hesitated a bit then asked, "By the way, where are you staying in Nigeria?"

"I am staying with a friend of mine called Bose Archibong. Bose and I were at St Magdalene's together and, out of the blue, we met again in Aberdeen. That was when the idea of a trip to Nigeria came up. She has a wonderful family, and they have been so good to me. I'm not sure yet, but I am seriously looking into gaining admission into a university over here. Who knows, if I am offered a place and it all works out, you could come over when I graduate."

Angela didn't know what to say. If only Josie could see how difficult it was for her to take all this in; the pain she felt when her daughter said she was staying with another family and considering university education in a third world country when she could have easily been accepted in a top university in the UK.

"Hello Mum, are you still there?" Josie quizzed.

"I am still here my dear. You look after yourself, and please stay in touch. Extend our greetings to Bose's parents. Maybe the next time you call, I can say thank you to them personally for taking good care of you. I am giving the phone back to your brother now."

Bruce didn't know what to say when his mother handed him the phone, especially after his rant earlier on. After all that Josie had done, Bruce found himself wondering if he ever really knew her. He never in his wildest dreams would have thought that his gentle sister would be bold enough to do something like this.

Finally, Bruce found the courage to say something.

"Josie, I know I may not understand how you feel, but please be careful out there and make sure you contact the British High Commission if you need any help. Is that okay?"
"Yes, big brother Bruce, but I know nothing will happen to me," Josie laughed. "Thank you for always looking out for me. I honestly appreciate you, and I miss you too. Like I told mum, I feel I have to do this to prove to myself and everyone that I am no longer a baby. Please try and understand "
"It's alright. Just make sure you take care of yourself, and if it's okay, can we call you every now and then?"
"That's fine. Bye Brucie." The tears began to flow down her cheeks as she dropped the phone.

Josie decided to stay in the quiet of her bedroom, that was until Bose came knocking.

"Oh, there you are. What's the matter?" Bose noticed her friend had been crying.
"BA, do you think I am doing the right thing? This whole staying and wanting to pursue a university degree over here rather than go back to England; do you think I am doing the right thing? I just spoke to my mum and my brother; I really miss them. Maybe I shouldn't have called them because now everything just looks hazy."
"Well, I won't pretend to understand what you're going through, but I think you should pray about it. That's what my mum taught us to do when we were young, and it always seems to work."

Josie had not forgotten how to pray. Just like Bose, she had also been brought up in a household where prayer was of the utmost importance, but because of everything she was going through she had relegated her relationship with God to the back burner. Even now, she was not sure if she would heed her friend's advice.

Josie put on a brave face as both of them made their way downstairs. By this time, the Dadas had arrived and were sitting in the family lounge having drinks with Bose's parents. When the girls entered the lounge, Bose knelt down to greet the visitors leaving Josie looking confused, unsure of what to do. Everyone realised Josie's dilemma and smiled. Josie finally found a way to say hello to the Dadas and also seized the opportunity to say a big thank you to Mrs Dada for everything she did for her on the flight.

Later while they were all seated at the dining table, Josie found herself talking to Mrs Dada, or auntie Mo as Bose fondly called her. It reminded her of the time they spent together in Glasgow. As Josie had come to realise, she was a very thoughtful and kind person with a listening ear; maybe this was why Josie enjoyed their conversations so much.

"So, Josie, I know you have only been in Lagos for two days, but how has it been so far?" auntie Maureen enquired.
"Well, so far so good. I am loving the weather, and I have also enjoyed eating some delicious Nigerian dishes like jolloff rice, moin-moin and dodo, which were prepared by Bose's mum." Josie smiled remembering the after effect of rushing those tasty dishes.
"My dear, you need to be careful not to put on too much weight. Our food is very rich and can easily have an adverse effect on your figure," Mrs Dada laughed.
"I will, but after losing so much weight when I was ill, I think it's time I filled out a bit." Josie smiled, but deep down inside she resented the man that had put her through all that pain and agony.

Apart from her family, Josie hadn't told anyone about what she had been through, and she planned to keep it that way. The rape, her baby and how her baby was given away to the very man who raped her were thoughts that continually haunted her. But now more than ever she was determined to rise above her past.

She planned to stick to her decision not to return to England until she had that degree certificate in her hand. Then, and only then would she return home and maybe apply to do a Masters in a British university. Josie Kimberley was intent on surprising the Michael Doland's of this world; she was also determined to reveal the truth about them.

After dinner, the men sat in the lounge and started talking about politics, a topic which the ladies, as well as Josie, Bose and her younger brother Tope, were not exactly keen on. So, they stayed in the dining room.

"Josie, I was wondering if you have had a chance to speak to your parents yet?" Kathleen Archibong asked.
"Oh yes, I have. I was on the phone to them before I came down for dinner. My mum sends her greetings. She said she would like to speak to you the next time I call."
"Fantastic! I would love to speak with her too. At least then I can assure her that her daughter is in safe hands. I know that if I were in her shoes, I would be distraught. Any mother would!"
"Oh, are you some kind of fugitive?" Tope asked abruptly.
"How many times have I told you to mind your own business and stop poking your nose in when adults are talking. Little brat!" Bose shouted and looked angrily at her brother through squinted eyes.
"Take it easy Bose, I was only joking. Anyway, I'm sure your friend hasn't lost her tongue, so she can answer the question herself," Tope shouted back at his sister.

"Now Tope, stop being rude," his mum swiftly butted in. "Josie is our guest, and as long as she is in this house, you will learn to respect her, do you hear me. What do they teach you in that American school of yours anyway?"

"I'm sorry mum," Tope looked like a puppy whose bone had been snatched away.

"Well, I am not the one you should be apologising to, young man."

Tope looked up at Josie.

"I am sorry if I offended you; I didn't mean to. It's all my sister's fault really, she has a way of bringing out the worst in me. I just wish my big sister was here; she and dad are the only ones who actually understand me in this house."

Everyone laughed at how Tope's apology has suddenly turned into a 'feel sorry for myself' rant. Being their only son, Mr and Mrs Archibong would do almost anything to make him happy, which was most likely the reason why he had the tendency to behave like a spoilt child every now and then. However, he was a pleasant boy, and from what Josie heard later on, he was also very brilliant and one day planned to be a pilot.

Mr Dada took a look at his watch and let out a shriek of surprise, he had no idea that time had flown by so quickly. He and Mr Archibong tried to round up their political discussion as they slowly walked over to the dining table.

Mrs Dada noticed her husband approaching and knew that it was time to leave. They said their goodbyes and made Bose promise to bring Josie over to theirs sooner rather than later.

After seeing their guests off, Mr and Mrs Archibong walked back to the dining table where Josie and Bose were still chatting away.

"Sorry to barge in, but I may have some good news for you, Josie."

Josie's eyes suddenly lit up. Mr Archibong continued.

"While Wale, Mr Dada that is, and I were talking I mentioned that you were looking at enrolling for a degree over here. Well, it turns out that he knows the Vice-Chancellor of the University of Lagos; to be specific, they are actually related. Anyway, to cut a long story short, Wale promised to discuss your situation with the Vice-Chancellor and hopefully work something out with regards to your admission into the University."

"Thank you so much, sir, I am so grateful," Josie was ecstatic. "Hopefully one day I will be able to repay the kindness you have shown me."

"Josie, there is no need for that. Any friend of a child of mine, is like my child. We are more than happy to have you here. However, now I think the two of you should go to bed," Chris Archibong smiled. "Meanwhile, I will be travelling to Abuja tomorrow and will most likely be away for two days so my driver will be available to take you young ladies wherever you need to go."

"Thank you, daddy, and have a safe trip," Bose said with a wide grin.

14.
Tension

*C*hris Archibong had only just returned from Abuja when he got a call from his friend, Wale Dada. As promised, Mr Dada had spoken to the Vice-Chancellor, Professor Bode Davies who had asked to meet Josie. The only issue was that, due to his hectic schedule he would only have time to see her today.

Professor Davies spoke to Josie, who had been accompanied to his office by Mr Archibong and Mr Dada, about the history and the ethos of the university before asking her a few questions like, the course she was thinking of studying and why she wanted to do her first degree in Nigeria. The conversation went surprisingly well; Josie seemed to have the right answer for every question, and from his reaction the Vice-Chancellor seemed very impressed.

Since Josie wanted to study International Relations and Strategic Studies, Professor Davies had asked them to go to the Faculty of Social Sciences where the Dean, who had already been briefed about Josie's peculiar situation, would explain what they would need to do next.

While Mr Archibong and Mr Dada looked on, the Dean of the Faculty of Social Sciences gave Josie a concise summary of the interview process. Then he politely asked the two gentlemen to wait outside his office while he interviewed Josie. About an hour later the Dean opened the door and Josie walked out looking both excited and exhausted.

"So, how did it go?" Mr Archibong asked, looking at Josie expectantly.

Josie shrugged her shoulders and smiled, "I think it was okay."

Mr Dada walked over to the Dean; he only had one question to ask.

"So, what is the verdict?" he asked anxiously.
"One step at a time," the Dean smiled. "Though I must say that she has potential and I believe she should be able to cope, but I will have to discuss this at length with the Vice-Chancellor. I am sure he will contact you once a decision has been made."

Mr Dada wanted an immediate response; he wanted to know if Josie had been accepted right there and then but taking into consideration that he was asking for a massive favour, waiting a few days was a small price to pay.

Angela Kimberley had told her husband about the telephone conversation she and Bruce had with Josie, and about the fact that she was now in Nigeria. John Kimberley could not believe his ears, and being more a man of action than words, he decided that he was going to find a way to put a stop to the 'nonsense' he had just heard. He wondered how Josie had managed to talk both her mother and brother into believing that she was in good hands.

"I mean, how can she be in good hands when she's in a place she has never been before?" John quizzed himself.

He was intent on drawing the curtains on this mess once and for all. As fate would have it, the week before while he was at the Chelsea club, he ran into his good friend, James Eastwood, who just happened to be the British Deputy High Commissioner in Lagos.

John knew that James could help repatriate his daughter back home, but first he needed to talk to him, and since James had told him that he planned to fly back to Lagos over the weekend, he needed to move quickly.

The more John thought about the mess Josie had gotten herself into, the angrier he became. He disdained and poopooed the idea of his daughter enrolling in a third world University.

"What has come over her? What makes a young girl, brought up in a loving, middle-class home, suddenly behave like an orphan?" he wondered. At that point John reached for his phone and called James.

The next day, John Kimberley and James Eastwood met at the Chelsea Club. As they sat down, John went straight to the point.

"James, I need to tell you something really important. It's about my daughter, Josie."
"What about her? I hope she is okay", James replied, shifting uncomfortably in his chair.
"From what I heard, she claims to be fine, but I have my doubts."
"What do you mean by, 'she claims to be fine'? John what is wrong with your daughter; is she sick or what?"
"James, apart from members of my family, no one knows anything about what I am about to tell you. But you have always been a good friend and I believe I can trust you."

James looked worried. Was he ready to hear what his friend had to say? Well, ready or not, he was about to be told.

"About two years ago, on Josie's sixteenth birthday, the son of a very prominent member of society broke into my daughter's room, raped her and left her for dead on the college grounds. By the time the paramedics rushed her to the hospital she was in a coma. It was while she was in this comatose state the medical staff discovered that my daughter was pregnant. Some months later when Josie came out of the coma we told her about the baby. Initially I thought that terminating the pregnancy wouldn't be an issue, but I was wrong. After going through the emotional ups and downs of what to do about the pregnancy, Josie, out of nowhere, decided that she wanted to keep the baby. I didn't agree with her decision but after everything she had been through, I was prepared to do anything for my daughter."

A tear rolled down John's cheek. James leaned over and gave his friend a comforting pat on the back.

"Don't beat yourself up, John. You did what any loving father would have done."
"But James, I watched her go through that painful pregnancy. My daughter almost died giving birth to that child. It just did not feel right. I won't lie James, I am still picking up the pieces of my broken heart. My marriage was almost ruined, and my family has never been the same."
"I'm not even going to pretend to understand what you are going through my friend, but your daughter was raped by the son of someone you obviously knew. Why did you not have him arrested? Why?" James looked confused.
"At the time, I did not want to get the law involved. I was the one who, in a way stopped the police from charging that animal. I had my reasons then, but now..." John's head drooped.
"So, I guess you and Angela look after the baby while Josie is in school; I take it she is back in school, right?"

John shook his head.

"Angela and I did something that we will most likely regret

for the rest of our lives. I also believe that it is the reason why Josie ran away. First, she went to my sister in law's place in Aberdeen, and a couple of days ago we found out that she was in Nigeria. I don't understand how she got there. Who issued her the visa? How was she allowed to travel on her own without parental consent for Christ's sake?"

"Okay John, calm down. I will answer your questions one at a time. So, by my calculations, Josie is about eighteen years old right? That means she can go wherever she likes, whenever she likes without parental consent. Going by what you said, since Josie was in Scotland she most likely applied for a visa through the Nigerian Consulate in Glasgow, unless she did it in London without your knowledge. So, you can see how easy it would have been for Josie to travel out of the country. We need to understand that the children of nowadays are a lot more street savvy than we were. Anyway, I will make the relevant enquiries. Since she most likely entered Nigeria on her British passport I am sure we should be able to trace her somehow."

"Okay, I would appreciate it if you could. Hopefully we will be able to identify the family that 'kidnapped' my daughter. Once that is confirmed, I will make the necessary arrangements," John's face lit up.

"Hold on John; don't you think you are overreacting? What makes you think that Josie was kidnapped, and if she was, how was she smuggled out of the United Kingdom? From my experience, most Nigerians are lovely, hospitable people. So, don't make the mistake of believing everything you read in the papers. Remember, there are good and bad people everywhere, and I am sure that you of all people would know that."

John sighed. Unfortunately, he agreed with everything James had said, but whatever the case he felt he had made his point. Once James found out where Josie was staying he planned to fly out there and possibly get a court order that would enforce Josie's return to

England.

John felt his phone vibrate. The caller ID was unknown, but he answered it anyway.

"Hello daddy," Josie's voice was trembling.
"Josie… is that you?" the shock was evident in John's voice. "What have they done to you? Are you okay? Who are these people who took you to Africa? Do you know what they want?"
"Daddy, I am fine. I really am, and by the way, I came here of my own accord. Anyway, I just called to tell you that I have been granted admission to study International Relations and Strategic Studies at the University of Lagos."

The line went silent. John couldn't believe what he had just heard. What was she talking about?

"You what?" John yelled.
"Not to worry daddy, I don't expect you to understand. Please give my love to mum, Bruce and the girls. Bye daddy, I love you."

Josie hung up.

"Well, talk of the angel," James smiled half-heartedly. "So, what was all the shouting about, I thought you would be happy to hear her voice?"
"James, I think my daughter has been brainwashed. She said she has been admitted to some university over there. Can you imagine; my own daughter! What will people say?"
"Come on John, listen to yourself. Remember, Josie is no baby and any interference from you might make my job extremely difficult. As a friend, I would advise you to back off. This situation may not be as bad as you think it is."

As they left the club, James promised to call John once he arrived in Nigeria, but in the meantime, he advised him to take things easy.

John felt his world falling apart. He cursed Michael Doland under his breath. More than ever before, he was determined to get his daughter back, even if he had to resort to using underhand tactics. He needed to talk to his wife, but somehow, he suspected that she would not agree with him.

When John Kimberley got home, everyone was out, except Bruce. He told his son about the conversation he had with Josie, but to John's surprise, Bruce did not flinch. The truth was, even though Bruce was shocked to hear about Josie's latest stunt, he was beginning to realise that his sister was full of surprises hence the reason why he didn't look perturbed. Whatever the case, Bruce had made up his mind that nothing was going to stop him from bringing her back home.

"Bruce, how come you do not look surprised?" John quizzed. "Did you know about this all along?"
"Come on dad, do you think if I knew I wouldn't have told you? I am as worried and anxious as everyone else. Remember, I was the one who went chasing after her in the first place."
"Where is your mother?"
"Mum and the girls went to the supermarket."

Bruce was curious to find out how his father's conversation with Josie had ended.

"So, dad, what did you say to Josie when she told you that she was going to start University in Nigeria?"
"Well, she hung up on me before I could say anything. Although, to be fair, my initial reaction did not exactly help

matters. My friend James Eastwood was with me at the time. He is flying back to Lagos over the weekend and, after giving him a summarised version of what happened, he promised to inquire about Josie's whereabouts."

"But Dad, I thought we agreed not to tell anyone?"

John and Bruce were still having their discussion when they heard the front door open. Lois and Daphne burst in as usual, their mother following close behind. Angela took one look at Bruce and her husband; she knew straight away that something was wrong.

Angela told the girls to go upstairs and do their homework, and once they were safely in their rooms she turned to her husband.

"So, what's with the sombre look?" She asked.

Words failed John Kimberley. He didn't know how to express the thoughts that were currently running through his head.

"What is it John? Bruce, what is going on? Have you heard from Josie? Is she alright?"

"Yes mum, Josie is fine," Bruce answered. "She called dad to tell him that she had been admitted to a Nigerian university. Obviously, dad wasn't too happy about it, and even though he hasn't told me yet, I think voices were raised."

Angela heaved a sigh of relief and began to laugh. Both her husband and son looked at her like she had lost her mind.

"Angela, what is so funny?" John interjected. "In case you have not realised, this is a serious matter, so if you have something to say do go ahead and say it."

"Listen to yourself, John Kimberley. I hope you know that Josie gets her stubbornness from you?"

John was left speechless. He did not appreciate the tone of his wife's voice. Bruce could feel the tension rising and tried to diffuse it.

"Okay mum, is there something you want to say?"
"Yes, there is actually. So, a daughter calls her father to tell him that she has been offered a place to study the course of her choice in a Nigerian university, and he blows up because the university is in the 'wrong' country. What is the matter with you? You should be happy that she even told you in the first place. What would you have done if she just went ahead without letting you know, or worse still, she did something to disgrace the family name? I just think that it is a pity that you do not understand your own daughter. My advice to both of you is to let Josie be and pray that someday she will come back to us."

Angela turned and stormed out of the room leaving both her husband and son staring open-mouthed at her departing figure.

15

Secret Revealed

osie's interview with the Dean had gone extremely well, so it came as no surprise when she was offered unconditional admission to study International Relations and Strategic Studies at the University of Lagos.

When Bose's father gave Josie the good news she could not hide her joy. She ran over to Bose, who just happened to be in the room at the time and gave her a great big hug.

Bose was genuinely happy for her friend, but she still could not understand why Josie did not want to let her in on her secret. Was it that Josie didn't trust her? One way or the other Bose was intent on getting to the bottom of this. She planned to wait until the time was right and then she would ask Josie again.

As fate would have it, that night as Bose was about to crawl into bed, she heard a knock on the door. It was Josie.

"So, BA, are we going to live on campus or are we staying at home?" Josie asked, a wide smile written all over her face as she poked her head around the door. She was still bubbling with excitement. "Though I wouldn't mind the comfort of going to university from home, I really don't want it to look like I am taking things for granted."
"Nonsense!" Bose replied. "Apart from that, I'm sure my parents would not want us to live in a university hostel when there is more than enough room in the house. The only snag I can see is the perennial traffic, but that simply means that we will have to make the small sacrifice of waking up earlier than usual." Both of them laughed.

It suddenly crossed Bose's mind that this just might be a good time to ask Josie about what she was hiding up her sleeve.

"Josie," Bose began, "I get the feeling there is something you're not telling me?"

"What's that supposed to mean?" Josie looked puzzled.

"I mean, after what happened at St Magdalene's you just disappeared. And then out of the blue I bump into you in a Chinese restaurant in Aberdeen. It's all just a bit strange. Josie, I hope you know that you can trust me?" The sympathy was evident in Bose's voice.

"BA", Josie sighed, "I don't want you to think that I am ungrateful and that I don't appreciate everything you have done for me."

"So, what is it Josie? What aren't you telling me?"

Bose was not trying to be nosey. She just felt that after everything she and Josie had been through, the time had come to lay bare all secrets.

Josie sat down on Bose's bed. She covered her face and tried to hold back the tears. She hadn't planned to hide anything from her friend, she just didn't know how or what to say. Finally, Josie raised her wet face and looked straight into Bose's eyes. If there was ever a time to be strong it was now.

As she sniffed and snuffled, Bose handed her some tissue to wipe her face, but did not say a word; she waited patiently. Finally, Josie broke the silence.

"Yes, it is true, I left St Magdalene's, but that was mainly because I was in the hospital being treated for the injuries I sustained after being attacked on the school premises."

"Hmm. Now it all makes sense," Bose sighed. "There were rumours about what had happened, but the school authorities suppressed them, and the teachers were not allowed to say a word."

"My parents told me that I was comatose for months and that they even feared for my life. BA, I was raped! Do you remember the extramural Ancient Greek Mythology, Roman and Hebrew Literature class for those of us studying Latin?"

Bose nodded slowly. She remembered that class all too well. They all had a teenage crush on the teacher, Mr Michael Doland. "But, he was married with children. Surely it could not have been him, or was it?" Bose thought.

Suddenly the conversation was becoming a bit uncomfortable.

"It was him BA," Josie's voice was shaking. She could see it in her friend's eyes; Bose knew who she was talking about. Josie looked away as she continued. "He raped me and left me for dead by the shed. If the school gardener had not found me that morning...,"

Josie shook her head, tears running freely down her cheeks, the memories once again flooding her mind.

"Josie, I am so sorry. I can't even begin to imagine what you have been through," Bose whispered. "You don't have to tell me any more if you don't want to."
"BA, apart from my family, no one else knows what happened after the night of my sixteenth birthday. The burden of this secret has become so heavy; I needed to share it with someone and I am glad that someone is you."

Josie paused for a moment as if she had remembered something, then she continued.

"I guess it was partly my fault, I was so naive. There I was enjoying the attention he was showering on me, letting him regale me with tales of the Greek islands and all the myths that surrounded the exotic places that I used to think were fairy tales. Like a dog, I lapped it all up. Not once did it cross my mind that he might have an ulterior motive. I was so foolish!" Josie shook her head.

"Don't beat yourself up Josie. It could have happened to any one of us. We were all smitten by Michael Doland. There was just something about him that made him so likeable. I am so sorry you have had to go through so much pain, but I want you to know that your secret is safe with me."

As they hugged each other, tears trickling down their faces, they promised to always look out for each other. The burden had finally been lifted, and for the first time in what seemed like forever Josie felt a certain kind of freedom.

She smiled, stood up and was about to leave Bose's room, when she stopped.

"BA, your mum has been so good to me and I would really like to get her a little something as a token of my appreciation. Any suggestions?"

"Don't be silly Josie. There really is no need for all that," Bose replied. "You are my friend, and as far as my mum and dad are concerned, you are more or less part of the family. So, whatever applies to me, applies to you; both the good and the bad!" Bose chuckled.

Josie couldn't help but feel a sense of amazement and wondered if an English family would be this generous and accommodating, especially to someone from a different cultural background.

"Is this really how all Nigerians are?" She asked.

"Well, pretty much," Bose laughed. "You will soon realise that even though we can be bitchy and full of tribal sentiments towards each other, most of us are very hospitable."

Suddenly Josie wore a concerned look.

"The other day I was reading an article on the internet about what happens on Nigerian university campuses; things like cultism and ritual killings. Are these for real?"
"Well, I have also heard about these ungodly acts, but I don't think we need to worry," Bose assured her. "I will however have a word with my dad and hear what he has to say."

Bose caught a glimpse of the time on her wall clock.

"Wow! It's past midnight already. Would you like to come to church with us tomorrow morning? The service starts at nine, but we usually leave home at about eight thirty to avoid the traffic." Bose noticed the look of surprise in her friend's eyes. "Yes, even on Sundays the roads get congested because almost everyone leaves for church at the same time."

Josie could not remember the last time she stepped into a church building, and all of a sudden, she found herself torn between showing appreciation for the goodwill the Archibongs had so kindly shown her and her own personal struggle.

Since that dreadful day she had gradually drifted away from God. She found it hard to come to terms with why He had let her go through such a traumatic experience at such a tender age. However, deep down in her heart she knew that sooner or later she would need to get her act together and renew the relationship she once cherished and shared with Him.

Bose noticed Josie's reluctance and immediately told her not to feel obliged in any way.

"I think I'll pass this time around, but thanks a lot for the invitation," Josie said. "Good night BA." On that note, Josie walked out of Bose's bedroom and gently closed the door behind her.

As soon as Josie closed the door, Bose fell on her knees and prayed for her friend. She asked God to visit Josie that night and help her change her perception of Him. Even though she knew that Josie was hurting and had every right to, she felt that her friend was too young to let one ugly experience haunt her for the rest of her life.

That night Josie tossed and turned and found herself sweating even though the air conditioning was on full blast. No matter how hard she tried she just couldn't sleep. Finally, she got up and had a shower hoping that it would help. It did.

When she eventually fell asleep she found herself dreaming; one dream after another. But frustratingly when she woke up in the early hours of Sunday morning she realised that the dreams were so disjointed that she couldn't make any sense of them.

Finally, at seven in the morning, Josie gave up trying to figure out what the dreams meant, if they meant anything at all, and decided to surprise Bose. Before jumping into the shower, she carefully laid out what she was going to wear on her bed along with the shoes that aunt Jacqui had bought her. Josie remembered how, out of guilt she almost didn't pack them, but they were just too beautiful to leave behind. "Today would be a nice day to wear them," she thought to herself.

Once she was ready, Josie quietly crept down the stairs and waited in the living room for the rest of the family. It was Mr Archibong who came down first and he was quite surprised to see her all dressed up.

"Oh, I did not know that you were coming with us this morning."

"I didn't know either until a few hours ago," Josie smiled sheepishly.

At that moment Bose came downstairs. When she saw Josie, she couldn't hide her surprise as well as her excitement and she started laughing.

"And what's so funny?" Josie asked. "After all you did ask me to come to church with you."
"But I thought you said you weren't coming?"
"Well, a girl is allowed to change her mind, isn't she?"
"Yes, she is," Bose replied with a wide smile.

Bose couldn't believe it but God had actually answered her prayer.

"Thank you, Lord," Bose whispered under her breath.

16
Memory Lane

$\mathcal{I}$t was a week to the University Matriculation. Bose's father came back from work on Monday afternoon and walked straight into his study. Before closing the door, he called his daughter. There was an air of seriousness in his voice, and Bose knew immediately that something was wrong.

As she approached the study door, she wondered what she could have done to get into her father's bad books, but nothing came to mind. Bose opened the door.

"Hello dad."

"Good afternoon Bose," her father replied with a cold, stern look. "Before I left the office I had a call from Mr Dada. He told me that the Vice-Chancellor had received a call from the British High Commission asking about the whereabouts of your friend. Is there something I need to know?"

"Why are they asking questions about Josie?" Bose looked confused. "I am pretty sure that she has done nothing wrong."

"Look young lady, I do not think you understand. If your friend left England without telling her parents, and they just happen to be worried because they do not know where their daughter is, then it could cause a diplomatic uproar and Wale could get into trouble for issuing her a Nigerian visa. Do you know if Josie had parental consent?"

"Dad, Josie's almost nineteen. Does she actually need parental consent to travel alone?" Bose asked.

"Bose, I have got to say that it is disappointing hearing you sound so naive. Would you leave home without telling us?"

Bose looked away, trying desperately not to meet her father's gaze.

"Well, it was uncle Wale's responsibility to ask Josie the relevant questions before issuing the visa in the first place. He wasn't cajoled into this. So, what does he want you to do about it?" Bose was determined to protect Josie. The last thing she wanted was for her friend to feel betrayed and start running again.

Bose's father on the other hand was taken aback by his daughter's response, and just as he was about to answer her perceived, insolent question his wife opened the door. The look in her husband's eyes and the relief on her daughter's face, told her all she needed to know; she had walked in just in time.

Kathleen Archibong was a British national. She worked part-time at the High Commission where she was in charge of British Council Affairs pertaining to applicants and their families. She also oversaw examinations taken by students planning to study in the United Kingdom and liaised with the High Commission to obtain permits for them. Kathleen had a good working relationship with the wife of the Deputy High Commissioner; they were not just old schoolmates, they were very good friends.

Mr Archibong knew that his wife was in a better position to handle this situation, not just because of her role with the High Commission and her friendship with the Deputy High Commissioner's wife, but because she had been through this before.

Kathleen was born to a white English mother, Irene Boswell and a black Nigerian father, Segun Akinjide who happened to be a student in the United Kingdom at the time. When her mother's family found out about their daughter's relationship they kicked against it and promised to disinherit her if she did not end it immediately.

The story goes that the two lovers pleaded with Irene's parents to allow them to get married, but when they threatened to deport and blacklist Segun, Kathleen's parents eloped to Germany where they got married.

Segun finished medical school in Germany while Irene studied German and International Politics. Four years later, Kathleen's dad was offered a job in the Premier University hospital in the ancient city of Ibadan, Oyo State in Western Nigeria. This was where Kathleen's older sister and brother were born.

Kathleen recalled how the Boswells, realising that they had crossed the line, had asked their daughter to visit them so they could sort things out. At the time, Irene was twenty-six and pregnant with Kathleen. Less than twenty-four hours after landing in the United Kingdom to see her parents, Irene went into premature labour and was rushed to the hospital.

Kathleen learnt that she had to stay in an incubator for close to two months before her mother could finally take her home. It was after Kathleen's birth that the bridge building between her mother and her grandparents actually began. Kathleen was nine months old when she and her mother returned to Nigeria and Irene was once again reconciled with her husband and her two little ones.

Kathleen's father passed away when she was only three years old, but she could still remember how she longed for his strong, protective hands to carry her and wipe her tears away each time she cried. When he died, she cried like everyone else but she didn't really understand why they were weeping, and why people were trooping in and out of the house.

So, Irene became a widow at the young age of twenty-nine in a foreign land; the husband of her youth snuffed out before her very eyes. With her soulmate and best friend gone, her mum became a shadow of herself. Many of Segun's friends wanted her as a second wife so that they could supposedly take care of her, but she did not entertain their silly proposals.

After everything she had been through with her husband, Irene could not see herself remarrying. He might be dead and gone, but his spirit and memory would always be with her. She purposed in her heart to do all she could to bring up their three children as he would if he was still alive.

Kathleen somehow remembered everything her mother had told them; it was so clear in her mind. How she decided to send her children to England to live with her parents about a year after her husband's death. They had asked her to come home with the children where they would have all the care they needed, but Irene was determined to try and do it her way, musing that her husband would have preferred it that way. Then one day, when she could no longer cope with the financial hardship, as well as the constant harassment from her husband's relatives and male friends, she left for the United Kingdom with the kids.

Her husband's relatives were not aware of her departure, and when she called them from England it did not go down too well. They were not pleased and demanded to know why she had left the country without informing them. They also reminded her that, according to African tradition the children belonged to their father's family.

This misunderstanding with the in-laws constantly brought Irene to tears, but there was no way she was taking the children back to Nigeria until she had sorted herself out financially. She made up her mind that she and her children would never be a burden on anyone.

About ten years later Kathleen's mum decided that it was time to go back to Nigeria. Interestingly, this coincided with the time her mother-in-law was critically ill and had asked her father-in-law to contact her. She wanted to see Irene and the grandchildren, and hopefully make amends before she died. Unsurprisingly, the Boswells did not support their daughter's plan to take the children back to Nigeria.

As usual, Irene's mum did not hesitate to make her feelings known and suggested that her daughter should leave the children behind if she intended to embark on this futile trip. But that simply wasn't an option. So, on that cold December night, Irene and the children left for Nigeria.

When they arrived in Lagos Irene felt a sense of relief. Conflict with her in-laws was the last thing she wanted, but at the time it seemed unavoidable. Even though her in-laws were not perfect, they had at least received her with open arms when their son introduced her as his wife.

Their old house was still there and it looked almost the same as the day she last saw it. Her father-in-law had kept it well maintained. He had also rented it out to university lecturers and saved every penny of the rent collected hoping that one day his daughter-in-law and the grandchildren would return. So, on hearing that Irene was coming home with the children, he gave the tenants adequate notice to vacate the property so that it would be available for the rightful owners.

Walking through the front door brought back fond memories of the good old days that they had shared as a family and looking through the lounge window at the bright sun hanging in the rich blue sky with the fluffy white clouds made her remember how she loved the beautiful Nigerian weather. In a funny way, it felt good to be back home.

And so, they started their new life in Nigeria. Kathleen remembered how her brother and sister were enrolled in the University secondary school while she was placed in the elementary school, and how they would all walk to school together since their house was within walking distance of the university. Kathleen really enjoyed her school days, and because of her bubbly personality, she made friends easily. This was when she met Nkechi Maureen Obiekwe.

Kathleen and Nkechi were birds of a feather and could easily have passed for sisters. They were both light in complexion and were almost the same height. The only real difference was their hair. While Kathleen's was curly and long, Nkechi's was cut short. She remembered how they were favoured by most of the teachers, and how they would gang up against the other children who tried to pick on them out of jealousy.

Saying that Nkechi's family was quite well off was a bit of an understatement. Her father was a sought-after university lecturer while her mother was a businesswoman, who traded in fancy fabrics.

Looking back, Kathleen was grateful for the insight of her paternal grandparents. The money from the rent came in very handy as it made sure they had more than enough, so her mum had no need to work or worry about money. Nevertheless, Irene decided that she was way too young to sit down and mope around the house. She got herself a job as a part-time lecturer in the university taking extramural courses for those who wished to learn the German language. She did this for four years, three days a week; she said it gave her a sense of fulfilment.

The memories kept flooding through Kathleen's mind. She remembered how her maternal grandparents started clamouring for them to come back to England just before she finished secondary school at Queens College in Lagos. They thought it was a no-brainer, but it was not that straightforward. By this time, they had settled into the Nigerian way of life and Kathleen's mum had decided that Nigeria was where they belonged.

It was going to take some convincing to change Irene's mind, but then her mother-in-law died. Even though she had been diagnosed with a terminal illness she refused to give up the ghost. She even outlived her husband who unfortunately died of prostate cancer.

It was after the death of her husband that she had a massive stroke which left her paralysed on the left side. Though she could still talk, she could only move around with a wheelchair. In fact, because she was used to being so active, it was actually the frustration of not being able to do things herself that eventually led to her death. Kathleen still remembered that day.

It was a bright, sunny morning during the school holiday. They were all at home when her grandmother's house help burst into the house crying and screaming, "Mummy don die o, mummy don die!" They all ran to grandma's place, which was just down the road. It was Kathleen's mum who went in first to check if the old woman was actually dead. While they all waited quietly, Kathleen found herself overwhelmed by everything that was going on. For some reason her grandma's death had triggered memories of her father.

"Why was it that those who loved her and those she loved had to die?" Kathleen thought. She had started crying inconsolably and even though her siblings tried to calm her down, they couldn't. Kathleen ran to her mum as she stepped out of grandma's room.

"Please don't die mummy. Please don't leave me," she cried holding her tight with all her might.

Holding Kathleen at arm's length, Irene wiped the tears from her daughter's face.

"Kath dear, look at me. I am not sick and I am definitely not dying. I still have you, your brother and your sister to look after. So, the good Lord willing, I won't be going anywhere any time soon. Is that okay?" She smiled as she consoled her daughter.

"Yes mummy," Kathleen had replied.

On that day, Kathleen decided in her sixteen-year-old mind that she would look after her mother and do all she could to make sure that she didn't die. During that period Kathleen watched her mother like a hawk; not once did she let her out of her sight.

Irene and her husband's younger brother, made arrangements for grandma Akinjide's body to be taken to the mortuary, and the funeral preparations were set in motion.

The funeral was a happy-sad occasion, but the one thing she never forgot was how it brought members of the family who had not seen each other for years, together. She remembered the flow of food and drinks, the dance groups and different cultural troupes, not to talk of the *aso ebi*[1] worn by members of the family.

Not too long after grandma Akinjide's burial, Irene confessed that one of the main reasons why she had stayed in Nigeria was because of her mother-in-law. However, now that she was dead Irene was strongly considering going back to England, at least for the sake of her children. Apart from the constant hounding from her parents, Irene wasn't a fan of the constant strikes and disruption in Nigerian universities. As this was having an adverse effect on Kathleen's older siblings, Irene concluded that it made no sense for the children to suffer, especially since there was an alternative.

As Kathleen pondered all this, she found herself identifying with why Josie would want to be left alone. After all, even she had rebelled.

---

[1] *A uniform attire traditionally worn in Nigeria and some West African cultures to show solidarity during ceremonies and festive periods.*

When they got back to the United Kingdom, Kathleen's older siblings were enrolled in universities quite some distance away from where they lived in West Hampstead, while she was admitted to a school nearby. That was when something snapped and Kathleen found herself on a path of discovery, searching for her true identity.

She started drinking and partying away; a lifestyle that made her mother very miserable, but Kathleen didn't care. She felt that her life had been run by other people for too long; she had finally had enough of others making decisions on her behalf without asking for her opinion.

Kathleen was a brilliant student so her academics didn't really suffer at first, but the constant late nights with friends began to take their toll on her health and eventually her studies. She ran away from home and moved in with some new-found Nigerian friends whose extremely rich parents were not resident in England. Kathleen's new friends specialised in living large. They didn't drink or smoke, but they were addicted to shoplifting.

These new friends of hers didn't need the money, after all they lived in a massive, mortgage-free house, and when Kathleen asked why they did it when they didn't have to, they simply told her that it all had to do with the buzz of not getting caught. They urged her to join in the fun, and even though she was reluctant initially, she found herself going with the flow. "If you can't beat them, join them," she told herself.

Kathleen was still lost in thought when her husband walked into the room. He immediately noticed his wife's watery eyes.

"What's the matter dear?" he asked.
"It is nothing important," she replied in between sniffles and smiles. "Right now, we have got an important decision to make concerning Josie."

17

Matriculation Day

osie jumped out of bed. She had an excited spring in her step and why not; it was Matriculation day! This was the day that the 'freshers' as they were called, would invite family and friends to witness the first day of the next phase of their lives.

Josie obviously had no one to invite, but she knew that Bose's family as well as Mr and Mrs Dada, would be there to cheer her on and she was determined not to let them down, especially after everything they had done for her.

However, more importantly she wanted to do her own family proud. After running away from home, she knew her folks would have little faith in her, but even if they didn't believe in her she believed in herself. Even if they considered her to be rebellious, she would prove to them that she was responsible. Josie had her mind set on not throwing her future away.

Singing happily as she came out of the bathroom, it crossed Josie's mind that even though she had only been in Nigeria for three months, she had already gotten used to the chaotic lifestyle, and in a funny way she was actually enjoying it. As she got dressed she found herself humming uplifting songs that she thought she had forgotten; songs that her rebellious times had tried to stifle; songs that brought back sweet memories of the relationship she once shared with God. For a second her head dropped, but nothing was going to take away the joy she felt today.

Josie ran downstairs smiling and bubbling with excitement. She felt on top of the world. She could see herself going through university, graduating, taking on her first job, and making it big in the corporate world. The thought of pursuing a Masters, maybe in England where she would most likely have better options, crossed her mind, but she immediately crushed the thought and refocussed.

"Don't get ahead of yourself Josie. Just take it one step at a time," Josie muttered to herself.

Josie was surprised to see uncle Chris and auntie Kath in the living room, and immediately sensed that there was something wrong.

"Good morning Josie. How are you feeling today? I hope you are looking forward to your matriculation?" Mr Archibong flashed a tentative smile.
"Yes, I am, uncle," Josie replied still trying to figure out what was wrong.

Then Mrs Archibong, in a low, soft voice asked Josie to sit down. This confirmed what Josie was feeling. She tried to think about what she might have done to upset this lovely couple, but nothing came to mind. She slowly slid into the chair opposite Bose's parents.

"Josie," Bose's mum began. "Since you arrived we haven't asked you any questions. We simply accepted that you were Bose's friend and that you had travelled to Nigeria because, like you said, you wanted to 'spread your wings'. The truth is we do not mind you staying with us for as long as you like. However, there seems to be a bit of an issue regarding your status here in Nigeria. Does the name Mr James Eastwood ring a bell?"
"No. Should it?" Josie looked confused as she shook her head.
"Maybe he is a family friend," Mrs Archibong tried to jog Josie's memory.
"I remember! I remember Mr Eastwood. He is a close friend of my dad's. If I remember correctly they both studied Law

at Cambridge University. What has he got to do with this anyway?" Josie queried.

"Well my dear, Mr Eastwood just happens to be the British Deputy High Commissioner here in Lagos. Apparently, he got wind of your recent admission to the University of Lagos and contacted the Vice-Chancellor to find out how that was possible. Anyway, to cut a long story short, Mr Eastwood would like to have a word with you."

Bose's mum looked at Josie, waiting for a reaction.

Josie couldn't believe that even in far away Nigeria her family was still bent on interfering with her life. She felt a surge of defiance rise up within her. She lifted her head, all fear and intimidation gone.

"I want to thank you both for all you have done for me since I arrived here. You have taken me in wholeheartedly, treated me like a member of your family and made me feel at home. You have respected my privacy, even though I know there are questions you want to ask, and all I can say is that I sincerely appreciate you. I just hope that one day I can repay the kind gesture."

Then Josie got out of her chair, and out of nowhere began to tell Mr and Mrs Archibong everything she had been through. She didn't miss anything out, and by the time she finished telling her emotional story Bose's mother had broken down in tears. She stood up and gathered Josie in her arms.

Kathleen could see herself in this spirited young English girl. She understood exactly what Josie was going through, especially when she mentioned the part about running away from home because she felt decisions were being made on her behalf without taking her feelings into consideration. "Why do we adults make the same mistake over and over again?" she thought.

When Kathleen and Chris got married they both decided that they would give their children relative independence, but also make sure that the children did not cross the boundaries set for them. What made this more straightforward was the fact that both of them shared the same values when it came to bringing up children. Kathleen was grateful to God that, so far, their children had turned out better than both she and Chris had expected; she knew that it was all by the grace of God.

Both Kathleen and Josie were still teary-eyed when Bose walked into the living room. She had overheard part of what Josie had told her parents, and even though she was surprised, she was relieved that the secret was finally out in the open.

Mr Archibong looked at his watch and reluctantly broke up the emotional moment.

"Alright everyone, we have a matriculation ceremony to catch."

Kathleen wiped away Josie's tears and told her to go and wash her face. By the time Josie came back downstairs, they were all ready to go. They jumped into the car and started the journey through the persistent Lagos traffic.

On the way to the university Mr Archibong decided that he would try and arrange a meeting with Mr Eastwood at his Victoria Island office.

"Tomorrow would be good; the sooner the better," he whispered to himself.

Even though the traffic was a bit heavier than normal, they arrived just in time for the programme. Before the day, each fresher paid a refundable deposit to the Bursar's office so that they could pick up a matriculation gown accompanied by a declaration which they would read on the day.

The programme was scheduled to start at nine in the morning, and just like the ones before, the freshers lined up outside the University Senate Building all gowned up. After reading the declaration, they were called out one by one and presented with a rolled scroll confirming their acceptance into the university.

During the declaration something outstandingly peculiar took place; something that had never happened before in the history of the university. Due to the increase in cult activity on the campus the authorities had decided that as part of the declaration the students would also swear an oath in the presence of their parents that any involvement in cultism, in any manner or form, would result in immediate expulsion from the university.

As Josie's name was called, she got up and made her way towards the stage. Interestingly, Mr James Eastwood, who had somehow learnt about the programme, also stood up from where he was sitting and made his way to the front to represent Josie's parents.

Both Chris and Kathleen were surprised to see Mr Eastwood, even though they knew that he would have made enquiries about when and where the matriculation was going to take place. After all, he had lived here for quite some time, so apart from being aware of Nigeria's political and economic climate, he also made it his business to keep track of British nationals living in the country, and Josie was a special case.

Bose's dad was about to get up and challenge Mr Eastwood, but Kathleen gently tugged on her husband's hand urging him not to.

"Chris, let him go," Kathleen whispered. "He is obviously in touch with Josie's parents, so in a sense he just might be doing us a favour by keeping them updated with their daughter's progress."

Mr Archibong agreed with his wife's words of wisdom and settled back into his seat.

Immediately after the ceremony, which lasted a little over three hours, Josie, in a bid to clear the air once and for all and hopefully put her parent's minds at rest, introduced Mr Eastwood to the Archibongs.

"Hello James, I must say that I am surprised to see you here," said Chris.
"Well let's just say I came to see how these things are done in Nigerian Universities," James replied trying to play down his presence at the occasion, but Mr Archibong didn't fall for it.
"Come on James, we all know that a Nigerian university matriculation hardly ever attracts international attention, unless of course you are here for something else," Chris looked at James through prying eyes.

Realising that he wasn't going to wriggle free of Mr Archibong's invisible hold, Mr Eastwood responded.

"Well, the truth is while Josie is here in Nigeria I have been mandated by her family to look out for her. I met up with Josie's father, who just happens to be an old friend of mine, while I was on holiday and he briefed me on what he knew about his daughter's situation. Understandably, since they found out that Josie was staying with a friend in Nigeria, Josie's parents have been anxious to find out how she is doing. I'm sure you would feel the same way if you found out that your daughter had relocated to a foreign country without your knowledge, right?"

Mr Archibong did not appreciate the condescending nature of Mr

Eastwood's tone, but before he could give him a piece of his mind Mr Eastwood turned his attention to Bose.

"Hello you must be Bose, Josie's friend. How are you?
"Fine, thank you," Bose replied.
"Well, thank you for taking good care of Josie. I guess now I can tell the Kimberleys that their daughter is in the good hands of a family I know and trust." James smiled then turned to Mrs Archibong, and in a subtle reprimanding tone said, "Surely Kathleen, I thought we trusted each other. If you had told me about Josie I am sure we could have avoided this uncomfortable situation."
"James, I am not sure you would have listened to me if I had brought up this matter. Most likely you would have told me how the British laws and regulations still applied to Josie even though she was in Nigeria. Most likely you would have insisted that we send the young lady back to England. With you, the law is the law and must be upheld even if an injustice is being perpetrated." Kathleen finished her mild rant.

Mr Eastwood could see the direction in which the discussion was going and immediately tried to lighten the atmosphere.

James knew the Archibongs; they were a family that stood for integrity, one of the few families he could vouch for, and he had no plans of messing up the friendship they had built over the years. After all, Josie was doing something positive with her life and from what he could see the Archibongs were helping her achieve her goal.

"Well, from what I can see Josie is happy, and she seems to be moving on with her life, thanks to you and Chris. That is good enough for me," James concluded.

And just like that, to Josie's relief, the matter was resolved.

"Thanks for coming for my matriculation, Mr Eastwood. I do appreciate it. I don't know what my dad told you, but the truth is I needed to find myself and make something of my life. If I fail, then so be it; at least I'd have no one to blame but myself."

Before Mr Archibong could say anything in response to Josie's statement, James Eastwood extended his hand towards him.

"Truce?"
"Of course," Chris smiled as both he and James shook hands. "If it is okay with Kathleen and yourself I would like to invite Josie and Bose over to mine for dinner one of these days. I am sure my wife would be very happy to have them over."
"Well, that would be up to Josie," Chris replied.

Josie realised that all eyes were on her as they waited for her response to Mr Eastwood's invitation.

"Bose and I would love that," she turned and smiled at Bose.

They all said their goodbyes and once again James Eastwood and Chris Archibong shook hands promising to meet at the club later on in the week for a game of golf.

Campus Mayhem

They had barely spent three weeks in university when Josie and Bose witnessed their first campus cult clash. From what they heard it was all because of a girl.

The girlfriend of the leader of one of the most notorious campus cults had jilted him and was now going out with another student. Even though it had not been proven, the Don, as the cult leader was often called, was said to be a notorious killer both on and off campus and was feared by both students and the University authorities alike. The rumour was that he was being shielded by one of the top professors in the University, also suspected to be a member of the fraternity, therefore making him almost untouchable. Now the Don was hell-bent on taking out this student who dared to hook up with his ex-girlfriend, and it seemed no one could stop him.

On this particular day, the cult members lay in wait for the couple, ready to inflict the maximum pain on them, as instructed. However, luckily one of the gang members, who happened to be a close friend of the Don's ex-girlfriend had tipped her off.

After waiting in vain for the couple to pass by the boys became restless and a false alarm about an altercation with some other cult members on the other side of campus was all it took for them to spring into action. They senselessly dashed over there and began to beat and maim whoever crossed their path. As it happened, by the time the police showed up, some ordinary passers-by who got caught up in the scuffle had been seriously injured, and some were feared to have died before they could be rushed to the hospital.

Mr Archibong's driver was on his way to drop Josie and Bose

for their classes when he heard gunshots being fired. He spotted the melee ahead and being aware of the cult issues on campus it took him a split second to figure out what was happening. He immediately threw the car into reverse and quickly turned around trying his best not to alarm the girls.

Josie turned to Bose, her face was fear-stricken.

"What was that?" Josie asked.
"Trust me," Bose replied, "you don't want to know. Let's just say that this is one of the reasons why my dad said no to us living on campus."

Josie didn't quite understand what her friend meant, but what she said did little to alleviate her fears.

"That scuffle looked rather violent." Josie's voice was trembling. "BA, what is going to happen to our lectures? One of my lecturers actually insisted that I submit an assignment today."
"I wouldn't worry too much about submitting any assignments right now. I suspect there won't be any lectures until further notice," Bose declared to her bewildered friend.

Josie began to wonder if this adventure of hers had been born out of naivety and sheer stupidity. "What would happen if this didn't work out?" she thought.

Josie cast her mind back to the night when she had dinner with the Eastwoods.

Unfortunately, Bose had been unable to make dinner with the Eastwoods, which made things a bit awkward for Josie. When Josie and the Eastwoods spoke after dinner she had tried to tilt the conversation in her favour telling her hosts that the reason why she had chosen this path was to somehow try and persuade her sceptic family members that she had what it took to make something of herself. But that didn't stop James from grilling her about her choice of university, and trying to discourage her stay in Nigeria. That was when Josie decided to go on the offensive.

"But James, you have lived here for more than four years," Josie started. "If it is really that bad then why haven't you asked for a transfer back to the United Kingdom?"

Mr Eastwood was taken aback by Josie's question and was suddenly lost for words. He of all people knew about the perks that came with the job, and how they outweighed the negatives. After all, there was no need to throw the baby out with the bathwater.

James' response when it finally came, was feeble and even he didn't sound convinced.

"Well Josie, my case is a bit different," he stumbled, "I am a Civil Servant working in the Foreign Office so I go wherever I am sent. Whether I like the place or not, I don't exactly have a choice."
"Really?" Josie began. "I seem to remember my friend's dad who also worked in the Foreign Office. He turned down a transfer to Kosovo, and one of the reasons he gave for his refusal, apart from not speaking the language, was that he did not agree with the policies of that nation towards ethnic Albanians. Anyway, it doesn't matter because I plan to finish my degree here before returning to England. That is what I told my dad the last time I spoke to him, and that is exactly what I intend to do."

Now, as Mr Archibong's driver drove her and Bose back to the house, Josie found herself asking if her decision to study in Nigeria was the right choice.

As soon as they got home, Bose turned on the television. There it was, the news she had been dreading all along. The authorities had closed the university and ordered all students to leave campus until further notice. The reporter also announced that the University authorities had expelled all the students who participated in one way or the other in the mayhem that happened earlier on.

Bose was pacing up and down the living room when Josie walked in. Josie noticed that her friend wasn't her usual boisterous self; she seemed agitated about something.

"What is wrong BA?" she asked.
"Nothing much. I'm just thinking about what happened today," Bose replied.

Though Bose had, in her own way, tried to explain the enormity of the cult problem faced in some universities across the country, she had not told Josie about the bloodshed that accompanied these bust-ups. Even now she could not bring herself to tell her about the multiple lives that had been lost that afternoon. Instead she decided to wait for her parents to come home before saying a word about it. Hopefully they would have heard about it by then.

It also dawned on her that the High Commission would have been briefed about the cult clash that had resulted in the university's closure. This made Bose fear for her English friend knowing that Mr Eastwood would most likely place undue pressure on Josie to return to England at once.

Sure enough, when Bose's mum came home, she told the girls that there had been a heated discussion between her and the Deputy High Commissioner and that a decision had not yet been reached. Kathleen then explained to Josie what had actually happened earlier and the possible effects it could have on her studies and her stay in Nigeria. She also told Josie that the choice to return to England was solely hers, and that she should not be pressured by anyone into doing something she did not want to do.

That night before going to bed, Josie asked Bose's father what he thought she should do.

"Well, I would suggest that you should be patient and see what the university authorities come up with. In reality they cannot afford to close the university indefinitely. So, let us just wait and see."

"Thank you, uncle Chris. I also wanted to ask what your thoughts were about private tutoring until school reopens?" Josie asked.

"Coincidentally, I was actually thinking of looking into the possibility of some private tutoring for you and Bose to at least keep your minds alert. My nephew's wife just happens to be a lecturer. Let me have a word with her and see what she has to say."

Josie said, "Good night" and was on her way to her room when Mr Archibong called her back.

"Josie, you do know that you and Bose are mature, young ladies and I trust both of you. So even though I have told you what I think, at the end of the day the choice is yours! I hope you understand what I mean?"

Josie smiled and nodded her head.

"Thank you, uncle. I am really grateful. Good night."
"Good night my dear, and don't worry too much. We know that God works all things together for good when it comes to His children."

Josie ran upstairs, straight to Bose's room and excitedly shared the discussion she just had with her dad. Bose tried to share Josie's enthusiasm, but the truth was she was really angry with the university system; a system that condoned strikes and consistently failed to eradicate a cult culture that was taking over universities and destabilising the lives of students. With all this negativity around she was not sure what the future held for Josie and herself. Bose felt the urge to pray.

"Josie, I don't really want to put a damper on everything you have said, but do you mind if we prayed?"

"About what?" Josie replied looking a bit confused.

"Well, I was thinking that it just might be a good idea to talk to God about our current predicament; ask Him to intervene in this university situation that we find ourselves in."

"Okay then," Josie shrugged her shoulders resignedly.

Bose knelt by her bedside and started a prayer of thanksgiving. She thanked God for ensuring that they did not get caught up in the earlier violence and bloodshed. She thanked Him for giving their driver the wisdom to do the right thing at the time, and she also gave thanks for her dad; for his advice and for his plan to help them with their studies during this lull period. Finally, Bose made a promise to God that both she and Josie would be good girls and try not to disappoint Him.

When Bose finished praying they both said, "Amen."

19

Drastic Action

*T*he University Senate had a closed-door meeting exactly fourteen days after the violent cult attack and they had decided, by a fifteen to five majority vote, to reopen the University. One of the objectors was Professor Wodu; the professor many believed was backing the cult.

Professor Wodu, educated in America, was a world-renowned writer and a playwright who had written quite a few plays that had been adapted into films. He was known for his penchant for snubbing those who did not agree with his opinions and did not hide his distaste when the university's Vice-Chancellor was appointed.

According to him, Professor Davies' appointment was purely political and it was the wrong decision for the university. He also did not appreciate being overlooked for the position himself, especially as he thought he was more qualified. He made his feelings clear at the slightest opportunity, and on numerous occasions even threatened to unleash his minions on the campus daring the Vice-Chancellor to sack him if he could.

Wodu was intent on showing everyone that Professor Davies was incapable of controlling the university and thanks to his cult-like following both on and off campus, along with his gift of the gab which he consistently used to manipulate situations to his benefit, he seemed to be doing a good job at it.

So, when later that day the Vice-Chancellor summoned the eminent professor to his office, the writing was on the wall.

"Professor Wodu, taking into consideration our decision to reopen the university and the volatile atmosphere, which I am sure you are well aware of, I would appreciate your maximum cooperation. We need to put the ill feeling between us to one side and put the university first; we owe it to our students. For the record, I have asked the same of all the other members of the Senate who opposed the decision and their response has been positive. So, are you on board or do you plan to persist with your belligerent behaviour?"

"Well, it appears to me that once again you seem to be chasing after shadows," the professor replied. "For the record I would have you know that I had no prior knowledge nor did I have a hand in what happened between the rival cult groups a fortnight ago."

Professor Wodu was known for turning whatever he disagreed with into an argument, or collateral that he could use against another. So, Professor Davies decided that he would not continue the conversation without a third-party present.

The professor was feared mainly because he had eyes and ears all over the place, and it was no secret that he had students who spied for him in return for good grades. As a result, a number of lecturers felt intimidated. But Professor Davies had just about had enough of Wodu and his ways, and he was intent on doing something about it once and for all.

The Vice-Chancellor stood up, walked over to the door and held it open.

"I don't think there is anything else to talk about. I have made my point; this discussion is over. Good day Professor and thank you for your time."

The Professor was shocked by the Vice-Chancellor's unusual

reaction. Most of the time he would do almost anything to avoid a rift between them. Wodu found himself walking out of the office like a zombie, leaving the room without uttering another word. Wodu needed to know what card this man had up his sleeve, and who better to ask other than Tunde, the Vice-Chancellor's secretary; one of Wodu's loyalists.

After the professor left his office, Professor Davies sent for his secretary and asked him to take a seat. Tunde had seen Professor Wodu leave his boss's office but did not know what had transpired between them as the Professor hadn't stopped to brief him.

Tunde had played a part in the fracas that led to the university's closure but had not envisaged that it would turn into a bloodbath. While the brawl was ongoing he ran away from the scene and took shelter in the cult's hiding place in the ghettoes of Bariga to avoid being implicated when the police came along. He returned a week later while his boss was still away at a conference.

Tunde sat down quietly waiting to hear what the Vice-Chancellor had to say. Considering the latest development, he assumed he had been called in to take a dictation which would be circulated to the students on their return to campus.

"So, Tunde, I understand you were not in the office while I was away. May I ask where you were?"

This question caught the secretary unawares. Tunde considered his boss to be a laid-back weakling and as a result he abused the man's trust by becoming a traitor. He had forgotten how this same man had rescued him and his family from poverty and employed him so that he could help his aged parents.

"*Oga*[2], I beg. I went to see my parents. I heard that my

---

[2] *'Boss' or 'Master' in the Nigerian Yoruba language*

mother was not feeling well, so I took some medication to her and stayed to lend my father a hand. I am sorry sir."

"Tunde, you are a bloody liar! You see, on my way back from the conference, I took the opportunity to visit your parents. I didn't see you there and they told me you haven't been home in two years."

"Oga, I beg. I am not lying. I went to see them. Maybe I hadn't arrived when you went there and they forgot to tell you that I was coming."

Tunde's mind was running wild. Suddenly he felt hot all over and started sweating. He had picked the wrong alibi to explain his absence, he should have known that his boss was on to him.

"It's alright Tunde. I have taken the liberty of changing the locks to the office. I have also informed the security personnel that you are no longer an employee of this university. They are waiting outside to escort you off the premises. They have also been instructed to take you home and retrieve all university property in your possession. Your salary, less the week you took off without approval, will be paid at the end of the month. I would advise that you do not leave town as I am sure the police will want to bring you in for questioning. Goodbye".

Tunde had often thought he was indispensable, and because his boss had a soft spot for his parents, he would keep his job no matter what he did. He was wrong! His world was crashing down right before his very eyes. He knew that professor Wodu would not offer him a job. As much as he liked the man, he knew that he was a very selfish person with a mean streak.

He fell at his boss's feet and asked him to please give him another chance, promising never to abscond again, but it was all in vain.

"Come on Tunde, do you actually think I am sacking

you because of a week's absence? No, it is because of your ingratitude. Since you have chosen to make your bed with the devil, you might as well go ahead and lie with him."

Tunde, still on his knees, looked up. He was dumbfounded.

"Did you think I would not find out? I have often wondered how memos from my office often got quoted against me at Senate meetings. Initially I suspected other junior staff, but when I started giving out false information which only you and I were privy to, I was faced with the painful truth. Please, leave my office now before I ask security to remove you forcibly," Professor Davies yelled.

Tunde held on to the Vice-Chancellor's legs weeping, pleading for forgiveness. So, Davies called in the security guards and asked them to escort his secretary out of the building once he had cleared his desk.

One by one the Vice-Chancellor got rid of all the undesirables; all those who were not loyal to him and his office, and by the time he was done seven of the eleven members of staff attached to his office either had their employment terminated or were transferred to other departments with immediate effect.

At the end of the week Professor Davies called a staff meeting where he spelt out what was expected and required of each one of them. He also encouraged all the staff to read the University Constitution as it would serve as a perfect guide and reminder.

Because of the seriousness of what had led to the closure of the university, lecturers were more than willing to cooperate especially as many of them had children studying there. By the time Davies brought the meeting to a close all those present had promised their full cooperation.

Professor Wodu was conveniently absent from the meeting, which explained the peaceful atmosphere. This just went to confirm what the Vice-Chancellor had always known; Professor Wodu was not just a bad influence on the students, but also among the teaching and non-academic staff.

Professor Davies knew what he had to do, but his immediate task was to reopen the campus and hope that the State Commissioner of Police would honour his promise to provide more police reinforcement on campus. Hopefully a more visible police presence would make a difference. Also, each parent would be asked to sign an undertaking, that from now on if their ward was found to be part of or linked to a cult in any way, they would be expelled from the University with immediate effect.

Once the university was up and running again, he would appoint a team of honest and diligent staff to be his eyes and ears on campus, to help maintain peace among the students. But he and the team could only do so much; to make this university the learning place it was always meant to be he needed the assistance and cooperation of both the staff and the parents.

For the first time since his encounter with Professor Wodu, Bode Davies had a smile on his face as he whistled along to his favourite Jim Reeves song, "This World Is Not My Own, I'm Just Passing Through..." He knew that the students deserved a lot more than what they were getting, and he believed that if he and his team could successfully implement the planned changes they would create a comfortable, conducive environment where students would excel and succeed.

Professor Davies felt assured that as long as there were still members of staff, like him, who were willing to give their time for the success of the students and the university, then there was cause to smile and give glory to the Lord.

He was still in a jaunty mood as he drove home. He knew it would not be easy but being a man of faith and determination, he was dead set on once again making the university a place of academic excellence.

"Where there is a will, and where there is faith, there is a way," he whispered under his breath.

"Dear God,
I know I am most likely the last person
You want to hear from right now
but please heal my wounded spirit
and forgive me for running away.
I just did not know what else to do."

Reunited

wo weeks after the announcement the University was formally reopened. The students started flooding in, and in line with what was agreed with the Vice-Chancellor at the staff meeting, lectures started immediately. Assignments were handed in and some of the senior students had their exams rescheduled within two weeks of resumption.

The students also noticed notable changes in the manner by which the lecturers conducted their lectures, with more emphasis on the students actually understanding what they were being taught. They noticed that the Vice-Chancellor was more visible, approachable and occasionally he even interacted with the students. On one occasion he came into the dining hall, sat down and ate with them. Interestingly the quality of food being served in the canteen also seemed to have improved considerably. In fact the students were so impressed that they joked about having more closures if that is what it took to see an improvement.

But not all of the students were happy with the changes, and some did not enjoy seeing the Vice-Chancellor roaming around; they saw it as a form of intrusion. This small group of students even approached the Student Union president urging him to advise the Vice-Chancellor that they were not comfortable with his new approach. But considering that most of the students, parents and staff, even those that were often at loggerheads with the Vice-Chancellor, liked what they saw, no one bothered to launch a complaint.

All of a sudden, the campus became a place of tranquillity and discipline, so much so that even those who lived close to the campus noticed the difference; students were no longer seen loitering around the joints on the campus outskirts.

It seemed like everyone was determined to make a success of the new campus lifestyle. Some students thought it was too good to be true and wondered if it was simply the calm before the storm, but still they were willing to give it a go.

It was the last day of the semester, time for the Christmas holidays, and so far, peace had prevailed. Earlier in the week the Vice-Chancellor had sent out a memo to all departmental heads asking them to inform their students that he would like to meet with them at noon on the last day of the semester.

As the students gathered around the Senate building, Professor Davies pleaded with them to keep up the good work and continue with the same attitude and discipline. He also admonished them to be wary of bad influences during the holidays. Finally, he wished them all a Merry Christmas and a happy New Year and said that he was looking forward to seeing them in three weeks' time.

After the speech, as he approached his office, he noticed some students, about twenty of them, waiting in the hallway.

"Ladies and gentlemen, what can I do for you?"

He noticed that most of them were holding gifts which he soon found out were tokens of their appreciation for his believing in the university and also believing in them.

Though Professor Davies was touched by their kind gesture, he found himself in a catch-22 situation. On the one hand he was determined to stamp out this kind of patronage, but on the other hand he didn't want to appear to be ungrateful. Anyway, on this occasion he decided to accept the gifts, and as he thanked each of the students with a heartwarming smile, he reminded them that their gift would not grant them an unfair advantage.

He had realised that Josie and Bose were among the students and he took time to ask about their welfare. Both of them responded positively saying they were enjoying their lectures and the other changes that had recently been implemented on campus. Josie also told him that even though she was still trying to adjust to the Nigerian teaching system, she was sure that she would soon grow accustomed to it.

When all the students finally left, Davies asked his deputy into his office and showed him the gifts that the students had brought as a show of their appreciation for the university's 'new' look.

"It looks like we must be doing something right," the deputy Vice-Chancellor smiled.
"Well, thank God for that. I think we should give the gifts to the members of staff. What do you think?"
"Sounds like a good idea to me," the deputy replied.

Bose and Josie were in a jovial mood when they finally left for home. They had scored top grades in their coursework, which proved that the two weeks of private tutoring had paid off. With these encouraging results, the girls felt confident about their written exams.

They waited until after dinner before saying anything about their results. It was Bose who excitedly broke the news of their coursework, explaining to her parents that both she and Josie had done much better than anticipated.

"So, girls, what are your plans for the three-week holiday," Mr Archibong asked.

Bose and Josie looked at each other and shrugged their shoulders.

"Well Bose, your dad and I were thinking of spending Christmas in Calabar which traditionally means the whole family will be going," Mrs Archibong said. "Margaret is also flying in from Aberdeen, and after talking with her fiancé's family, we decided that we might as well celebrate the traditional wedding ceremony while we are there. In fact, Josie, you can come with us too, unless you have something better to do?"

"No, I definitely have nothing planned; I would love to come, and it will be nice to finally meet Margaret," Josie said excitedly.

The Archibongs had decided to fly rather than drive to Calabar. The tickets were booked such that the family was split into two; Mr Archibong and his daughters, Bose and Margaret were on one flight while his wife, Kathleen, their son Tope, and Josie were on another.

Josie couldn't help but wonder why they weren't all travelling on the same flight and decided to ask Mrs Archibong.

"Auntie Kath, is there any particular reason why we are not all on the same flight?" Josie asked, a puzzled look on her face.

"Not really Josie," Mrs Archibong replied. "Let us just say that it is more of superstition than anything else. I know it sounds a bit ridiculous, but I can assure you that there is nothing to worry about," Mrs Archibong smiled.

Josie didn't exactly understand what Mrs Archibong meant but decided not to think about it.

Unfortunately, both flights were delayed due to bad weather, the harsh harmattan causing disruption to both local and international flights. Initially Mr Archibong thought about getting everyone something to eat, but considering how unreliable the local flights could be, he quickly decided against it.

He was now beginning to regret not driving down, but that was obviously no longer an option. So, they were simply going to have to wait, and wait patiently.

Finally, Chris' flight, which should have departed at eleven in the morning took off at almost four in the afternoon, while Kathleen's departed a whole hour and a half later. By the time they touched down at Calabar Airport they were all tired, hungry and grumpy.

Luckily, they did not have to wait long to pick up their luggage, and since the drivers were waiting outside to drive them home, they all piled into the two waiting vehicles. Surprisingly, there was hardly any traffic on the roads and they arrived at the Archibongs country home within an hour.

As they drove into the compound Josie immediately realised that this house was a lot bigger than the one in Lagos; there were seven massive rooms all of which had en-suite facilities. There was also a three bedroom boys' quarters around the back which housed the drivers and the maids.

Josie was shown to her room, and just as Bose had said, the rooms were enormous, and the decor was lovely. As she lay on her bed staring at the ceiling she felt a tinge of sadness. For the first time in quite a while she actually missed the banter she shared with her mother and younger sisters. Josie decided that once she finished unpacking she would call home. Her thoughts were interrupted by a gentle knock. Josie opened the door and there stood Margaret, Bose's elder sister.

Since arriving from Aberdeen, Margaret hadn't really spoken to Josie but had already taken a liking to her. Without asking any questions, she had treated Josie as part of the family, but now Josie wondered why she was standing outside her door.

"Hi Josie, I know we haven't exactly had a chance to catch up since I arrived so I thought now would be as good a time as ever, if it's okay with you?"
"Definitely," Josie replied.

Josie and Margaret both sat on the bed.

"I'm not sure, but did mum and Bose tell you about the traditional wedding plans?
"Yes, they did." Josie smiled.
"Well, I'm not going to lie, even though it's meant to be lots of fun, it also has the tendency to be very stressful. It is like a week of ceremonial activities which ultimately lead to the traditional wedding itself. Then of course there's the boat regatta, the traditional fattening room experience, the age mate dance and the elders' forum meeting to determine the suitability of my husband to be. In other words, he is going to be initiated into the decision-making forum as an in-law."
Margaret laughed.

Being someone who enjoyed photography, Josie asked Margaret if it was okay for her to take pictures during the various ceremonies.

"That shouldn't be an issue, but I don't think you will be allowed into the elders' forum. It is normally an all-male affair."
"That's okay," Josie replied.
"Anyway, I trust Bose, Tope and my parents have been taking good care of you?" Margaret asked.
"Of course, and to be honest I couldn't have asked for a more hospitable family. You guys are great!"

"Oh, thanks Josie," Margaret blushed. "Well, as part of the family, you have the option of wearing our native ensemble. Of course, the choice is yours; you don't have to if you don't want to. Mum, Bose and I are going to see our seamstress tomorrow, so if you are interested you can tag along."
"I would love that," Josie replied excitedly.

They were still chatting away when Margaret's phone rang; her attention was needed elsewhere.

"Well Josie, I've got to run. It has been nice getting to know you, and by the way dinner is normally served at six," Margaret whispered.
"Thank you, Margaret," Josie whispered back.

The time was already five thirty so she only had a few minutes to get ready. Then out of nowhere Josie was overwhelmed by sadness. She fell to her knees and silently began to weep. If only what happened hadn't happened, she would be living happily with her mum, dad, Bruce and the girls. It dawned on her that even though she was lucky to have come across such a wonderful family, she was still just a stranger in a foreign land. Then Josie, who hadn't prayed in ages said a prayer.

"Dear God, I know I am most likely the last person you want to hear from right now but please heal my wounded spirit and forgive me for running away. I just did not know what else to do. Help me make something of myself in this foreign land. Also, give me the peace of mind to forgive my parents. Lord, I need You now more than ever before," she prayed.

Josie slowly got up, went to the bathroom, washed her face, and changed her top. Then she picked up the phone and called her mum. The phone rang but there was no response. She dialled her mum's number again but still there was no answer. Finally, Josie ran out of patience and was beginning to wish that she hadn't bothered in the first place. Then, just as she was about to leave her room, her phone rang. She picked it up assuming that it was Bose calling her to come downstairs for dinner.

"Hello."

"Hello, Josie." It was her mum.

"Hello mum," Josie replied, pleasantly surprised. "How are you? How is everyone?"

"We are all fine my dear. Sorry I didn't answer when you called earlier; I was in the kitchen and by the time I got to the phone it had stopped ringing. Anyway, how are you, and how are you getting on with your studies?"

"I am fine, mum. I really am. I am living with a wonderful family and they are taking very good care of me. At times they actually remind me of you guys."

"Well, that's good. By the way, your dad spoke to Mr Eastwood the other day. He said he was at your matriculation ceremony and that he had the opportunity to meet the family you are staying with. He also said something about a heated conversation."

"Actually mum, everything is okay now. I had lunch with Mr Eastwood the other day and after explaining everything he admitted that he had made a mountain out of a molehill. He now understands that I do have a plan and that I do not need to be treated like a little child."

"Okay Josie, I will take your word for it."

"Thank you, mum. So, how are dad, Bruce and the girls?"

"Well, your dad travelled to Lichtenstein two days ago for a meeting. He should be back tomorrow. And Bruce took the girls out to watch a movie. So, I am home alone."

Josie could hear the sadness in her mum's voice and she could feel the tears coming to her own eyes.

"Alright mum, I will call again tomorrow and then hopefully

I will be able to speak to everyone. Thanks so much for your prayers and support, it really means a lot to me."

Josie paused for a brief moment.

"Mum, I am so sorry for everything I have put you through; for the sorrow I brought to you and dad. I just pray that I don't let you down."

"It is okay my dear. All I ask is that you let me know if you ever need anything."

"I will mum."

"Anyway, you take good care of yourself and I look forward to speaking with you again tomorrow. I love you."

"I love you too, mum. By the way, are you still having therapy? What have the doctors said about your condition?"

"Yes, I had a therapy appointment the day before yesterday and the prognosis was very positive. Apart from the occasional tiredness, which was because of the treatment anyway, I am fine. In fact, I have been told that now I only need to pop in for regular check-ups. So, there is nothing to worry about."

"Okay mum. I will be praying for you. Please stay strong, we don't want to lose you," Josie was trying hard to hold back her tears.

"It is okay Josie, I am fine, really. I would have told you if I wasn't."

Josie heard footsteps coming up the stairs. She looked at the time; it was half-past six! She hurriedly said goodbye to her mother, dropped the phone and opened her door just as Bose was about to knock.

"I am really sorry."

"It's okay Josie. I just wanted to make sure you were alright."

"Thanks BA."

The girls joined everyone else at the dining table, and as Josie was about to apologise for keeping everyone waiting, Mr Archibong asked her to say the grace. Josie was taken aback by his request. She shut her eyes tight and stuttered through the prayer wondering if this was some kind of punishment for being late for dinner.

Mrs Archibong noticed the bewildered look in Josie's eyes.

"Josie, are you alright? I hope you like your room? Is the air conditioning working?"
"Yes, I am fine auntie Kath. The room is lovely. I must apologise for coming down late. I lost track of time while speaking to my mum. She sends her regards by the way."
"I hope everything is okay back home? I know it is only natural, but I hope that they are not too worried about you?"
"Everything is okay," Josie replied reluctantly.

Josie went on to tell them about the conversation she had with her mum; what Mr Eastwood had told her father about the matriculation day and her having lunch with the Eastwoods. For the first time, she also told them about her mother's health, but assured them that her mum was feeling a lot better.

The Archibongs promised to remember Josie's mum in their prayers. Then the conversation gradually turned to Margaret's upcoming traditional wedding ceremony.

There was a lot of excitement about the ceremony, especially as Margaret was Chris and Kathleen's first-born; their first daughter and the first in the Archibong family to get married. Bose had hinted that no expense would be spared on this ceremony, and from the little she knew about the Archibongs, Josie understood exactly what that meant.

They were expecting quite a few guests at the wedding ceremony, and with three days to go a lot of preparation and attention to detail was required. Canopies had been hired, the food and drinks had been ordered, and accommodation for their guests had been booked. However, the one thing they had no control over was the weather.

They had already experienced its bitter taste when their flights to Calabar were delayed. All they could do was leave it in the hands of God.

To avoid the unpredictable weather situation, Margaret's bridesmaids had decided to drive down rather than risk travelling by air, and they brought along an unexpected but pleasant surprise.

Margaret was told that her other sister Francesca Eyo wouldn't be able to make the ceremony because she was currently sitting her exams, but to Margaret's surprise, as the bridesmaids alighted from their cars, there she was. Margaret ran and gave her sister a great big hug.

"Mum said you couldn't make it," Margaret exclaimed.
"Well, I flew in from the States yesterday evening. I wouldn't miss this for the world," Francesca Eyo giggled.

Margaret suddenly remembered that she hadn't even said hello to her bridesmaids, but they understood. All of Margaret's bridesmaids were her friends; some she grew up with in Lagos while the others were friends she made in Aberdeen. The plan was for all of them to stay in the family house and help make sure that everything ran smoothly.

The Archibong family house was buzzing with excitement as guests trooped in and out of the building. Josie snapped away excitedly taking picture after picture. She had never witnessed anything like this before and she was glad that she had chosen to come to Calabar with the Archibongs. By the time the last guest left they were all shattered, but with the wedding just a day away none of them could rest on their laurels.

Before the day finally came to an end Josie was introduced to Eyo, as she was fondly called. She was only two years older than Bose but came across a lot older, maybe because she only spoke when she was addressed personally. Though she was not as loud as Bose, and appeared to be on the shy side, she was a fiery debater with a passion for politics.

Eyo was the prettiest of the Archibong girls, according to Josie. When she walked she glided like a peacock, an air of quiet confidence surrounding her. She also had a way of tilting her head towards her right shoulder when she spoke. Even though Josie didn't quite know what to make of Eyo, she liked her and funnily enough, they seemed to get on well together.

Unconsciously when Josie got to her room she found herself tilting her head towards her right shoulder and gliding just like Eyo, and even if it wasn't obvious to Josie it was definitely obvious to her friend. As Bose walked into Josie's room she immediately noticed the transformation and couldn't help but laugh.

"What's so funny BA?" Josie asked.
"I'm just wondering why you are walking like that, and what's with the head tilt? Are you trying to imitate my sister?" Bose asked. She was still giggling.
"I do not know what you are talking about," Josie replied, her head still tilted to the right.

Try as she could, Bose couldn't stop laughing, but unknown to her, Josie was beginning to get upset.

"Bose, why are you making fun of me?" she began, "How I choose to walk and talk is no one's business."

Josie turned and left the room slamming the door behind her.

Overnight the skies seemed to clear a little and better weather was forecast for the rest of the week. Flights were landing more frequently and dignitaries arriving for the wedding were picked up from Calabar airport and chauffeured to their respective hotels. And so it was all through the day.

That evening, the eve of the wedding, the heavens opened. To some this was a good omen as the rain was a sign that the wedding day would be peaceful, and it would usher in a fresh, new beginning for the couple.

While it was still raining, Josie had the pleasure of meeting Margaret's husband-to-be, Emmanuel Okezie, for the first time. Emmanuel was accompanied by his brother, who was his best man, and three of his friends. They had all flown in from Lagos that afternoon. At first glance Josie thought the groom-to-be looked like an older version of Tope, Bose's brother, and she wasn't the only one who thought so. Almost everyone who saw him commented on the resemblance.

Emmanuel Okezie who was of Igbo parentage, told them about the day he knew he was going to marry Margaret. He was walking along a particular street in Lagos when he saw some boys playing football on a nearby field. Emmanuel, being an avid football lover had decided to have a kick around with the boys. He got carried away showing off his skills and teaching the youngsters new tricks, and it was only when some of the boys said they had to go home that he realised how late it was.

That was when he noticed a pretty, young lady standing by the fence; she had come to pick up her little brother. There was just something about her that struck a chord in his heart and somehow, he knew that one day they would share something special together. That was four years ago!

One thing led to another, they started talking and eventually became friends. That was when they realised that they were both Aberdeen-bound; Margaret for a Master's Degree and Emmanuel on a posting to an Aberdeen based oil company. While they were in Aberdeen their relationship blossomed and one day Emmanuel found himself on one knee asking Margaret to marry him. The rest was history.

From the little Josie had seen, both Margaret and Emmanuel had different temperaments. Margaret was more of a go-getter, a perfectionist, and though at times she came across as impatient, she had a heart of gold. Emmanuel on the other hand seemed laid back. He preferred to mind his own business and let people be whatever or whoever they chose to be, and he only offered advice when asked. However, one thing was for sure; Margaret and Emmanuel were truly in love!

21

Wedding Bells

*I*t was a beautiful day. The sun was high and there was a cool ocean breeze flowing from the Bight of Biafra. It was the perfect day for a wedding!

Josie had not seen Margaret the day before the wedding and when she enquired, she was told that the bride-to-be was in a secluded place called the fattening room. Apparently, this was a place where she was being pampered, waited upon and fed so that she could, believe it or not, put on some weight. Josie didn't exactly understand the reason why Margaret wanted to put on the extra pounds. She had a lovely, envious, slender figure like her mother and her sisters Bosede and Eyo, but if that's what Margaret wanted, then who was she to question her.

The atmosphere was buzzing and Josie with her manual, compact kodak camera to hand, was looking forward to the ceremony. From around eleven o'clock that morning the in-laws, Emmanuel's folks, started arriving and within half an hour, most of the chairs under the canopies were occupied. All the while, a live band had been playing music in the background.

Suddenly they upped the sound and tempo of the music; the bride's parents had arrived. The Archibongs swayed to the music as they were ushered to their table and once they were seated, the Chairman opened the ceremony with a prayer. He prayed for good weather, and for God to take full control of the ceremony. Finally, he prayed that God would bless the new couple with His love, wisdom and understanding, and fill their quiver with many sons and daughters. There was a resounding "Amen". Then the chairman handed the microphone to the emcee, who was a friend of the groom.

The emcee was a funny chap and the jokes rolled off his tongue with ease. He told the story of how the couple had met on a football field and then joked that their first son would therefore naturally be more famous than David Beckham. The guests clapped and burst out laughing. After cracking a few more jokes some of which received a standing ovation, it was finally time to introduce the bride and groom.

The band started playing high tempo music as the bridesmaids and groomsmen danced joyfully to their seats. Then the emcee ushered in the groom. Emmanuel and his brother came out dancing and after showing off a few choice steps they took their seats and waited for the beautiful bride.

The emcee's voice boomed out over the microphone as he announced the arrival of the bride. The band reacted by playing a tune that brought the guests to their feet. Then Margaret appeared. "She looks stunning," Josie thought. The people clapped and danced along with her until she was handed a cup filled with wine. The tradition was for Margaret to carry the glass of wine to her husband-to-be, bypassing every other young man along the way.

Eventually, when she finally managed to get through the crowd of men, she saw a handsome young man seated, grinning from ear to ear. She knelt down and handed the glass of wine to her fiancé. Emmanuel took a sip then gave the rest back to Margaret, and to the joy and amusement of the guests, helped his wife-to-be to her feet.

Then both Emmanuel and Margaret made their way to where the family head, the elders and Margaret's father, were seated and knelt down. One by one, the elders blessed and prayed for the couple according to the rites and traditions of the family.

The Archibongs originated from the Mbiabong family of Duke Town in Calabar and the family tradition was that the bride's first dance would be with the family head. After this rite of recognition had been performed, the emcee announced that a buffet had been prepared and that the guests at each table would be directed by the waiters in an orderly manner.

Josie was hungry and thankfully, as she was seated with the Archibongs, a designated waiter brought food to the table. As she looked around she struggled to remember the last time she had seen so much food and drink in one place; maybe because it was a sight she had never seen before. There was just so much of it. The guests were milling around either talking and getting reacquainted with those they had lost touch with or making new friends and exchanging details.

Once everyone was seated the speeches started flowing. Josie concluded that Nigerians simply could not be rushed. It seemed to her that everyone had something to say, but no one was in any hurry to say it; each person spoke as if they had all the time in the world. Thankfully, after a while, the emcee started hurrying up the speakers reminding them that some of the guests had travelled some distance and because of the dangers associated with travelling at night compounded by the state of the roads, it would be expedient to round things up at a reasonable time.

There was some more singing and dancing before the fathers of the bride and groom, Mr Chris Archibong and Dr Emmanuel Okezie Senior, asked for everyone's attention. After exchanging pleasantries, they spoke about how both families had hit it off from the very beginning and how they were grateful for the union of their children. They both warned the couple against entertaining strange women or men as such people only brought untold problems and prayed that both Margaret and Emmanuel would associate themselves with the right people and seek the face of God at all times.

Once the prayers from both parents were concluded, Emmanuel thanked everyone who had gone out of their way to make their day so special. Then, turning to his father-in-law, he promised not to let the Archibong family down, and that with all he had within him he would look after their daughter; his special friend! Once again Emmanuel turned to the guests and told them that their church wedding would take place in Dubai, three months from that day. There was a gasp from some of the guests as the announcement took them by surprise.

After Emmanuel's vote of thanks, Margaret was handed over to the Okezie family as traditionally this was seen as the real wedding; a time when both families acknowledged each other, sampled each other's cuisines and traditions, and forged an eternal connection as both families became as one.

Bosede and Mrs Archibong found it hard to hold back the tears when the time finally came for Margaret to leave with her in-laws. The Archibongs were very close and watching Margaret go felt like they were losing a member of the family. As Margaret consoled her family she reminded her mum of how she had always prayed that her first daughter would get married before the age of twenty-six.

"Well mum, you are witnessing an answer to your prayer."
"I guess so," her mum smiled as she dabbed away the tears from her eyes.

Margaret hugged her family one last time while the driver placed her suitcases in the car that would soon take her and Emmanuel to the airport to catch their Lagos flight. Margaret's returning to Lagos with her in-laws was simply to signify that she had been handed over to the Okezie family. However, as they were yet to have the church blessing, the couple had decided not to live together just yet. Instead, as soon they arrived in Lagos, Margaret would stay in Ikeja GRA with Emmanuel's parents, while Emmanuel would stay with one of his friends in the Festac Area of Lagos.

The Archibongs planned to return home after the Christmas celebrations. They had never stayed in their Calabar country home for the New Year because they always attended the New Year crossover service at their local church in Lagos.

The time in Calabar seemed to go by so quickly; a bit too quick for Josie who was only just beginning to enjoy her stay. On Christmas day, lots of family members and friends came to pay their respects to the Archibongs, and also exchanged gifts. If nothing else, Josie was glad that she came and thanked Bosede's family repeatedly for inviting her.

"Thank you, thank you, thank you so much for inviting me on this trip. I have really enjoyed myself," Josie exclaimed.

Kathleen couldn't help but laugh as she watched Josie.

"Josie, I am happy that you have had so much fun. To be honest, with all that has been going on I wasn't too sure you would. I hope you know that you are a part of this family and hopefully one day, we will meet your family in England," Kathleen said.
"The wedding was lovely, and now I can hardly wait for the one in Dubai," Josie giggled. "By the way, I spoke with my parents and my siblings. I just wanted to wish them all a Merry Christmas, but we spoke for a while and I am so glad we did." Josie's head dropped. "I believe that my coming to Nigeria was all part of God's plan. He has given me another chance and I have my friend Bose to thank for that. The last few years have been hard, but now I think I can actually say that I have forgiven my parents, and more importantly I

believe I am ready to move on."

"I am so glad to hear that you have made up with your family. You have made a very wise decision and I believe that from now on the joy you feel inside will be real. Well done my dear."

Kathleen Archibong then told Josie that they would be leaving for Lagos the day after. However, this time around, while everyone else flew home, Kathleen would be travelling by road because she wanted to buy some food items along the way. Seeing that Josie was looking confused, she explained that food items were usually a lot cheaper when bought from the mini markets along the route than in the city markets, especially when buying in bulk.

On departure day, while everyone was still fast asleep, Kathleen Archibong, her maids and one of the drivers set off on their journey back to Lagos. The other driver would follow on later after dropping the rest of the family at the airport.

As there was hardly any traffic on the road, Kathleen got to the Onitsha end of the Niger Bridge in Anambra State before ten that morning. From there they travelled until they got to the small village of Umunede in Delta State where they stopped to buy food items like garri, yam, coconuts, snails and palm oil. They then continued on to Benin city where they stopped to buy fruits and vegetables. This also gave them another opportunity to stretch their legs, fill the car with petrol and grab a bite to eat. They eventually left Benin City at about one in the afternoon and because the road between there and Ore town in Ondo State had just been tarred, the drive was smooth and uninterrupted.

However, things were quite different when they started the last leg of their journey. The stretch of road between Ore and Lagos had been badly maintained, but even though it had potholes all over the place the driver carefully navigated his way through to make the ride as comfortable as possible.

They finally made it on to the Lagos-Ibadan expressway just before three that afternoon and entered what one would call the war zone of crazy driving. On this road, drivers threw patience out of the window and all caution to the wind. This road, though designed with three lanes, was usually turned into six as drivers of lorries, trucks, vans and cars drove as if they did not have a care in the world. But then considering that most of them did not have a driving licence, it wasn't that much of a surprise. What made matters worse was that some of the vehicles were not even roadworthy; faulty brakes, worn out tyres, and as long as their palms were sufficiently greased by the violators, the vehicle inspection officers simply turned a blind eye.

But apart from the faulty vehicles without insurance, the spate of accidents was caused by a lack of road maintenance.

It was a few minutes past five and after weaving through the crazy Lagos traffic, Mrs Archibong finally drove up the driveway to her Victoria Island home. To her surprise her husband and the girls were just carrying their cases from the car which made her assume that they had only just arrived. When she asked Eyo what took them so long, she told her mum that they ran into heavy traffic after they left the airport.

Kathleen smiled, looked heavenwards and thanked God for bringing the family home safely.

Family Affairs

The new year was now almost a week old and things were getting back to normal in the Archibong household. It was Bose and Josie's first day back at university while Margaret and Eyo were flying back to Aberdeen and California respectively to resume their studies.

Tope, their little brother was off to Abuja to start his first year in sixth form at St Ignatius of Loyola School, one of the best schools in the Federal Capital. Chris and Kathleen both believed that Catholic schools were more disciplined than private or missionary schools and Tope, being their only son needed that boarding school discipline; something they knew he would never get if he stayed in a school near home.

Normally, while all their other children were studying overseas, Tope was the one who always lent his parents a helping hand, so they were going to miss him, but with Bose gaining admission to the University of Lagos the onus was now squarely on her. But Bose did not really mind; she was more than willing to help, and with Josie around she was sure they would cope.

Of all the Archibong children, Eyo was the most interesting. It was always difficult to tell what was on her mind. She just seemed to live in her own little world. However, like her siblings, she was very brilliant and she hardly ever got into trouble. This was Eyo's final year, and if Chris and Kathleen had their way, their daughter would either be returning to Nigeria or staying with her sister in Aberdeen.

It was also Mrs Archibong's first day back at work. On her way to the office she made a slight detour to her shop just to check up on her shop assistants and confirm that the shop was open and ready for business.

When she finally got to work she spent almost half an hour greeting her colleagues before opening the glass door to her office and sitting behind her neatly set table. As she scrolled through her emails her mind went back to the traditional wedding ceremony. It brought a smile to her face. Then she remembered her father's family.

Surprisingly none of them came for the traditional wedding even though she had personally given them an invitation. She thought she could at least vouch for auntie Aduke, her father's younger sister. They were very close, so for Kathleen not to hear from her was odd. She decided that she would travel to Ibadan to see them, and as the working day drew to a close Kathleen made preparations for her trip next day. But, it was not to be.

That evening when she came back from work, she was told that her auntie Aduke was waiting for her in the lounge. Kathleen had an uneasy feeling inside. "I hope everything is okay," she whispered to herself.

> "Good evening auntie Aduke," Kathleen greeted with a traditional bow of the knee. "I hope all is well? I had actually made arrangements for tomorrow to come and visit you in Ibadan; I thought that no one showing up for Margaret's wedding was rather odd."

Auntie Aduke sighed. Kathleen saw the deep lines around her auntie's eyes and wondered what was going on. She waited for her to speak, and when she did, the tears fell unhindered from her eyes.

> "It is my husband, Dapo. He has been diagnosed with

aggressive prostate cancer and has been given less than three months to live."

Kathleen jumped up, ran over to her aunt and hugged her, crying at the same time. Uncle Dapo was such a nice man; he had always been good and loving to them, and he never forgot about her mother. This news was heart-breaking.

She remembered the part that uncle Dapo had played in reconciling her mother with her father's younger brother. She remembered how he scolded him and reminded him of all the good her father had done for the family; how he had helped them with admission into schools in the United Kingdom, as well as paid their tuition fees when they couldn't afford to. Uncle Dapo then told her father's younger brother to apologise to her mum.

"Is there nothing that can be done? At least we should get a second opinion, if necessary outside the country?"
"Well, his company has been informed, and due to his position within the firm, they are willing to cover the costs to send him to America for a proper check-up. They have also agreed to cover operation costs if necessary. I just hope we haven't left it too late," Aduke shook her head.
"Don't give up auntie. Have any arrangements been made?"
"They have contacted the hospital in the States and should be flying him out within the next two weeks. I thought I should come and tell you personally so that you would know the reason why we did not show up for Margaret's wedding. Also, I was hoping Dapo and I could stay with you for a day or two to sort out my visa, before flying out to the States?"
"Of course, auntie, you are more than welcome. I will get the ground floor en-suite bedroom ready as soon as possible. At least that will remove the need to use the stairs."

Kathleen paused and looked at her aunt. The poor woman must be hungry, she thought.

"Auntie, let me get you something to eat."
"Thank you, Kathleen."

As Kathleen walked to the kitchen all kinds of thoughts crossed her mind. She had tried not to look too bothered, but deep down inside she knew that prostate cancer was a deadly disease, especially if it wasn't diagnosed on time. Another thought that weighed heavily on her mind was how to break this worrying news to her mother and her siblings.

Telling her brother and sister would be difficult but pretty straightforward. However, she wasn't sure how her mother would take this devastating news considering the close relationship she shared with uncle Dapo. As Kathleen rustled up something for auntie Aduke to eat she decided that she would run it by Chris; maybe he could proffer a solution or at least offer some much-needed advice.

Chris came back from work while the two ladies were eating at the dining table. As soon as he saw Aduke he knew something was wrong, but he resisted the urge to ask any questions. Instead he smiled, greeted both of them then excused himself as he needed to make an important phone call.

Later on, after auntie Aduke had retired to bed, Kathleen broke the sad news to her husband. Chris could not believe his ears. He knew something was wrong but that his good friend Dapo had been diagnosed with prostate cancer and had less than three months to live, was the last thing he expected to hear.

"How could this happen to such a good man," Chris asked himself as he shook his head.
"Chris, if you don't mind, I would like to travel to Ibadan with auntie Aduke tomorrow."
"That is fine with me," her husband replied. "We may have

driver situation though. Fred is taking the girls to school, and Mohammed called in sick today so most likely he will not be in tomorrow."

"Maybe I should call Segun and see if I can hire his taxi service for the day."

"That is an option, but I'm not too sure he will be available at such short notice."

"Well, I guess there is only one way to find out."

Kathleen picked up the phone and called Segun. He had helped them in the past, and apart from being an experienced driver he was also a very polite and honest young man. So, unsurprisingly there was a high demand for his services, but as fate would have it, he just happened to be available. Once again Kathleen apologised for calling so late in the evening and thanked him immensely before hanging up. Then she turned to Chris, and as if he hadn't heard a word of her conversation, told him that Segun had agreed to drive her to Ibadan and back.

The next morning, as agreed, Segun arrived at the Archibong residence at half past seven on the dot. Kathleen and Chris had decided that if she was to spend some quality time with her uncle and aunt, and since she only worked three days a week anyway, she might as well take the rest of the week off.

So, Kathleen called her office and left a message to let them know that she would be away for the rest of the week due to a family emergency.

Kathleen and auntie Aduke left Lagos at exactly nine that morning. The journey was going well until they approached the dreaded Oworonsoki bypass. Once again there was an accident at the bypass which as usual had affected most surrounding routes. The trail of traffic was horrendous and the ladies found themselves caught up in it for close to three hours.

When they finally managed to make their way through the Oworonsoki traffic, the rest of the journey was quite smooth and they were able to get to the city of Ibadan before the rush hour started. By the time they eventually got to auntie's house they were tired, hot and sticky partly because the air conditioning in the hired cab had failed and also because a journey that should have taken no more than two hours had taken close to six.

Kathleen was taken aback by the gaunt appearance of her aunt's husband but she just about managed to stifle her emotions so as not to break down. She walked over to where uncle Dapo sat and gave him a big, warm hug. After exchanging pleasantries and asking after her husband and the children, Dapo jokingly enquired after the *oyinbo*[3] girl and how she was getting on.

In between their conversation Kathleen noticed how he coughed and gasped for air, a sight that was quite terrifying. Kathleen assumed that this was one of the side effects of the illness and so as not to create too much of a fuss, she decided that she would talk to auntie Aduke about it when both of them were alone. Also, uncle Dapo no longer had an appetite for food. He hardly ate anything, and the little he did eat he eventually threw up. So, auntie Aduke made sure that he was taking in a lot of fluids.

Watching all this was a terrible experience for Kathleen who had known this man since she was little. She called Chris and told him about the condition uncle Dapo was in and how she didn't feel comfortable leaving the couple here on their own.

"Do whatever you think is right dear. The girls and I will be fine. By the way, Bose and Josie are home tomorrow because their university is being used as a polling station for the elections."
"Which election is this?" Kathleen asked.

---

[3] *A word generally used in Nigerian Pidgin, Igbo and Yoruba to refer to Caucasians*

"I am not sure if you remember, but the senator representing that part of Lagos mainland died about three months ago. Hence the by-election, to elect a replacement."

"O yes, I remember."

Kathleen eventually told her husband that she would be back on Sunday. Hopefully by then she would have ascertained the full extent of uncle Dapo's illness.

She had also planned to convince the couple to come to Lagos with her but uncle Dapo promptly turned down the offer as he and his wife did not want to be a burden. Kathleen tried all she could to persuade them highlighting all the advantages and benefits she could come up with but her words fell on deaf ears. The couple had decided to stay put until Thursday, less than seventy-two hours before they were scheduled to fly out.

So, on Sunday morning Kathleen left Ibadan alone but at least she had an assurance that uncle Dapo was not going to die anytime soon. Unlike the journey to Ibadan, the traffic on the way back to Lagos was quite mild and Segun, the cab driver dropped her at home before noon.

Throughout the week following her Ibadan trip, Kathleen was not her usual cheerful self. She seemed to withdraw into a shell, and she stayed that way until the morning the Akinwales arrived. After helping them settle in, Kathleen accompanied auntie Aduke to the American Embassy to pick up her passport before going to Prince Ebeano supermarket in Lekki to buy some items that the Akinwales would need in America. She also took the opportunity to call her siblings, Samantha and Jeff, and her mother. Kathleen was relieved when she did not get through to her siblings and conveniently left them voice messages. However, when her mother picked up the phone she knew that dreaded moment was upon her.

Just like she thought her mother was totally distraught when she told her about uncle Dapo and said she would be in Nigeria as soon as possible. Even when auntie Aduke told her that she and Dapo would be travelling to the States within the next forty-eight hours she still insisted on coming to Nigeria, even if it meant spending some quality time with the other members of her husband's family.

Mr Akinwale's condition seemed to have improved since Sunday. Apart from his gaunt look, his wits and sense of humour had not left him and he teased both Bose and Josie non-stop, calling them *aje butter pikin*[4]. This left Josie looking bemused, but once Bose interpreted the phrase they both burst out laughing. Then Josie in her feigned Nigerian accent replied, "Ah uncle, no be so o. Me I no be butter pikin o!"

Two days later, the Akinwales left for the States. Sadly, that was the last time any of them would see uncle Dapo as he died within the first week of their arrival in America. He passed away in the presence of his wife and son who was resident there.

It was a very dark and mournful time in the Archibong household, especially for Kathleen. She thought uncle Dapo at least had three months, and with the surgery, maybe a bit longer. But to hear that he was dead; it was a bitter pill to swallow.

Kathleen's siblings and her mother, Irene arrived in Lagos a few days after uncle Dapo died. They would have preferred to have been reunited under different circumstances but here they were comforting each other over the loss of their dearly beloved uncle.

Samantha, Jeff and Kathleen had been watching their mother and how she had surprisingly managed to hold herself together. However, they knew that sooner or later she would need a shoulder to cry on and they intended to be there for her. So, when out of the blue she said she was going to Ibadan to help with the funeral arrangements, Samantha immediately offered to go with her.

---

[4] *A phrase used generally in Nigeria to refer to a wealthy or spoilt child*

Initially Irene quite adamantly said that she wanted to go alone, but she eventually gave in when she realised that her daughter wasn't budging.

While they were in Ibadan Kathleen called to let them know that they were in the process of transporting uncle Dapo's corpse back to Nigeria and if all went according to plan their flight from the States would touchdown in Lagos in three days' time.

As expected, uncle Dapo's corpse arrived in Lagos accompanied by his wife and their son and was taken to Ibadan where the funeral was planned to take place. Five days later, after Dapo Akinwale's body had been interred, the Archibongs returned to Lagos along with Kathleen's siblings, while their mother opted to stay in Ibadan to keep her sister in law company.

That night before they all went to bed, Kathleen accosted Samantha and Jeff asking them why they did not show up for their niece's traditional wedding despite being aware of it well ahead of time. "At least out of courtesy they could have told me that they weren't going to make it," she thought.

> "Kath," Samantha looked apologetic, "I am so sorry if you still feel bad about my absence, but I did say that there was a possibility I would not be there. My husband insisted that we go to Lokoja because he wanted to inform his friends and family that he was planning to enter the gubernatorial race for Kogi State. My hands were tied; I really couldn't do anything about it. How did it go anyway? I am sure it went well."
>
> "Yes, it went very well actually," Kathleen replied bluntly. Then she turned to Jeff. "And what happened to you because I don't recall you telling me that you wouldn't be able to make it?"

Jeff's head dropped.

"Kath, there is something I have not told either you or Samantha; my marriage with Olivia is over!"

"What!" the sisters chorused.

"Yes, it is over. When I told mum before we left London she said she wasn't exactly surprised. Apparently, she had seen the writing on the wall for quite some time. I guess I was stupid not to listen to the advice you guys gave me."

The brief silence was broken by Kathleen.

"So, what happens to the children?"

"Well, we are not quite sure yet, but in the meantime, I have decided to relocate back to Nigeria. The children will stay with their mum until they complete their university education, which hopefully should be sometime next year. Then maybe they will come over here and do their National Youth Service."

"I don't know what to say," Samantha replied. "But this will surely affect both girls considering that their loyalties will most likely be divided between you and Olivia".

"Well, I guess so, but there isn't much we can do about that now."

Then he looked at his younger sister.

"So, Kath that's the reason why I couldn't make it to the wedding."

"I understand Jeff," the shock still evident on her face.

"By the way, when is the Church wedding and where is it taking place?" Jeff asked.

"The couple has chosen to tie the knot in Dubai, during the Easter period," Kathleen replied.

"Wow! that is actually less than three months away. God willing, I will be there. Maybe I can even bring the girls with me; they should be on holiday then. Anyway, let's see how it goes."

As a lecturer at the University of Abuja, Samantha could not afford to stay any longer and had booked a seat on the first Abuja flight out of Lagos. She bade everyone good night and went to bed hoping to get a good night's sleep. Jeff who himself wanted to see some of his former colleagues in Abuja, had decided to travel with his sister, and from there maybe fly back to London.

Meanwhile, both Josie and Bose planned to hit the ground running regarding their lectures. These had been interrupted because of uncle Dapo's funeral, but now that they had said their farewells to the good uncle, it was time to resume their studies with renewed vigour.

Cotonou

The last couple of years had really gone well for Josie. To a certain extent she had reconciled with her family especially with her mum and her siblings, but her father still did not approve of the path his daughter's life had taken and constantly made this clear whenever she spoke to him over the phone. She had stayed in touch with the Eastwoods mostly to keep her dad happy and also because, after getting to know them, they were actually a very nice family.

Josie recalled Margaret and Emmanuel's wedding in Dubai and how chuffed she had felt when Margaret asked her to be one of her bridesmaids. They spent four days in Dubai. The weather was extremely hot, and though it was a lot of fun, everyone was glad that the wedding was taking place indoors where the cool air from the air conditioner was truly refreshing.

All in all, it was a lovely, enjoyable holiday for everyone; the family members, the couple's friends from Aberdeen, and the bridesmaids and groomsmen who, going by all the teasing and flirting that went on between them, seemed to enjoy each other's company very much. She remembered everyone being exhausted when they finally got back to Lagos and how they spent the days that followed lazing around.

It was now Josie's fourth year in Nigeria and she was looking forward to July; the month when she would finally complete her Bachelor's Degree programme. For now, however they had just resumed lectures and her focus was on preparing for her mock examinations.

Everything seemed to be going pretty well until that fateful day, February twenty third to be precise, when without any warning the Academic Staff Union of Universities (ASUU), issued the Federal Government an ultimatum to meet their demand for higher wages. ASUU had been in protracted negotiations with the Government for some time but as it seemed the government had no regard for their grievances, they had decided to give the government, represented by the Minister of Education who himself used to be an ASUU member, a two-week ultimatum.

If their demands were not met within the requested time period they would embark on an indefinite strike. As students read the ASUU posters pasted on notice boards across the campus, there was a palpable fear of the unknown. Going by what had happened in the past, whenever the Academic staff went on strike it often took about six months for them to call it off. This often led to students being pushed into circumstances that were not of their own making.

When the girls got home that day they sadly informed Bose's dad about the situation that was about to erupt within the university. Mr Archibong could hear the uncertainty in their voices and he knew that considering they were meant to wrap up their degrees in July, they were afraid of what would happen if the lecturers were to go ahead with the strike. Even though he was concerned about his daughter, Chris was beginning to wonder what was going through Josie's mind.

Josie had endured electricity fluctuations, horrendous traffic and the ever worsening condition of the roads, and she always seemed to make light of the constant disorganisation she witnessed. But if this strike went ahead, would it be the last straw that would break the camel's back?

Bose's dad was still in a despondent mood when his wife came back from her boutique. She could sense there was something on her husband's mind.

"What is the matter dear?"
"I am not too sure if you heard, but the girls told me that ASUU has issued the government a two-week ultimatum to meet their demands, and if they don't they plan to strike indefinitely."
"That is news to me. I thought both parties were going to settle this issue amicably."
"I really hope they do settle this because I am concerned about Josie. Her mind is set on finishing her degree programme in July, so if the lecturers go ahead with the strike how do you think she will take it? What are we going to do?"

It was not every day that Kathleen saw her husband in a state of panic. She could see that he was genuinely bothered and wondered what to do to allay his concerns.

"Do you remember how Cynthia, auntie Aduke's daughter moved to the Republic of Benin during the last six-month ASUU strike?

Chris nodded.

"Well, while she was there she learnt how to speak French and that helped get her a job with Total, the oil and gas company. If the strike does go ahead we could encourage the girls to do something similar. What do you think?"

Chris wasn't convinced.

"Dear, it is easy for us to do that for our own child, but I am not sure about Josie."
"I am not suggesting that we force her into doing something

she doesn't want to do. Look, Josie is twenty-two years old, she can choose to do whatever she wants. She may have other plans, but one thing I know is that she will not want to return to England without her degree."

"Well, that is true."

"Who knows, maybe ASUU and the government might come to some sort of agreement," a tinge of hope in Kathleen's voice.

"Are you for real!" Chris exclaimed. "When was the last time the Federal Government actually listened to the demands of any union? Never! And I do not think they will start anytime soon"

"All I am saying is, let us wait and see. It just might be a storm in a teacup!"

Two weeks later, their fears became a reality. The government chose not to meet ASUU's demands and the lecturers in all the Federal Universities in the country downed tools and started an indefinite strike. The Archibongs were not exactly caught off guard. Even though they prayed and hoped it wouldn't happen, they had already discussed the various options with Bose and Josie should the strike go ahead. The girls had jumped at the idea of doing a French course in the Republic of Benin, and now that the strike was confirmed they were both excited about the adventure that lay ahead.

Mr Archibong had already advised Josie that if the strike went ahead she would have to inform Mr Eastwood of her plans. So, as Josie made her way to the British High Commission Office reception desk, that is exactly what she planned to do.

When Josie asked for Mr Eastwood, she was told that he had just left for Abuja but should be back the following day and suggested that she could come and see him tomorrow afternoon. Josie was torn in two minds; to leave for the Benin Republic and entreat Mrs

Archibong to tell him on her behalf, or to simply come back the next day. However, considering that Mr Eastwood had constantly shown care and concern for her well-being during her stay in Nigeria, she decided that it was only polite for her to tell him herself.

As she was just about to leave the High Commission premises, to her surprise and delight, Mr Eastwood drove in. Apparently, he had forgotten an important document that he needed for his meeting with the High Commissioner in Abuja. He was surprised to see Josie and immediately thought that maybe she needed his assistance. He of course had heard about the university closure but having been in Nigeria for a while it was nothing new.

"Hello Josie, what are you doing here?"
"Hello Mr Eastwood, actually I came to see you, but I was told that you had just left for Abuja."
"Well, I was on my way when I remembered that I had forgotten something in the office. Do you need to see me urgently or can it wait until tomorrow because I am in a bit of a hurry?"
"I guess you have heard about the latest ASUU strike? Well, I just came to tell you that instead of sitting around waiting for them to call off their strike, I have enrolled for a French language course at the Ecole Professionnelle Specialisee la-cite University in Cotonou for the duration of the strike. I have always wanted to learn French and I think this would be the perfect opportunity to fulfil my French-speaking dream."

James Eastwood looked surprised but just about managed a smile.

"Well, what can I say? You are indeed your father's child. This is the sort of thing your father would have done; he never allowed a chance to excel pass him by. Have you told your parents?"

"No, not yet. But that's partly why I came to see you. We both know what my parents, especially my dad, will say if I tell them. I was hoping you could inform them on my behalf and also let them know that you gave the idea your stamp of approval. However, maybe we should leave out the part about university lecturers being on strike."

"By the way, are you and the Archibong girl going together?"

"Yes," Josie replied.

"I thought as much. So, was this an Archibong idea or yours? Come to think of it, it must have been theirs because how would you have known about the university in Cotonou?"

Josie was quiet. James continued.

"So, where are you going to stay, and how are you going to manage financially? Oh, don't tell me; everything is being taken care of by the Archibongs, right?!"

Mr Eastwood's words lacked diplomacy and tact, and Josie did not appreciate his sarcasm towards the Archibongs. She had already turned to walk away before it dawned on James that he may have hurt her feelings. To be fair, this family, though not connected to Josie in any way had treated her like family. So, there was really no need for him to be sarcastic. Maybe in some way he was jealous of the Archibongs because they had succeeded where he had failed.

"Josie, stop," James said in a little more than a whisper.

He gently pulled her back and apologised for his hurtful words. He also promised to speak to her parents and assure them that she was in good hands.

By the time Josie got back home it was past noon. She ran upstairs to finish packing what she needed for the Cotonou trip. Unsurprisingly, Bose was also going through her checklist, making sure that she hadn't forgotten anything. The girls planned to go to bed nice and early so that they would be ready to leave first thing in the morning. Hopefully leaving early would help avoid the traffic that usually built up around the Festac area on the way to Badagry.

Since Mohammed was going to drive them to Cotonou, Mr Archibong had asked him to spend the night at the family residence to make sure they left on time. Mohammed didn't bother arguing; he knew that his boss was a stickler for time.

Apart from a few potholes on the expressway, the journey to Cotonou was a pleasant one thanks to Mohammed's skilful driving. Bose and Josie could not hide their excitement; from the way they chatted and giggled during the journey it was obvious that they had high hopes for the adventure ahead. Apart from learning a new language there was also the prospect of exploring this ancient nation and visiting its rich capital, Porto-Novo.

Bose's mother had arranged everything including a student visa for Josie, something her daughter didn't need because she held an ECOWAS passport. Mohammed drove straight to the apartment which had been rented for the girls and while they settled in, Bose's father went to the Ecole Professionnelle Specialisee la-cite University Admissions office to sort out their tuition and all the other expenses for the next six months, hoping that the strike would be over by then. Even though he tried to hide it from his wife and daughter, Mr Archibong was still very anxious. He felt a heavy responsibility for Josie and prayed and hoped that no harm would come to her.

Mr Archibong booked himself and Mohammed into a nearby hotel, and later on that evening, he took Bose and Josie out for dinner where he advised them to concentrate on their studies and to mind the company they keep. After dinner, Mr Archibong dropped the girls off at their apartment, and once he was satisfied that all the doors were securely locked, he and Mohammed returned to their hotel.

As arranged the night before, Mr Archibong picked the girls up in the morning and dropped them at the university for their first French lesson before making his way back to Lagos. During the class the lecturer introduced Josie and Bose. Being the only white girl in the class, Josie knew that all eyes were on her; she could sense it. But she planned to enjoy and excel in this French course even if their gawking eyes stuck to her like glue.

After the lecture, as Josie and Bose walked out of the classroom, they overheard a few of the students whispering and were intrigued to find out that some of the girls who had been starring at Josie were actually nervous because it was their first day too. Then they bumped into two sisters who just happened to be students at the University of Lagos. Just like Josie and Bose, their parents had enrolled them immediately the ASUU strike was confirmed. All four girls hit it off immediately which came as a bit of a surprise to Josie because she knew Bose was quite reserved. However, she soon found out that the sisters' older brother used to be Eyo's boyfriend.

Over the following months Bose's parents visited them a couple of times and Josie even received a surprise call from Mr Eastwood. He asked after her welfare and how she was getting on with the French course. She was happy to tell him that after a few months of intensive learning she was confident with her oral and written French, and that being in a country where they actually spoke the language had helped a lot. Mr Eastwood assured her that he had not told her parents about the strike or the fact that she was in another country altogether to which Josie thanked him and promised not to let him or her parents down.

Time flew by and before they knew it the girls were preparing for exams. They had already spent more than five months in Cotonou yet there was still no resolution to the ongoing ASUU dispute. Interestingly, this did not bother Josie that much. She was really enjoying her French lessons and was already toying with the idea of taking on a French degree at the university if the ASUU strike went on indefinitely.

After all the hard work that Josie and Bose had put in, it came as no surprise that they topped their class. As if it had all been planned, the very day they received their results, was also the day an agreement was reached between the lecturers and the Federal Government to call off the strike.

To mark the end of the course, a formal party, to which all parents and guardians were invited, had been organised. During this party students were to be presented with their certificates and various awards would be given out. Only Bose's mum was able to attend the party as her dad was tied up in the office.

The party was well underway when Josie excused herself as she needed to use the ladies room. But just as she was about to open the door to the toilet she saw someone who looked like Peter Rowe, her brother's friend. At first, she thought she was seeing things, but as he and the young man he was talking to drew closer, she confirmed that it was him.

Realising that Peter had not seen her, she quickly opened the toilet door and hurried in, her heart beating rapidly. From what Bruce had told her Peter was meant to be studying for his PhD at the Warwick University, so what was he doing here of all places? She wondered.

After using the toilet and making sure that the coast was clear, she scurried back to the party hall and walked over to where Bose and her other classmates were standing. Then she turned to Bose and asked if she was aware of any other event taking place at the university.

"Why?" Bose noticed that Josie was looking shaken. "What's the matter, Josie?"

Before Josie could articulate a response, the Dean of Foreign Studies cleared his throat and spoke into the microphone.

"Bonjour Mesdames et Messieurs. Good day Ladies and gentlemen, may I have your attention please. Apart from saying thank you to our outgoing students, we also have with us some students from the University of Warwick in the United Kingdom who are here as part of our ongoing University exchange programme. We would like to use this opportunity to show our appreciation and gratitude to them for taking out two months to sit and study with our Engineering students."

The Dean waited for the applause to die down before continuing.

"We look forward to this time next year when some of our students from the Faculty of Engineering will also be going over to Warwick."

There was a massive uproar when the Dean mentioned this as some of the students wanted to know why the exchange programme was limited to engineering students. But Josie didn't really care about that. For her, the Dean's speech had answered the question that was on her mind.

"So that's the reason why Peter is here," Josie hadn't realised that she was speaking out loud.
"What are you talking about? Who is Peter?" Bose asked.

"BA, please I need your help. One of the students on the exchange programme happens to be my brother's friend. I saw him on my way to the ladies, but fortunately he didn't see me. If he finds out that I am here he will tell my family and we both know what will happen next."

All this time Bose's mum had been engaged in a conversation with a friend whose daughter was also in the French class, but she somehow overheard Josie's last statement. She turned to Josie.

"Josie, is everything okay?"
"Everything is okay, mum," Bose replied.

At first, Mrs Archibong looked a bit confused wondering why her daughter had answered when she was actually talking to Josie, but then her friend dragged her back into their conversation.

"Phew! That was close," Bose whispered. "But Josie, what happens when they call your name during the certificate presentation ceremony?"
"Well, that is where you come in BA. I need you to help me distract those young Warwick men. You know what I mean," Josie winked.
"Eh, what exactly do you mean by 'distract'? I don't even know them."
"Oh, come on BA. I need your help. Please!"
"Why does this feel like déjà vu?" Bose wasn't too happy with the situation, but she had to help her friend. "Alright, but you're going to have to point him out because there are close to twenty-five of them in that corner."

Josie pointed Peter out to Bose.

"So, what exactly do you want me to do again?"
"Anything! I don't really care. I just need you to make sure that he doesn't hear my name when the Dean calls me out"

"Okay, I will try my best."

About ten minutes later, after the necessary protocols had been observed, the Dean began to call out the names of the students receiving certificates starting with those who studied English as a foreign language. From there, he went on to call out their French counterparts; Josie and Bose's class.

Bose's name was called the first time, then a second but she was nowhere to be found. Her mother asked Josie if she knew where her daughter was, but Josie feigned ignorance. When Bose's name was called a third time Mrs Archibong stepped forward and apologetically collected the certificate on behalf of her daughter.

Meanwhile, Bose had moved surreptitiously to where the Warwick students were standing. Then she started a conversation with one of their female students pretending to want to know more about the University and when they would be going back. As she did this, she also listened out for the names being called out. When Bose heard the Dean call out the name before Josie's she made a sudden lunge towards Peter Rowe.

Both Bose and Peter fell to the ground and before anyone could offer any help Bose jumped up and proffered an apology to him. Everyone including Peter assumed she was drunk and flashed pitiful glances at her. Bose felt so embarrassed but she had to play it out. "I'm going to kill that friend of mine," she thought to herself.

While Bose was wreaking havoc, the Dean had presented Josie with her certificate and she was safely seated beside Mrs Archibong who had not noticed the fracas in the visiting students' section. When at last Bose returned her mum did not hide her displeasure.

"Bose, where were you?" her mum asked. "You should have at least told either Josie or myself that you needed the toilet. The Dean called your name three times and, in the end, I

had to collect your certificate for you."
"I am so sorry mum."

Josie did not utter a word while Mrs Archibong told her daughter
off. She knew that Bose wasn't happy with what she had made her
do and Josie planned to apologise but at the moment there was
something more urgent that she needed to take care of.

Josie knew Peter, he was a gentleman and most likely he would
come looking for Bose just to make sure that she was alright, and
she had no intention of being there if he came. After giving it some
thought, she concluded that since she and Bose had collected their
certificates there was really nothing stopping them from leaving.
Now all she needed to do was find the perfect excuse.

Josie tapped Mrs Archibong's shoulder.

"Auntie Kath, I think I need to go back to the apartment?"
"Why Josie? What is the matter?"
"I have got a really bad migraine and could do with a lie-
down," Josie lied.

Mrs Archibong hesitated for a second before calling the driver.
Then she turned to Josie.

"Alright Josie, Mohammed will take you back to the
apartment. Do you want us to bring you some food on our
way back?"
"Thank you, auntie Kath, but I am not really hungry."

While all this was going on Bose remained conspicuously quiet.
This unusual behaviour had not gone unnoticed by her mother
who wondered what had happened between them. So, after Josie
had left Kathleen looked at her daughter and demanded to know
what the matter was.

"Nothing's the matter mum," Bose snapped.

"Don't give me that attitude young lady," Kathleen replied her daughter in a stern, firm voice. "Do you think I was born yesterday? I noticed how you reacted when Josie complained of having a headache".

"Mum, now is not the time to read something into nothing. Can't we just sit back and enjoy the ceremony?"

"Yes, we can after you tell me what happened between the two of you."

Bose looked away and did not say a word. So, her mother continued hounding.

"Well, whatever happened between both of you, just remember that Josie is not just your friend, she is our guest."

"Yes, blame it all on me. I am sure you did not notice me making a fool of myself all because of our sweet, precious Josie." Bose's voice was shaking. "Do you know that she asked me to do something really embarrassing simply because she was trying to avoid someone who happens to be her brother's friend? And there I was falling all over a young man while those around laughed at me and my clumsiness. In all my life I have never felt so humiliated."

"Bose, how do you know they were laughing at you?" her mum asked. "Sometimes it is just so hard to understand you young people."

Bose could not believe her ears. "Is she for real?" Her mum was starting to irritate her.

"Mum, I want to go back to the apartment," Bose said angrily.

"And how do you intend to get there? I am sure you remember that Mohammed just took Josie home. What is the matter with you, Bose? Can you just try and behave yourself?"

Bose's attitude did not change and she sulked until the driver got back. The car was uncomfortably quiet as Kathleen and her daughter drove back to the apartment. Bose was angry. She felt let down by her mum. "How could she take Josie's side even after she told her what had happened?" Kathleen on the other hand was disappointed with her daughter's childish behaviour especially after everything she and Chris had taught their children about hospitality.

Mrs Archibong remembered a scripture in the bible that said, "Do not let the sun go down on your anger" and decided to settle whatever was going on between the girls that very night, before they went to sleep. So, as soon as they entered the apartment, Mrs Archibong called Josie while she and her daughter sat and waited in the living room. When Josie finally emerged from her room Mrs Archibong told her to take a seat. She wasn't in the mood to mince words.

"Now ladies, I need you both to tell me what the problem is."
"Auntie Kath," Josie began, "it is all my fault. I shouldn't have asked Bose to do my dirty work. I guess I panicked when I saw my brother's friend. I just wasn't thinking straight."

Then Josie turned to Bose.

"BA, I am so sorry. Please, forgive me for putting you in such an awkward position. I just didn't know what else to do."
"It's alright Josie," Bose replied. "I am sorry I reacted the way I did. Even though it was quite humiliating, I guess I didn't have to do it."
"Now girls, listen to me," said Mrs Archibong. "This was nothing but a little test of your friendship, and from my experience it is bound to happen again, and again. It is therefore up to both of you to learn from this experience

and determine that next time it happens the outcome will be different. Do you understand what I am saying?"

"Yes, we understand," they chorused.

"Now then, we all need an early night so we can leave at the crack of dawn. Hopefully we can avoid the traffic around the Seme border because it was pretty bad when we were coming this morning."

After they all said their good nights and Bose had gone to her room, Mrs Archibong noticed Josie lingering behind.

"Josie, what is the matter?"

"I'm fine auntie Kath. I just want to say thank you for what you did. Please believe me when I say I didn't mean to hurt Bose. I just hope she can forgive me."

"Don't worry my dear, I know my daughter, I can assure you that she has forgiven you, and eventually she will put this whole episode behind her. Now, you get some sleep."

"Good night auntie Kath. I love you."

"I love you too Josie. We all do."

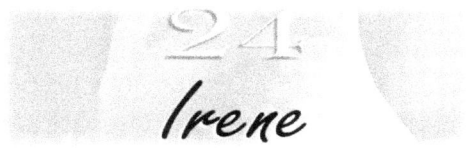

24.
Irene

*A*bout a month after the ASUU strike was called off the University of Lagos was reopened, and students were immediately told to prepare for their exams. However, the students objected, arguing that after spending over six months without any lectures it would be unfair for the authorities to test them on things they had most likely forgotten. Sensing that this could become another issue, the University Senate decided to give the students extra time to study and finish their curriculum for the semester.

The exam boards were duly informed and exams were put off until May the following year. The new timetable did not exempt students from class work and mock examinations, much of which would count towards the final examinations.

As usual, Bose and Josie were determined to make the best use of their time and studied really hard. They also practised speaking French to one another as frequently as possible. Most of their friends were surprised to hear them speaking French wondering where they had learnt it, and when they heard that during the strike both of them actually attended a French course in a school in Cotonou some regretted not doing something similar themselves.

At the end of that year, when really, they should have graduated, the students started hearing rumours that the Federal Government had reneged on their promise to ASUU and there was a possibility that it would cause further disruption. When Josie heard about it she was distraught and concluded that if this was truly the case she just might have to throw in the towel and return to the United Kingdom. But until it was confirmed she would study as if her life depended on it.

Unlike the year before, it looked like this year's Christmas was going to be uneventful as the Archibongs had decided to stay in Lagos. They were however expecting Margaret, her husband, Emmanuel and Eyo to travel down. Tope was already back from school, and there were also plans in place to host some family friends, as well as some of Mr Archibong's associates. So, maybe Christmas would not be that boring after all.

Josie called her family to wish them a wonderful Christmas. She had spoken to her sisters and her mother. Then she braced herself as her mum handed the phone over to Josie's dad.

"Merry Christmas daddy."
"Same to you Josie. How are you?"
"I'm very good, thank you."
"That's great. By the way, I meant to ask, when are you graduating? I thought you enrolled for a three-year course. Is this not the fourth year?"

Josie knew what her father was up to, and she had envisaged that he might bring it up.

"Well, I took some time out to study French as a second language. Considering that a lot of corporations nowadays are Multi-national, I thought it might come in handy in the near future. But not to worry, by the grace of God, I will be graduating next year."

Josie was about to drop the phone when her father asked her how she was doing financially, considering that since she left England she had not asked them for a penny.

"I am fine, daddy. If I need anything I promise to ask either you or mummy. But for now, I am doing just fine."

Josie didn't want to continue the conversation any longer because she knew her father would eventually go off on another one of his tirades. She wanted this call to end peacefully for once. She always enjoyed speaking to her mum who had overcome her initial objection to the stance her daughter had taken. They had both rebuilt broken fences and now Josie's mother was her greatest encourager.

Bruce was her greatest challenge; there was always one excuse or the other as to why he could not come to the phone and speak to her. This bothered Josie a lot especially when she thought about the close bond of friendship they once shared. She wished Bruce would answer her calls but he remained intractable preferring to speak to her either through their mum or her sisters.

Thinking back, she also wished she hadn't taken her relationship with aunt Jacqueline for granted. She had thought about calling her a few times, but the longer she left it the harder it became to call to try and make up for the wrong she had done. It was all her fault and she knew it; if only she had confided in her.

At the time, Josie was only interested in her own survival. She didn't want her family to interfere with her plans and she feared that anything she told her aunt would ultimately be relayed back to her parents. In hindsight, Josie knew that because of the kind of person aunt Jacqueline was, she most likely would have supported her even if it caused a bit of family friction.

Maybe now was a good time to try and reopen the lines of communication with her aunt. After all, it was Christmas, a festive season of joy, Josie thought. So, she picked up the phone and called her aunt Jacqueline in Scotland.

The phone rang for some time then went to voice mail. Knowing her aunt, Josie suspected that she was out shopping, so she left her a voice message apologising and asking her to please forgive her bad behaviour. Josie also left her phone number and promised to call her back soon.

Having done that, Josie decided to call Lily Ann. The last time they spoke was when she called her from Cotonou. Josie had told Lily about the French course she was enrolled in and how she was really enjoying the Benin culture. She had also tried to explain the ongoing problem with universities in Nigeria, and even though Lily didn't quite understand, she had been very supportive and encouraged Josie without being judgmental. Lily did however ask Josie to make sure she stayed in touch with her family because from what she had observed, they were still quite worried about her. At the time Josie had assured her friend that everything was under control.

Lily Ann answered the phone excitedly. She always enjoyed her girly chats with Josie and today was no different. She told her that she had met someone in university, and how she believed their relationship was serious. She wanted to know if Josie had met a tall, dark and handsome young man and teased her about the many Nigerian young men who must be falling head over heels for her. However, Josie told Lily explicitly that she was not interested in any frivolous relationship with any member of the opposite sex, and that her sole priority and focus were her studies.

Even though Josie didn't voice it, she felt that all men were the same; all they wanted to do was prey on a woman's body and she was having none of that. Thanks, but no thanks, she was doing just fine and even if it meant dying an old maid, she was okay living the single life.

"Oh Josie, what has come over you?" Lily Ann scolded her friend. "The fact that you had a misfortune doesn't mean that all men are the same."
"Thanks for the advice Lily. Remind me to call on you if I ever need a matchmaker or marriage counsellor," Josie retorted, wishing she hadn't even bothered to call her friend.

Lily realised that Josie was getting upset and quickly changed the topic.

"Did I tell you that I am thinking of joining my dad's law firm when I graduate?
"No, you didn't," Josie responded abruptly.
"Well that's the plan, but before I start working I'm thinking of taking a break. What is the weather like in Nigeria? Would you say it's a nice holiday location?"
"Lily, if you're thinking of holidaying in Nigeria I would advise you to do so during the rainy season; the weather is a lot cooler then."

Josie went on to tell Lily about some of the exciting tourist attractions like Bar Beach, Banana Island, Kuramo Waters and Tarkwa Bay, and by the time she finished she felt a lot better. They talked for a while and afterwards she realised that she was still tetchy about her encounter with Michael Doland. Considering it happened over six years ago, Josie wondered how long she would continue to feel this way about what happened. She knew that even if she tried she could not run away from it, and unless she confronted it head on the ghost would always haunt her. But, first things first, there was no returning to England until she held that degree certificate in her hands. It was a task that she had to accomplish.

It was two days to Christmas and as a hungry Josie made her way down the stairs she could smell the sweet, irresistible aroma of baking coming from the kitchen. Baking cakes for her friends and extended family members was a Christmas tradition for Bose's mum and as Josie walked into the kitchen she saw Bose and her mum putting finishing touches to the cakes.

"Hello Josie, I am sure you must be hungry," Mrs Archibong said teasingly. "Why don't you help yourself to something to eat. We have some beans in that pot over there and Bose just made your favourite dish, fried plantain."

Kathleen smiled then turned to her daughter and asked her to help Josie with some chicken from the oven.

"Not to worry, I can do that myself auntie Kath," Josie replied.

They were still talking about how the cakes were going to be distributed when the front doorbell rang. One of the maids opened the door to welcome Kathleen's mother. Bose's grandmother Mrs Irene Akinjide nee Boswell had not returned to England since her sister in law's husband's funeral and only really come to Lagos to spend Christmas with her grandchildren.

"Good afternoon ma," the maid, Gift greeted Kathleen's mum.
"Good afternoon my dear," Irene replied. "Please help me bring my suitcase inside. Where is everyone?"
"Madam dey for kitchen with sister Bose and her friend. Dem dey bake cake. Madam don tell me say make I carry your box go room wey dey downstairs."
"Ok. Thank you, Gift."

The old lady made her way to the kitchen where her daughter and granddaughter were busy decorating cakes.

Bose ran and embraced her grandmother. Then Kathleen came over and also hugged her.

"How was the journey from Ibadan, mum?"
"It was not bad. I was actually surprised that the traffic was so light."

Irene Akinjide was a beauty when she was young and it still reflected in the way she carried herself even at the tender age of seventy-seven. As she sat down on one of the kitchen chairs, Kathleen noticed something about her mother's gait that troubled her.

"Are you alright, mother?" Kathleen asked.
"Of course, I am," the old lady replied. "Why do you ask?"
"Apart from looking tired, it seems to me that you have lost some weight. I was just a bit concerned really, but if you say you are okay then that is alright with me."

Irene reassured her daughter that she was fine and promptly changed the subject.

"So, are Margaret and her husband coming for Christmas?" Irene asked.
"Yes, they are," Bose replied. "The driver should be picking them up from the airport anytime from now."

Kathleen Archibong was just about to ask her mother if she was hungry when she heard some commotion at the front door; it was Tope yelling at the top of his voice because the dog had chewed on his expensive t-shirt. Then he saw his grandmother and immediately went to greet her.

"Sorry about that, grandma. No one told me that you had arrived. No one tells me anything in this house and now even the dog is treating me like a stranger. The wicked thing has chewed up my..."

His tantrum was interrupted by his father who walked into the kitchen with his sister, Eyo; you could trust her to make her usual grand entrance. She ran straight to her grandmother, gave her a big hug and then immediately asked if there was anything to eat because she was starving. Josie, being a big admirer of Bose's sister, asked Eyo if she would like some beans and fried plantain. However, to Josie's consternation Eyo told her that she no longer ate that kind of food as it was too heavy for her, but she wouldn't mind some salad and chicken if there were any available.

One thing was for sure, Eyo did not intend to get the food herself; she expected someone else to do it and once again Josie obliged her. Bose knew her sister well enough to know that she was not the best at helping others and was a bit annoyed to see Josie pandering to her every whim. She made a mental note to discuss this with her friend later on.

After sitting down in the kitchen for a while, Irene excused herself saying she needed to lie down as she felt a bit tired after her trip from Ibadan. However, before leaving she cracked everyone up when she said they should remember to wake her up for dinner.

Not too long after she left, Chris asked his wife if she had noticed the way her mother looked and the way she walked. Kathleen said she had but her mother had assured her that she was okay.

"My dear, I think you need to ask her again," Chris suggested. "Maybe she didn't want to talk about it while the children were around."

When Kathleen entered her mum's bedroom, the first thing she noticed was that though the air was humid, the air conditioner was off. She noticed her mum shivering in her sleep. Kathleen gently tapped her mother's shoulder and asked her what the matter was.

"I have had a very bad bout of malaria which I have been trying to shake off for the last three weeks or so but it just seems to be getting worse. But do not worry about me, with a little rest I should be fine."
"Mother, you do know that malaria is a very serious illness which should not be taken for granted? We need to have you checked out as soon as possible."
"Don't be silly Kathleen, and stop being melodramatic. It is

only malaria fever!"

"But mother you just said you have had it for three weeks and you haven't been able to shake it off, so how am I being melodramatic? I am going to tell Chris; we are going to St Nicholas right now."

Before Irene could object Kathleen was out of the room. She told Chris that as suspected her mother was ill.

Chris Archibong had always been fond of his mother in law, and considering what she went through, losing her husband at a very young age and raising three little children in a foreign land, he had the utmost respect for her. Of her three children, Kathleen was the closest to her mother yet when he asked Irene for the hand of her youngest daughter she had been very supportive even though she knew that he and Kathleen would be relocating to Nigeria.

Chris drove Kathleen and his reluctant mother in law to St Nicholas Hospital, and even though he had called ahead to let them know that he was on his way, they were very lucky to see the family doctor, considering that it was Christmas Eve.

After examining Irene, the doctor told them that he would have to run some tests because he was not satisfied with the initial examination. The tests were carried out and before they left the hospital, the doctor gave her some medication and promised to get back to her with the results of the tests within a week. He also assured Kathleen's mother not to worry but to make sure she gets as much rest as possible.

By the time they got back home Margaret and Emmanuel had arrived; the Archibong family was together once again, and grandma Irene was simply the cherry on the cake. The atmosphere was buzzing with excitement as everyone looked forward to a Christmas season they would never forget.

Christmas was a lot of fun but it was over before they knew it. Margaret and Emmanuel had left for Aberdeen, Tope had gone back to school in Abuja and Bose and Josie had resumed lectures, leaving Eyo and her grandmother to keep each other company. It soon became apparent that Chris and Kathleen did not want their daughter to go back to America. Left to them, since she had finished her course, she might as well stay in Nigeria and do her National Youth Service (NYSC). Eyo did not agree and she did not hesitate to make it clear to her parents.

"Mum, dad, I do not have any intention of staying in this country not to talk of doing the National Youth Service. And by the way, I thought the plan was for me to go and stay with Margaret in Aberdeen?" Eyo asked trying not to lose her cool.
"Well, that was obviously before your sister got married," Kathleen replied. "Don't you think it would be unfair to ask her to let you stay with them while they are still practically on their honeymoon?"

Eyo was about to respond but her father had heard enough.

"Eyo, do you know what? You can do whatever you want but if you are not going to listen to your mother and I then do not expect me to fund your allowance."

With that Chris turned and left for work while Kathleen retired to her bedroom.

Eyo could not believe her ears. "Was he really serious?" She thought about asking her grandmother for help but since her medical results had come back and the doctor had confirmed that she would need to be operated on, she didn't want to drag her into this little mess. To be fair, arrangements were already being made for her grandmother to return to England for a second opinion and since her mother would be accompanying her, it dawned on

Eyo that she might just have to stick around.

The flip side was that if her mother did travel with her grandmother then Eyo would be the lady of the house, meaning that she would have the maids at her beck and call. It would also give her a chance to teach that little sister of hers a much-needed lesson. So, staying in Nigeria wasn't all bad. Then come to think of it, why couldn't she be the one to accompany her grandmother to England?

With this in mind, Eyo ran upstairs and knocked on her parent's bedroom door.

"Who is it?"
"It's me, mum," Eyo replied bursting into the room. "Good morning mum, I am sorry about earlier on."
"That is okay my dear. What is on your mind now?"
"Well, I was thinking. What if I relieved you of the stress of accompanying grandmother to England? Why don't you let me go with her; I promise to take good care of grandma. You know I will."

Kathleen looked at her daughter and shook her head in amusement. Because of the special love Eyo had for her grandmother, Kathleen knew she would take good care of her mother, but she also knew that the only reason why Eyo was offering to help was simply because she wanted to wriggle out of staying in the country. To be fair Eyo wasn't really a troublesome child, she was just used to having her way, but that was not going to happen today.

"I am sorry my dear, but that is not an option. You see, your father has already started processing your National Youth Service attachment.
"But mum...", Eyo began.
"There are no buts Francesca Eyo! You are staying in Nigeria and you will do your bit for your fatherland," Kathleen responded in a stern tone.

Whenever Eyo heard her mother call her full name she knew there was no point pursuing the issue. Her mum was not like her dad who she could often wrap around her little finger. Even though he was a disciplinarian in his own unique way, her mother was the one who ran the house. Eyo decided to change the subject.

"Mum, do you know how long you will be away for?"
"No, not really," Kathleen replied. "It will all depend on your grandmother's medical test results, and if I need to return to Nigeria I am sure I can count on Margaret to help out."

Irene's condition seemed to get worse. She complained of incessant pains all over her body and she was also losing weight at an alarming rate. Chris had gone to see the family doctor at St Nicholas and picked up the detailed test results that Kathleen and her mother would need when they got to the United Kingdom. Because of Irene's rapidly deteriorating condition, Chris brought the flight forward so that Kathleen and her mum could leave as soon as possible.

As he drove them to the airport he asked his wife to check and make sure that she had the passports and all necessary documents. When they finally got to the airport Chris helped his mother in law into a wheelchair, and while checking them in he arranged for a British Airways official to wheel Irene, escorted by his wife, to the departure gate. He had booked them on a British Airways flight that was scheduled to leave at eleven thirty that night and also made the necessary arrangements for an ambulance to take Kathleen and her mother straight to the hospital once they arrived at London Heathrow the next morning.

Before they said their goodbyes, Kathleen took her husband by the hand and said, "Thank you". She also had a few other things she wanted to tell him.

"Chris, please look after the girls. I know you have a soft spot for Eyo but make sure she does not try and talk her way out of the NYSC programme, and that she doesn't take this opportunity to lord it over Bose and Josie."

"Don't worry dear, I have it all covered," Chris smiled.

"Also, you know my office gave me a two-week compassionate leave; well I don't know if we will be done by then, but whatever the case I will keep you posted."

"That's okay. By the way have you decided where you are going to stay?" Chris asked. "Maybe it would be better to stay in that hotel near the Cricket Grounds instead of your mother's place. It is a lot more central and also quite close to the hospital." Chris suggested.

"Well, that is true but I still need to go to mum's place and do some tidying up just in case. I guess it will depend on the initial assessment by the Oncologist. Let us just pray that everything goes well and even if there are any issues, the medical team will know what needs to be done. Emmanuel has promised to come over if I need any help, so I guess I should be alright. I am more concerned about you and the girls."

"So, are you saying I cannot take care of the family if you are not around? Don't worry about us, we will be fine, and unless the rumours are true, Bose and Josie will be busy preparing for their final exams anyway."

"What rumours?" Kathleen asked anxiously.

"Oh, I thought you knew. There have been rumours that there could be another nationwide university strike."

"Oh God, please not another one. The girls have worked so hard, another strike would devastate them to say the least. What are we going to do if that happens?"

Suddenly Chris wished he had not said anything about the strike. Even though he tried to reassure his wife that it most likely would not happen and that common sense would eventually prevail, he knew that she would not let it go.

Chris and Kathleen were still talking when the British Airways official who was going to wheel Irene to the departure gate arrived and kindly told them that it was time to go. Chris hugged his wife and gave Irene a kiss on the cheek and watched them as they went through the immigration section of the airport.

Kathleen and her mother boarded the aircraft and settled into their Business Class seats. By the time the cabin crew brought the pre-flight drinks Kathleen realised that her mother had fallen asleep, so she decided not to wake her up. Kathleen also felt tired, but even though the crew members were aware of her mother's condition, she tried to stay awake just in case her mother woke up and needed her attention. When the plane had stabilised at cruising altitude, Kathleen made sure her mother was comfortable then made a dash for the loo.

After cruising for over two hours the plane speaker bleeped and the pilot's voice told all the passengers to fasten their seatbelts because of the turbulence ahead. Kathleen adjusted their seat belts and began to pray. She did not really enjoy flying and she totally hated turbulence. However, to Kathleen's relief, the turbulence was minimal and the 'fasten your seat belt' light was soon turned off. After that, she dozed off and only woke up when they started the descent into London Heathrow airport. Her mum had slept all through the flight refusing to eat anything and only drinking a cup of tea and a glass of apple juice.

When the plane finally came to a standstill, Kathleen got her mother ready to disembark and noticed that she was sweating profusely even though the air conditioning was still on. She rightly attributed this to her mother's illness and made a mental note of it.

Irene was wheeled directly from the plane to where the ambulance was waiting and driven straight to the hospital where the medical team were ready and waiting. The doctor heading the team had come highly recommended by a colleague who now worked in one of the leading teaching hospitals in Nigeria.

The doctor read through Irene's medical notes then looked directly at the patient and proceeded to find out her level of awareness. To his amazement, the old lady knew exactly what was wrong with her and with a precise and analytical mind she told the consultant when and how it all began.

After carrying out an initial examination, the doctor told his secretary to book an appointment for Mrs Akinjide at their clinic on Harley Street for all the tests he had listed. Then he advised Kathleen and her mother to go home and that he would be in touch soon. Kathleen watched the doctor's facial expression and tried to decipher if the prognosis was good or bad but could not read anything from it. She decided that she would call him the following day when her mother was not with her.

While they were in the taxi to her mother's house in Enfield Kathleen sensed that she was uncharacteristically silent.

"Mum, are you okay?
"I feel the consultant was withholding information from us."

Kathleen had suspected this to be the case, but as she had already made up her mind to speak to the doctor the next day she did not want to say too much about it.

"Really? I don't think he was withholding anything. He simply told us what we need to know."
"Is that what you really think?" Irene looked at her daughter as if she knew exactly what was on her mind. "My dear Kathleen, I have learnt to accept whatever life dishes out to me. Since the death of your father there is really nothing that can shake me. I know who I trust to fight my battles for me."
Irene smiled and winked at her daughter.

By the time they reached the house in Enfield, Irene's younger sister, Edith had arrived from Ireland where she lived with her husband and their two children. Edith had a spare key to the house so she had already helped clean up. She had also switched the heating on so that the house was nice and warm, ready for her sister.

25

Angela and Kathleen

Kathleen had informed the rest of the family about her mother's medical examination results. They were not positive. The consultant had discovered a tumour embedded in Irene's throat which was diagnosed to be cancerous and he had advised surgery and chemotherapy treatment.

On hearing the news, the entire family came together to pray for Irene's health. Even though they were happy that the hospital had diagnosed the problem, they were apprehensive about what the outcome might be. No one dared voice it, but they feared that at her age, Irene might not make it through the treatment. Chris remembered how his mother in law had often said that she would hate to be put under any form of anaesthesia, words that were born out of a fear that she would not wake up. But there is nothing that God cannot do, he thought.

The surgery had been scheduled for the first week of March. Bose's mother had returned to Nigeria as she had only been granted two weeks of compassionate leave, leaving her mother in the safe hands of her younger sister. However, as the time for the surgery approached, Edith had asked if Kathleen could return as she needed to attend to an urgent family situation at home in Ireland.

So, Kathleen asked for an immediate leave of absence so she could return to the United Kingdom to look after her mother. This time however, Kathleen was not going alone. She was travelling with Samantha, her older sister who had also taken time off work to help with their mother's care.

Thankfully the surgery was successful and a week later, Irene was discharged. Apart from being given medication that she would need to use daily, Irene was told that she would also have to attend the outpatient clinic weekly for further observation that would aid her recovery.

It was on one of those afternoons, as Samantha and Kathleen were walking back to the outpatient clinic to take their mother home that Samantha heard someone shout her name. They both turned to see a lady scurrying towards them.

"Carol Pearce!" Samantha exclaimed as they hugged each other.
"Wow!" Carol gushed. "It has been how long now? Over nineteen years when we attended each other's weddings back in Liverpool. How are you, and how is your husband?"
"We are fine," Samantha smiled. "We moved back to Nigeria about ten years ago, and I am now a lecturer in one of the universities in Abuja. How are things with you and Declan?"
"Well, we moved to London almost immediately after our wedding. As you know, Declan was in the army. His unit was posted to Afghanistan and on their second military tour, the unit was ambushed by Taliban militants. Unfortunately, while Declan was defending the troops in his unit, he was cut down by a sniper's bullet. It was later discovered that one of the Afghan soldiers accompanying Declan's unit was a traitor. So, my dear, yours truly has been a widow for the past nine years. I was pregnant at the time and our daughter Emily was born the following year. One look at her and all those sweet memories of Declan come rushing back."
"Carol, I am so sorry about that. By the way, this is my younger sister, Kathleen. You met her at my wedding. Kath this is a friend of mine from back in the day. We both worked in the same office at the Department of Works and Pension in Liverpool."
"Of course, I remember Carol," Kathleen replied. "Lovely to

see you again."

"So, what brings you two here?" Carol asked.

"We came with our mother. She has an appointment with one of the consultants. We popped out briefly to grab a bite to eat and were just on our way back to the visitors' lounge on the first floor. What about you?" Samantha asked as they all waited for the lift.

The lift door opened and just as Carol was about to answer, they saw a lady who seemed to be calling Carol's name running towards them. Kathleen pressed the button to hold the door and released it when the lady was safely in. Carol smiled and as they all made their way to the first floor, she introduced her friend.

"Samantha and Kathleen, please meet Angela Kimberley. She is a good friend of mine."

"Nice to meet you," the sisters replied.

"Angela and I are here to visit a young girl who was recently admitted."

"I hope she is okay," Kathleen looked concerned.

"Let us just say that the worst is over," Carol responded.

Carol looked at Angela who was still trying to catch her breath, and apologised.

"Angela, I am really sorry. I got carried away talking to these two long, lost friends of mine and totally forgot that we were meant to meet up."

"That's alright Carol. Somehow, I don't think I am as fit as I used to be," Angela smiled breathing heavily.

Carol, Samantha and Kathleen were still laughing when the lift door opened on the first floor. They all stepped out and before they went their separate ways promised to meet up before the sisters left for Nigeria the following week.

After waiting in the visitor's lounge for about half an hour, Kathleen and Samantha went to meet their mother in the oncology department on the second floor. The consultant smiled assuringly as he told the sisters that he was pleased with the way their mother was responding to the treatment after the operation. He prescribed a specific drug and explained that it would help reduce the pain that Irene was feeling around the throat area. He also told them that he would need to see Irene again in the coming week, and assured them that barring unforeseen circumstances, it should be her last consultation.

As they made their way out of the lounge, Kathleen turned to her sister.

"Sis, do you recall the name of Carol's friend?" she asked.
"Yes, I think she said, Angela Kimberley."
"That is what I thought I heard too. It just might be a coincidence but that is the name of Josie's mother."
"Interestingly I can actually see a bit of a resemblance, and also the way her upper lip seemed to turn up when she spoke. Doesn't that remind you of Josie?" Samantha asked, curiosity in her eyes.
"You're right you know, but could she really be Josie's mother?" Kathleen replied.

Irene had been listening to this intriguing discussion between her daughters.

"So, why didn't you just ask?" Irene quizzed.
"It didn't ring a bell at the time," Kathleen replied.
"Well, we are planning to meet up with Carol and Angela next week," said Samantha excitedly. "We could ask her then."

During the week, Carol had called Samantha to set up their date and they had agreed to catch up during Samantha and Kathleen's mother's next consultation at the hospital. So, on that sunny day, the sisters left their mother and their aunt, who had since returned from Ireland, in the hospital reception and made their way to the Costa coffee shop across the road from the St John's Wood station. Even though they were a bit early, they were pleasantly surprised to see both Carol and Angela already seated. Carol waved them over.

As they manoeuvred their way through the maze of chairs and tables Kathleen was immediately struck by the striking resemblance between Mrs Kimberley and Josie. Now, more than ever she was eager to resolve this mystery.

When the sisters finally sat down Carol asked after their mother's welfare.

"She is doing quite well actually," Samantha smiled. "The consultant is satisfied with how she is responding to treatment and barring any complications, mum should be discharged from the outpatient clinic today. And how is the young girl you came to visit last week; is she better now?"
"Well, she has been mildly sedated mainly to take her mind off the trauma she has been through," Carol replied.
"If I may ask, what actually happened to her?" Kathleen asked.
"It is very uncomfortable to imagine but the poor girl was consistently being raped by her so-called father," Carol answered bitterly. "She is recovering gradually and the police are still investigating the case. I have been told that this time he will not get away with it."
"Oh no!" the sisters exclaimed in shock.

Kathleen's head dropped. She knew Josie's story and was praying that this young girl was not Josie's child; the little girl who Josie's parents had given to the abuser's family to look after. When she raised her head, she had tears in her eyes. Samantha was surprised at her sister's reaction and thought that now might be a good time to give Angela and her sister some space.

"Carol, do you mind if I could have a word in private?" Samantha asked.
"Sure," Carol replied.

The two friends excused themselves and went to the bathroom leaving Kathleen and Angela to get acquainted. As soon as they were out of earshot of the two women, Samantha asked her friend if Angela Kimberley had a daughter called Josie.

"Yes, she does. How did you know that?" Carol looked surprised. "Angela told me that her daughter ran away from home after she was raped by this same monster, and that even though they are still in contact with her they do not know when or if she will be coming back."

Samantha waited for a few seconds then sighed heavily.

"Josie lives with Kathleen in Lagos, Nigeria. In fact, she is in her final year in one of the universities in Lagos."
"No way!" There was shock written all over Carol's face.
"Yes. My sister and I noticed the resemblance when Angela ran into the lift last week, but it didn't occur to us to ask at the time."
"Oh my God," Carol exclaimed. "How on earth do we break this to Angela?"
"I wouldn't get too worked up, Carol. Josie is in touch with her family, especially her mum. So, Angela knows that her daughter is in Nigeria and she has an idea of what she is up to. What she doesn't know is that she is sitting across the lady who has looked after her daughter for the last few years."
"I wonder how she is going to take that?"
"I guess we will soon find out. So, tell me," Samantha continued, "is the young girl you went to visit related to Angela in any way?"

"Yes, she is Angela's granddaughter; Josie's daughter.
"What!" Samantha couldn't believe it.
"Incidentally her name is also Josie, even though she was christened Annabel Leah," Carol continued. "I am not sure if you know this, but when Josie was sixteen she was raped by this same brute; Annabel was the result of that abuse."
"What a tragedy. Both mother and child raped by the same man! I wonder how Josie would feel if she knew what her daughter had been through," Samantha shook her head, her eyes beginning to well up.
"Well, the good thing is that Annabel Leah is recovering gradually. The police are currently investigating the case and we have been assured that this time around that animal will not get away with it."

Kathleen had told Angela about her work with the British Council in Nigeria which made Angela ask her new-found friend if she knew the Deputy High Commissioner, Mr James Eastwood who happened to be a close family friend of theirs.

"Yes, of course I know Mr Eastwood," a chirpy Kathleen replied.

To their mutual surprise, both Angela and Kathleen realised that they had a lot in common especially when it came to art, antiquities, reading and travelling. Bose's mum still had not asked Mrs Kimberley if she was Josie's mum, but she suspected that Samantha would have asked Carol.

As Carol and Samantha approached the table they could see that Kathleen and Angela were deeply engrossed in discussion, so much so they did not even notice them coming. Kathleen was just about to invite Angela to visit Nigeria when her sister and Carol took their seats and immediately Carol turned to her friend Angela.

"Angela, do you know that Kathleen actually knows Josie?"

"What!" Angela exclaimed. "I had no idea. So, you know my Josie? When did you see her last? Do you know the family she is staying with?"

"Well, Josie and my youngest daughter just happen to be very good friends. They schooled together at St Magdalene's College."

"Are you saying what I think you're saying?"

"Yes, your daughter has been living with us since she came to Nigeria and I hope you will believe me when I say that she is hale and hearty."

"I would have called this a coincidence, but to meet the lady that has been taking such good care of my daughter is no coincidence. I believe this is the hand of God." Angela's face lit up. "How is my baby, and how is she getting on with her exams? She told me last week that she was preparing for her finals. I can't wait to see her again. We have missed her so much." Tears of joy were now flowing down Angela's cheeks.

"Well, this is wonderful!" Carol said, clapping her hands.

"Amazing," Kathleen replied, "and just to think that I was about to invite Angela over to Lagos on holiday."

Kathleen turned to Angela excitedly.

"Come to think of it, what do you say about the Kimberley family coming for Josie's graduation in August? I can keep it a secret if you want me to. I am sure it will come as a pleasant surprise to her."

"We will be there, God willing," Angela replied happily. "I shall tell my husband and children. Thankfully, the girls should be on holiday and I am sure Bruce, Josie's brother would love to see his sister. When are you going back to Nigeria?"

"We are leaving on Saturday morning."

"What about your mother, is she going with you?"

"No, she won't. She needs to recuperate. Fortunately, mum's

younger sister, my big brother and his family, as well as Margaret my eldest daughter and her husband are all on hand to take care of her. We are also making arrangements for a carer to check up on her from time to time."

They all exchanged phone numbers and promised to stay in touch. As they walked back to the hospital Kathleen asked if it was okay for them to see little Leah before picking up her mum, to which Angela kindly said, "Yes."

As Kathleen and Samantha approached Leah's room, they noticed the police presence. When they enquired, they were told that the protection was in place just in case the suspect or any member of the Doland family tried to pay Leah a visit. At the mention of the Doland name Angela became visibly angry and she reminded the police that if anything happened to her granddaughter, she would not be held responsible for her actions.

The Kimberleys had asked the police to intensify their presence on the ward as it had come to their notice that both Sir Ian and Lady Doland had recently arrived in the country from New Zealand. Knowing the kind of person that Lady Doland was, they did not want to take anything for granted. The police were also aware of John Kimberley's threat to expose their connivance with the Dolands which he believed to be the reason why investigations into their granddaughter's case had stalled.

With the other ladies listening in, Angela asked the attending doctor how the little girl was doing. What he told them was a big shock to their senses. Both Kathleen and her sister Samantha could not hold back the tears. Samantha whose youngest daughter was almost the same age as Leah seemed to feel the pain the most.

Poor Annabel Leah had been systematically raped repeatedly by her father so much so that her vaginal mucous membrane had been damaged. What puzzled the ladies the most was that all this happened in the same house where his wife lived, and she claimed not to know anything about it. It was simply repugnant to them!

As the four ladies surrounded little Leah's bed watching her drift in and out of sleep, they joined hands in prayer and asked God to heal the little girl's spirit, soul and body. They finally left the room when Leah was sound asleep, and the nurse attending to her told Carol, who had brought the little girl to the hospital in the first place, that she would let her know if there was any change in little Leah's condition.

When they left the hospital, the first question on their lips was how to break this tragic news to Josie. As she was about to sit her final exams, they all agreed that now was not the time to tell her. Kathleen was of the opinion that nothing should be said to Josie until she came back to the United Kingdom, something she planned to do after her graduation in August.

Kathleen also had a burning question on her lips, and just as she was about to voice it Angela Kimberley began to tell them how she got to know about little Leah and her condition.

One day Angela's friend Carol Pearce had asked if she could accompany her to the hospital; they were going to visit a young girl who had been sexually abused. On getting there and seeing the little girl's name, it dawned on her that this was the baby that she and her husband had relinquished responsibility for; their very own granddaughter!

She recounted how she had broken down in tears in the hospital reception filled with sadness, anguish and remorse; how she told herself that this would never have happened to little Leah if she and John had not been weak. She also knew that if Josie were to find out what had happened to her daughter, all the bitterness of the past that she was still trying to put behind her would resurface, and only God knows what would happen to her then.

Angela cried as she spoke, vividly remembering the look of betrayal on Josie's face when she realised what her parents had done. She told Carol, Kathleen and Samantha how they all woke up one day and Josie was gone She refused to tell them where she was or even call to speak to them. The first they heard about her whereabouts was when she called her younger sister, Jacqueline who lived in a village near Aberdeen to ask if she had heard from Josie. She went on to tell the ladies how Josie's older brother, Bruce had travelled to Aberdeen to plead with his sister and bring her back home but each time, Josie was one step ahead. Eventually even Jacqueline who she was meant to be staying with did not know when she decided to fly to Nigeria.

"I guess she met your daughter somewhere along the line," Angela concluded as she looked at Kathleen

"According to Josie she ran into Bose, my daughter in a restaurant in Aberdeen. I guess at the time they had no idea what they were getting into. From what Josie told me, she only decided to travel to Nigeria after she discovered that her brother had come looking for her; he wanted her to return home at once and told her to stop behaving foolishly. It was after this that she made up her mind that she was going to Nigeria no matter what it took. Apparently, at the time she felt that any place out of the reach of her immediate family would do, hence her journey to Lagos."

"You have to stop torturing yourself about the past," Samantha pleaded with Josie's mum. "The Josie I have come to know is a wonderful girl; very well-mannered and always willing to help others. My sister can bear witness to this. She is like family and I can assure you she is taking her studies seriously. She has matured into a confident, young lady; someone you would be proud of. I know it is little comfort but believe me when I say that you have nothing to worry about."

They hugged each other and once again promised to keep in touch.

With that, the sisters went to the second floor to see how their mother and her sister were doing. The plan was for all of them to go home together once the consultant had given their mum the all clear. When they got there, they were told that both women had left over an hour ago. When Samantha asked for the doctor who had treated their mother, she was told that he had also left for the day.

Both Samantha and Kathleen felt bad about the situation, after all they were meant to be there for their mother. Eventually they called her cell phone, and that was when she told them that she and Edith had decided to have lunch in the hospital restaurant instead of waiting for them in the reception.

Irene's daughters hurried down to the restaurant, waited for their mum and auntie Edith to finish lunch, then called a cab to take them to Enfield. The plan once they got home was to make sure their mum was comfortable, after which Kathleen would dash out to do some last-minute shopping for the trip back to Nigeria the next day. However, when they got home they were pleasantly surprised to find that Margaret and Emmanuel had arrived.

The couple had let themselves in using their spare set of keys and apart from cooking dinner, Margaret had done some shopping for the house, buying the things she felt her grandmother would need after her daughters had left for home.

When Kathleen finally left the house to do her shopping, Margaret offered to go with her because she also wanted to pick up a few things for Bose, Josie and Eyo.

"So, what about your father and Tope; aren't you going to buy them anything?" Kathleen asked her daughter.
"What can I get them? After all, you are here, and he is your husband; Tope is in school in faraway Abuja, so..." Margaret said lamely as she laughed.

"Excuses, excuses," Kathleen shook her head and smiled. "Meanwhile, guess what happened today?"

"What?" Margaret asked curiously.

Kathleen told her daughter how she had met Josie's mother through Samantha's friend. She regaled her daughter of everything that had happened; how they had visited little Annabel Leah who had been sexually abused by the same man who raped Josie. Margaret had heard about Josie's story and was in total shock when she learnt that the same brute of a man had made the lives of both mother and daughter a living hell. When she asked her mother if it would be alright to visit little Leah in the hospital, Kathleen promised to give her Angela Kimberley's phone number so she could ask for permission from her to arrange a visit.

It was quite late when they finally got back home. Margaret helped her mother pack for the Lagos trip before they all sat down for dinner. Since their flight was early the next morning and Samantha and Kathleen really did not want to disturb their mother that early, they all said their goodbyes on the dining table and promised to call once they touched down in Lagos.

Early the next morning Margaret and Emmanuel drove the two sisters to the airport and waited for them to check in before returning to Enfield. The couple had decided to keep grandma Irene company and help out with errands for the next three days after which they planned to drive back to Aberdeen.

"Tears still streaming down her face Josie turned to her big brother. She could see the forgiving look in his eyes as they embraced each other for what seemed like an eternity."

Dominic Parkes

There was relative calm on campus as the students prepared for their final examinations. Bose and Josie were well-prepared thanks to a little assistance from their private tutor. They were also spending quality time in the library which seemed to be paying off.

As they packed their books and exited the library it was obvious that the girls were a lot happier than normal, and who could blame them; Bose's mum was coming back today, and the girls could hardly wait to see her.

When the Akinjide sisters landed in Lagos they called their mother as promised after which Samantha boarded a local flight to Abuja while Mohammed, one of the family drivers, picked Kathleen up from Arrivals and drove her home.

Kathleen was impressed with how tidy the house had been kept and was about to thank Eyo for doing such a wonderful job when Chris told his wife that she had the two maids, Bose and Josie to thank for keeping the house spick and span. Chris told Kathleen how Eyo just sat back and bossed everyone around. The only work she actually did was pop over to the supermarket when they ran out of milk. Gift had done the main market shopping as well as most of the cooking.

When Bose and Josie got home the entire household was buzzing. Everyone had something to enthuse about; even Eyo who was usually indifferent was gushing about her gifts, especially the ones that her older sister, Margaret had bought for her. When Mrs Archibong gave Josie her own present which was a lovely skirt and top with a small bottle of perfume, she could hardly believe it. She gave Bose's mum a massive hug and screamed her appreciation.

"Thank you, auntie Kath. To be honest I wasn't expecting anything but I am extremely grateful. Thank you so much."
"You are welcome Josie, but remember, you are a big part of this family and for as long as you are here I will treat you just like one of my own."
"Hey Josie, if there is something you don't want I'll have it. I'm sure I'll know what to do with it," Eyo smirked.
"Don't bother Eyo," Josie replied laughing. "You keep yours and I'll keep mine."
"And by the way, that is called covetousness, Eyo", her father remarked jokingly, but Eyo didn't find it amusing.
"So, Bose and Josie, how is the revision coming along? Kathleen asked. "I know I was not here to monitor things but I hope you are taking your studies seriously?"
"Erm, what exactly is that supposed to mean?" Chris objected. "Girls, can you please tell my wife that she is not the only one who helps you out with your studies. Abi Bose, na lie?"
"Daddy, you no lie," Bose answered in pidgin English with a cheeky smile. "He actually got one of his lecturer friends to help us out."

It was nice having most of the family back together again, and the sound of laughter was very refreshing.

After everyone had gone to bed Chris finally had an opportunity to find out about his wife's trip. He sat back expecting to hear about his mother in law and how her treatment was going but was left dumbfounded when Kathleen told him about her encounter with Josie's mother. However, when she related the story of the young girl and what she had been through Chris was shocked to the core.

"What kind of animal does that to his own child?" Chris

exclaimed, shaking with anger.

Kathleen waited patiently for her husband to calm down a bit before asking him how and when he thought they should break this traumatic news to Josie.

"Well, we can't tell her now," Chris muttered. "We are going to have to wait till she finishes her exams, and even then, I am not too sure how to break it to her."

Meanwhile, in London a new Commissioner of the Metropolitan Police had been appointed. His name was Mr Dominic Parkes.

Mr Parkes had vowed to rid the capital of criminals irrespective of who they were or who they knew. The crime of sexual abuse was top on his priority list as he hated it with a passion and was one of the main reasons why he joined the force after graduating from Oxford University.

The memory of how he came back from a holiday one summer evening to discover that his little sister had been raped by his supposed best friend always weighed heavily on his mind.

His friend had taken advantage of his little sister's naivety and tried to intimidate her, but when it came to her giving evidence in court, she was able to point out the perpetrator and did a good job of crying so loud that everyone including the jury had pity on her. This as well as the astuteness of the legal team that his family had hired to help with the prosecution, had clinched the case.

Dominic remembered the anger he felt at the time and how, if he had gotten his hands on his so-called friend he would most likely be doing time himself. But that was when he made up his mind to join the force. He was impressed with the way the police had diligently investigated the case, considering the fact that his sister was traumatised after the whole experience and was not in the right frame of mind to identify or even name the individual who had raped her.

Dominic Parkes enrolled at the Police College in Hendon, where he studied all aspects of policing. He was prepared to learn all he could about detective work and how to carry out effective crime investigations. He was also determined not to succumb to bribery and corruption no matter the inducement. Dominic was enjoying being a policeman and what started out as a quest for revenge against his sister's molester had turned into something he had come to love and cherish.

He had rapidly risen through the ranks because of his steadfastness, diligence, integrity and his attention to the minutest detail. On his first promotion he had been appointed as a diplomatic policeman stationed in one of the Middle East embassies where he had witnessed a lot of wrongdoing.

He was also posted outside the country for a little over three years where he was involved in intelligence gathering with the Interpol. It was during this period while living in the French capital that he met and married his wife who was also a police officer. When his assignment was up he asked his Commander if he could return to England as his wife was expecting their first child. His request was granted, and now here he was, the new Metropolitan Police Commissioner.

The crime rate in the capital had become a great concern. As usual, politicians looking for someone to blame had laid the onus of bringing down the crime rate firmly on the police department's doorstep even though they did not intend to put a stop to the planned financial cuts. It had not been easy for Dominic's predecessor who was castigated as a weakling even though he had tried his best with the resources he had. He had warned the ruling party about the danger of the cuts being made within the force and how there was no way they could function effectively in the capital with such reduced numbers, but his words had fallen on deaf ears.

Since he took over, Dominic had seen further cuts to the men and women that made up the force and his comments with regards to this issue had been publicised. However, the politicians continually rebutted his statements even though the facts were there for anyone who cared to take a look. His friends had warned him to go easy in his press conferences, but Dominic preferred to keep it real and did not mind facing the consequences. After all, his job was to protect the people and keep the Capital safe.

Before Dominic Parkes assumed the mantle, his predecessor had told him about some delicate, high profile murder, rape, robbery and racial incitement cases. He also advised him about the rise of suspected terrorist activities involving certain ethnic and religious groups. So, the first thing he did on his appointment was to assemble a unit of seven intelligent, trustworthy officers who would deal with certain cold case files. Dominic had no intention of profiling any individual or ethnic or religious group until his newly formed unit gave him the green light.

It was while he was mulling over what he could do to make this unit even more effective that his eye caught sight of a large file with multiple red tags, which implied that it was important and urgent. He also noticed that the date on the file made the case about eight years old. He opened the file, and from the first page of the report realised that it was a rape case. The name of the victim had been taped over because she was a minor but the alleged attacker happened to be the son of an elite member of society. He felt that same anger, which he thought he had conquered, rise up inside him and he could not bring his mind to finish reading the report. He decided that he would hand the file over to his special unit so that they could investigate the case further.

Dominic didn't know who the young girl was but he was determined to fight for her. However, first they had to contact her family. Considering how long ago it happened, he hoped the family were still interested in bringing the perpetrator to justice. It would also serve as a warning that crimes of this nature were not statute barred. Dominic felt the adrenaline pumping through his veins, he was excited. As far as he was concerned, a rapist was a coward and a criminal and should be put in jail and the keys thrown away. But he also knew his own limitations as a police officer; he was neither the judge nor the jury. His duty was to carry out a proper investigation and from there it was sent to the Crown Prosecution Service (CPS). However, he was determined that any case he investigated that went to court would not end up with a 'not guilty' verdict; every case would be proven beyond reasonable doubt. He asked his secretary to schedule a meeting with his new squad. He planned to meet with them after his visit to the Mayor's Office.

By the time Dominic Parkes got back to his office in Victoria, the team was ready and waiting. He closed the door and told his secretary that he was not to be disturbed. As requested, there were three large cold case files on his desk. The first file was a negligence case where an unqualified doctor had operated on a patient. The second file was a murder case, more of an honour killing of a girl who had married someone who did not share her family's ethnicity or religion. The third file was the rape case that he had handed to the squad.

He split the team into three, with two officers in each group, and handed each group the case he wanted them to work on. The seventh officer, the team leader would oversee the investigations and report directly to him. After the meeting Dominic asked the team leader to wait behind while the others filed out of his office.

The Commissioner told him that it was of utmost importance

that the team handling the rape case interrogated every person mentioned in the file, and if possible visit the parents of the girl to get their side of the story. He also warned him about the need for discretion because it was an extremely sensitive case, and the last thing he wanted to do was jeopardise it in any way. Lastly, he told the team leader that he expected a daily report on each case no matter how minute the detail. Once he dismissed the young officer, he decided to embark on some discreet investigating of his own; he would start by tracking down the first officers who handled the case.

Interestingly it was while Dominic was talking to his wife after dinner that he had a eureka moment regarding the rape case. His wife had sensed something was bothering him as soon as he walked through the door but thought it would be wise to bring it up later. After dinner she put the children to sleep then sat beside her husband in the lounge.

"So, how was your meeting with the Mayor?"

"It was quite fruitful actually. He was very cooperative and even told me not to hesitate to contact his office if I needed any assistance with my plan to clean up the capital of its crimes and other misdemeanours."

"So, what is running through that mind of yours? You have looked preoccupied since you stepped through the front door."

"Well, I came across a cold case file last week and it sort of brought back memories. It was a..."

"Rape case," his wife concluded.

"Yes," Dominic replied looking surprised.

"Don't ask me how I knew, but I guessed as much. You need to give yourself a break. I hope you know you cannot change the world all alone. When are you going to stop thinking of rape cases every time? You cannot change the world alone!"

"I know, but that does not mean that I won't keep trying. I will do all I can to seek justice for the helpless, especially in those high-profile cases that have to do with the elite of our society."

"Talking of high profile cases, when I went for coffee with Carol today, she told me about a little girl that she had been visiting in the hospital who incidentally happens to be a rape victim too."

"Is this a recent case?" Dominic asked.

"I suppose so. From the way she said it sounded like they knew who the perpetrator was but he had not been apprehended because of his parent's status."

"Nonsense!" Dominic exploded. "Are the laws of the land meant only for the poor? I don't remember reading that in any of our statute books."

"She also told me that the little girl's mother was also raped, I think that was eight years ago, and this child was a result of the abuse. In fact, what makes the story even more devastating is that both the mother and child were sexually abused by the same man. So, it is actually a case of a father raping his own child!"

Dominic closed his eyes and shook his head, he found it hard to comprehend the horrific story he had just heard.

"Did Carol tell you the name of the minor who was raped eight years ago?" he asked in a menacing tone.

"If I remember correctly, I think Carol said her name was Josie Kimberley. Does her name ring a bell?"

"That is the name on the case file." Dominic could not believe it. "That young girl never got any justice, her case did not even sniff the doors of a courtroom, but in spite of all the pressure my predecessor refused to close the case."

Dominic smiled and hugged his wife.

"Thank you so much honey," he whispered in her ear. "What would I do without you!"

After a brief silence, Dominic heaved a sigh of relief.

"Honey, I know you are really busy with the kids but I need you to help me with this case, starting with your friend Carol. If you could get all the information you can from her I would really appreciate it."

Dominic couldn't believe his luck and he was somehow amused about the whole scenario. His wife was simply a blessing, always at the right place at the right time. At times he would laugh at her girlish ramblings, but the truth was that she cracked cases by simply talking to people. Even if they did not want to talk they eventually opened up to her. How she did it he did not know, but he knew his lovely wife was gifted.

It was a happy Commissioner who walked through the doors of his office the following day. He immediately called the team leader and gave him the family name of the rape victim. He advised the young officer to start by going to the school the girl attended at the time of the attack, and if possible question those who were still there. He knew he was treading on thin ice when he saw the name of the man who allegedly committed the crime, but he was equally mindful of the fact that if he let the perpetrator off, it would be contrary to everything he believed and stood for. He was prepared to sacrifice his career to see justice carried out on behalf of this mother and her child.

Dominic planned to call the individuals who were listed in the original case file, starting with his predecessor, the local priest and the Dean of the College where the incident took place. He was also beginning to wonder how he was going to approach the parents of the young girl when his phone rang. It was his wife.

"Dom, I just spoke to Carol and she offered to set up a meeting with Mrs Angela Kimberley, the girl's mother. She is looking at some time next week."

"That will be fantastic. Thank you, dear. You know I love you right?" He laughed.

"Yes, I know," she giggled.

27
Diligence Rewarded

*T*he University exams went smoothly amid fears that they would be cancelled. There had been rumours that certain cults from other institutions of higher learning were planning to instigate trouble on the university campus. Fortunately the authorities had been able to quench these plans by putting out feelers to other universities to help forestall whatever was being planned, and a contingent of mobile police units was drafted to various universities around the country where these cults were said to be based.

Students were encouraged by the various university authorities to go home once they had handed in their final papers and advised to keep checking their university websites for further information as to when results would be posted as well as the date for their respective graduation ceremonies.

Both Bose and Josie were more than content with their examination performance. While some of the girls had spent time flirting with lecturers to achieve exam success, they had studied hard and they believed their hard work would be rewarded with excellent grades. The girls were ecstatic that their university degrees were done and dusted and didn't even try to hide their excitement as Fred, one of the Archibong drivers, drove them home one last time.

While they waited for their examination results to be published, the girls decided that they wanted to visit Bose's aunt, Samantha and her family in Abuja. Josie had wanted them to travel by road so that she could take in the scenery of the countryside, but Mr

Archibong advised against it. He knew the dangers of travelling for miles by road in public transport without any security or protection. He also knew that Josie, being a white girl, would most likely attract unnecessary attention, so to him, it really wasn't worth the risk.

One of Chris' friends had suggested that if they really wanted to go to Abuja by road then the best option would be to travel in one of the ABC coaches. ABC transport was a top-notch transportation company that catered for the rich and middle class. The company boasted new, fully air-conditioned coaches with WiFi and offered guaranteed, top spec security that was second to none.

In the end, the compromise was that they would go by air and return by road in an ABC coach.

The day for the Abuja trip had finally arrived. Bubbling with excitement, Bose and Josie had placed their luggage in the boot and were about to leave for the airport when Bose's mum came rushing out of the house looking shaken. Apparently, the plane that the girls were scheduled to fly to Abuja had crashed a few miles from the airport.

They all stood, rooted to the spot; confused, not knowing what to do. Then suddenly the girls dashed into the house, stood in front of the television screen and watched as the news about the crash unfolded. Bose and Josie looked at each other, fear written on their faces, the same thought going through their minds: If the plane crash had happened on the way to Abuja they would have been in it!

Mrs Archibong instructed the driver to bring in the girls' luggage, and just in case they did not know already, she told her daughter and her friend that the trip to Abuja was off. This was particularly painful for Josie because even though she understood the reason why, she had been looking forward to going to Abuja for some time. She could have gone to Abuja earlier, after all she had been in the country for more than four years, but due to her own procrastination she hadn't.

Both of Bose's parents walked into the lounge, their eyes glued to the screen. What would they have done if Josie was on that flight? With James Eastwood breathing down their necks and constantly reminding them that Josie's welfare was ultimately his primary responsibility, they both knew that while she was living with them they could not afford for anything to go wrong.

Since the trip to Abuja had been cancelled, Chris and Kathleen found themselves struggling to keep Bose and Josie occupied. Each day they checked the university website but there was no indication that the results would be published any time soon. Chris thought that he might have to pay Professor Davies a visit to see if he could advise on when the exam results would be released, or better still find out if he could confirm Bose and Josie's grades.

The Archibongs had decided to invite Josie's family for their daughter's graduation. While making the necessary plans they were also beginning to realise how much they were going to miss Josie once she returned to England.

Considering the good influence she had been to both Bose and Eyo, and even to their son Tope, who had grown to like and appreciate Josie so much that he now called her 'sis', it was obvious that they were really going to miss her. However, inviting Josie's parents over to witness this special day was the least they could do. Kathleen and Chris sensed that it was what Josie desired, so, hopefully seeing her family would be a pleasant surprise.

As the days rolled by, Kathleen and Chris noticed that Josie was getting more and more restless, and once again she asked if she could revisit some of the tourist attractions that she had really enjoyed over the past four years. This time however she was quite specific.

"Uncle Chris, would it be possible for us to revisit a few places before I go back to England; places like Ile-Ife to see the ancient artworks and the fabric dyeing shops; Olumo rock so we can climb those man-made stairs that were carved out of it, and the National Museum in Benin city? Please!"
"Well, let us wait and see, Josie," Mr Archibong replied in a low, hesitant voice.

Chris was in a bit of a quandary because Josie would not let go. Like a dog with a bone she insistently went on about wanting to visit these attractions before going back home. He knew how she felt; she wanted to do as much as possible before leaving Nigeria. However, he was reluctant to let Josie and Bose visit these places without some kind of protection. If only he could take some time off work he would have accompanied the girls on their adventure himself but unfortunately now was a very busy time in the office.

Then there was the issue of the girls' grades. He was still quite concerned that the results had not been released especially as the graduation day was just around the corner. At least he needed to confirm that Josie's name was actually on the graduation list before inviting her parents over for the ceremony. So, time wasn't exactly on his side.

One day it all came to a head. Right there and then he made up his mind to talk to his friend Wale Dada and see if he could pull some strings at the University so he could confirm when the results would finally be released.

Unfortunately, Chris' phone call caught Wale at the wrong time as he was just about to step out of the house. His son, one of the twins, had decided to relocate back to Nigeria from the States and was arriving that day. Wale was in a hurry to leave for the airport to pick him up and had asked if Chris wouldn't mind coming over to his place later on in the evening to discuss what was on his mind.

As Chris dropped the phone he suddenly had an idea. Maybe Kehinde, Wale's son could accompany the girls on their planned tourist trips. Personally, he believed the girls needed a male figure with them and from what he knew about Kehinde, he was a responsible, respectable young man. So, if he could it would be an answer to prayer. Or so he thought.

Excitedly Chris called his wife.

"Kath, I think God may have answered our prayer."
"What do you mean? What prayer are you talking about exactly?"

Kathleen wasn't too sure she understood what her husband was going on about.

"I just got off the phone with Wale. He told me that Kehinde has decided to relocate back to Nigeria and that he was arriving today. He also invited me over to his house so I guess I'll discuss the issue of the girls' examination results with him."
"But why are you so interested in knowing their results before they are actually released? And what has this got to do with Wale's son? I am not sure I understand." Now Kathleen looked perplexed.
"Don't you see? Kehinde's return is very timely, he could accompany the girls on these trips that they want to go on."
"Are you sure? First of all, the young man is just coming back from America so I am not too sure that he will be conversant with all these places that Josie and Bose plan to visit. Then,

what makes you think that he will even be interested? Me I no dey there o," Kathleen replied breaking into pidgin English.

She paused for a second then continued.

"When was the last time you saw Kehinde? The young man has been in America for years; he may not be the same pleasant boy you used to know. I beg, leave this matter, I don dey tell you. Left to me the girls should stay at home and occupy themselves. And by the way, Eyo is here; I am sure they can all find something to do to while away the time."
"Oh, come on Kathleen, why do you have to be so negative? So, what if I haven't seen Kehinde for a while? Isn't his mother your very good friend, and he seemed okay to me when I saw him in America six years ago. Or do you know something that I don't?" Chris quizzed.
"Well, since you ask, rumour has it that he was found in possession of illegal drugs and was meant to be imprisoned, but Mr Dada's lawyer friend somehow managed to get him out on bail. I also heard that he actually skipped bail, hence his hurried return to Nigeria."
"Ah, *na wa o*[5]! These children of nowadays," Chris exclaimed. "Such a brilliant and intelligent young boy, why was he messing around with drugs? Now, for a moment of instant gratification and useless pleasure he has destroyed his bright future. But come o, you said it was just a rumour abi? So, it hasn't been confirmed?" her husband countered.
"*Na you sabi*[6]! All I know is that my daughter and Josie will not be going anywhere with him, and the fact that he is Maureen's son is irrelevant."

While they were talking, Josie came down to give Bose's mum the phone. It was James Eastwood.

---

[5] *An expression of surprise, joy, happiness, sadness, anger and despair used in the Nigerian Pidgin language*
[6] *"That's your business", in the Nigerian Pidgin language*

"Hello James, I hope everything is okay?"

"Yes, everything is fine, thank you. It's about Josie."

"What about her?"

"I was thinking that while she is waiting for her results I could get her a part-time job here at the High Commission. I ran it by my wife and she seemed to think it would be a good idea. What do you think?"

"Now, that would be brilliant. In fact, that will actually help resolve the dilemma we are currently facing. Chris and I have been thinking about how to keep the girls occupied during this period so this will be perfect. Thank you, James."

"You're welcome, Kathleen," James replied.

While she was on the phone Chris kept gesturing to Kathleen to tell him what she and James were talking about and was beginning to get frustrated. When she finally got off the phone, Kathleen told her eager looking husband about James Eastwood's proposal.

"So, what do you think?" she asked.

"Ah, this our God is good o! Here we were biting our nails, thinking about what to do. Meanwhile He had a solution already packaged. I think it is a wonderful suggestion if you ask me. I know James can be a bit pompous..."

"Ah, ah. You and James, na wa o!" Kathleen interjected laughing. "Anyway, I don't really care what you think about him, all I know is that right now he has saved us a major headache."

"Well, it is not done and dusted yet. We still have to convince Josie to accept the offer?"

"Don't worry, leave that with me. Besides, she is going to make some money; I am sure she won't complain about that."

Josie was over the moon when Mrs Archibong told her about the offer. She went ecstatic, dancing all over the place. Then she asked

Mrs Archibong when she was meant to start.

"First, let me tell Mr Eastwood that you are happy to accept the offer then we can discuss a start date, but I am pretty sure that he will want you to start as soon as possible."

In the midst of her excitement she suddenly realised that the job was only being offered to her. She and Bose had always done everything together so what was going to happen now? As the reality of the situation gradually dawned, her countenance drooped. Bose's mum noticed the sudden change and asked if she was having second thoughts.

"Not really auntie Kath, but what about Bose? Can't Mr Eastwood get her a job too?" Josie asked.
"My dear, do not worry about Bose. She can work in her father's office if she wants to. Or she can even help out at my boutique by supervising the shop assistants. Trust me, your friend will not be bored," Kathleen smiled.

Mr Eastwood expedited the paperwork so that Josie could resume the following Monday, the first day of June. Even though the British High Commission in Victoria Island wasn't that far from the Archibong residence, Josie enjoyed the luxury of being picked up and dropped off in a chauffeur-driven official car.

The days went by so quickly that even though Josie had only worked at the High Commission for a month and a half, it almost felt like she had been there for a year. She enjoyed the work and the thrill it gave her, and was over the moon when she received her first paycheck. She couldn't believe the amount she had been paid; it was more than she had anticipated since there really hadn't been any discussion about how much she was going to earn at the time of the appointment.

Even though she now earned a salary, Josie was not allowed to contribute anything and occasionally when she popped into the Shoprite Centre to buy some sausages, bread, butter, eggs and a few other things needed in the house, Bose's mum would tell her not to bother as it wasn't necessary.

One day she made up her mind that she was going to share part of her salary with everyone. She enclosed various amounts in enveloped 'Thank You' cards and waited until Sunday morning when everyone was getting ready to go to church. Then she and Tope slipped the envelopes into the ladies' handbags and into Mr Archibong's large agbada pocket without any of them knowing. Once this was all done, Josie and Tope gave each other a high five and whispered, "Mission accomplished." What they did not realise was that Eyo had been watching them all along.

It was the way they kept whispering to each other as well as their suspicious behaviour that attracted Eyo's attention. Even though she was amused at their immaturity, she gave Josie kudos for being so magnanimous in character and wanting to share her salary with the family. Eyo wondered if she would do the same had the ball been in her court and knew straight away that she wouldn't. She also knew that once everyone found out what was in the envelopes they would most likely return it to Josie promptly.

Kathleen didn't discover the mystery envelope in her handbag until lunchtime when she was taking out her cell phone. Out of curiosity she opened the envelope thinking that one of the ladies in her church group had placed it there, only to find a thank you card and some money from Josie.

Even though she was really touched by the young girl's gesture of love and appreciation, Mrs Archibong knew she could not keep the money. However, because she did not want to hurt Josie, she had devised a way to say thank you and at the same time give the money back. But first she needed to run it by Chris.

Bose came across her envelope at around the same time as her dad who looked confused when the envelope fell out of his pocket while he was changing. Just as he was showing his wife what he found, Bose, not sure what to do, ran over to tell her parents that Josie had given her some money. It soon dawned on Chris and Kathleen that Josie must have given each member of the family an envelope. So, they called Eyo and Tope and told them to hand over the mystery envelopes they had received.

Tope was not exactly chuffed that he had to give the envelope back especially as he knew what he was going to do with his share of the booty. Eyo on the other hand already knew why she was being called and simply handed her parents the envelope. She had no plans of spending the money anyway as she felt Josie deserved every penny and there was no need to give it to anyone. In a funny sense it reminded Eyo of how much she was going to miss Josie, especially as Josie seemed to understand her better than her own sister.

After collecting all the envelopes, Kathleen told them they were going to use the money to buy Nigerian fabric for Josie's family who they hoped would be coming over for her graduation. She also warned her children not to let Josie know as it was meant to be a surprise.

That afternoon while they all sat down for lunch, it was Mr Archibong who broached the topic of the mystery envelopes.

"Josie, thank you so much for the surprise packages that you gave us. We are really very grateful, but you know you did not have to do that. I have said it before and I will say it again, you are and always will be a part of our family, even when you go back to England."
"Thank you, uncle Chris. I have felt at home from the first day I arrived; the envelopes are just a token of my gratitude. After all I assure you that there is a lot more where that came

from," Josie laughed.

And that was the last they said about the envelopes.

In July, Wale and Chris, as discussed, went to see Professor Davies. It turned out that the university had just finished collating the students' results so he was able to show them Bose and Josie's. Both girls were among the thirty students who had graduated with first-class honours degrees in their various disciplines.

Chris was overjoyed, he hugged his friend and praised God. He was especially happy for Josie and knew that her parents would be so proud of what she had accomplished; that in spite of everything she had been through, she had shown that she was not going to be dragged down by circumstances and situations. He was also grateful to God, for using his family to give Josie a second chance.

He carefully wrote out their individual scores and grades and thanked the Vice-Chancellor for his kindness and cooperation. Professor Davies had played a big part in Josie's success as he had been very helpful and understanding when it came to accommodating Josie's peculiar situation while seeking admission to the university. Before leaving the Vice-Chancellor's office, Chris invited him for lunch. Professor Davies thanked Mr Archibong for the offer and promised to think about it.

Chris was so excited about the girls' results that he handed his car keys to Wale and asked if he wouldn't mind driving them home. It was while they were driving back to Victoria Island that Wale told Chris about his son Kehinde. It was a long, intriguing story but Wale insisted on telling him every single detail. He was obviously very disappointed with his son but he had taken consolation in the fact that Taiwo, Kehinde's twin brother had turned out to be what every father would be proud of.

Taiwo had completed his Master's degree and started his PhD

program. Wale also told his friend that Taiwo would be coming to Nigeria in August for a month as, to use his words, he wanted to find a wife.

Immediately Wale made that statement, Chris' mind went into overdrive. If he remembered correctly, Taiwo Dada was about twenty-seven years old which just might make him perfect for his daughter Eyo. He thought that, rather than mope around all day and surf the internet, the time might just be right for his second daughter to start thinking about marriage and marrying his friend's son didn't sound like a bad idea. But then, there was the little issue of Taiwo's twin brother.

"So, now that Kehinde is back, what does he intend to do?" Chris asked.

"Well, I have not asked him yet because I don't know where or how to start. Since he came back, all he does is eat and sleep and Maureen can't stop crying. You would have noticed that it has been a while since she last came over to yours and each time Kathleen calls her, she comes up with one silly excuse or another to explain why she is not available. I tell you, I am losing my patience with both of them!"

"*Haba!*[7] Take it easy my friend. I am sure you understand that no mother would enjoy seeing her child in that condition. Remember, whatever is in the house of a lizard is also found in the house of a rat. There is no complete family, including my own. Would it be okay if one of these days I came over to talk to him?"

"Why should I mind? Please feel free. In fact, anything that will help bring him out of the cuckoo land he has descended into is fine by me. Right now, I am more concerned about my wife."

"Okay, I will come over when I get back from Abuja on Friday.

---

[7] *An exclamation of astonishment or disappointment commonly used in the Nigerian Pidgin, Igbo, Yoruba and Hausa languages*

Wale pulled into the Archibong residence and thanked Chris for listening to him.

"Thank you for listening to me ramble on."
"No problem at all Wale, that's what true friends are for," Chris smiled and placed an assured hand on his friend's shoulder.

Wale gave Chris his car keys and they bade each other good night.

Kehinde

*C*hris Archibong arrived in Lagos on Friday afternoon and that evening, as promised, he drove down to the Dada residence to visit Wale's son. As the two friends relaxed on the patio, Chris asked Wale if he could first have a word with Maureen before talking to Kehinde. Wale did not say anything but nodded to confirm that it was okay.

Maureen came into the conservatory with a tray of snacks and drinks for the two men. She placed them on the table and just as she was about to leave Chris asked if she could please take a seat. From the look on Chris' face Maureen knew that whatever he wanted to say had to be very important.

"Maureen, your husband told me about what happened to Kehinde. I am still finding it hard to believe how my godson got involved in this illegal activity."

"I don't know how much Wale told you but all I can say is that your godson is no longer the sweet boy you used to know. I keep asking myself where we went wrong? Wale and I never denied Kehinde and his brother anything; we always paid their school fees on time and made sure we gave them an allowance that was more than enough just so they wouldn't get involved in things like this but look at how far that got us. I just don't know what to do," Maureen looked distraught as she shook her head.

"Don't torture yourself, Maureen; I am sure it has nothing to do with either you or Wale. The children of nowadays are very selfish; most of them are only interested in self-gratification."

Wale gave his wife a comforting hug.

"We can keep going back and forth," Chris opined, "but we cannot change the past. Now we need to pray for wisdom to salvage the situation and move forward. Maybe you need to ask him what his plans are for the future, apart from eating and sleeping. The Kehinde I knew was a brilliant young man who always strived for greatness. I am sure he regrets what he has done, and with a little encouragement I believe he can make something of himself now that he is back home."

"Well, personally I think that we sent them off to America way too early; they were too young to understand and..."

"Maureen, stop right there!" Wale interjected angrily as he looked at his wife. "Don't let us start with that silly excuse again. What do you want to say about Margaret, Eyo and even young Bosede? Were they not left in England while their parents came back to Nigeria? Look at what they made of themselves. Even take a look at our Taiwo, has he not done well for himself?"

Chris realised that the conversation was rapidly deteriorating. He knew he had to do something. He tried to calm the couple down and once again assured them that their son was not a lost cause. Then he told them about Josie's story; how she came to Nigeria of all places and was given a second chance at life and had become a university graduate because she was encouraged to take the bull by the horns. Then he reminded them that Josie's story would never have become a reality if not for the part that Wale and Maureen played in it. After all, it was Wale who initiated the process of the young English girl's sojourn to Nigeria.

"If you could sow such a seed into the life of a total stranger, then be rest assured that God has not forgotten you; He can turn Kehinde's situation around," Chris encouraged the couple.

Now, the patio just happened to be located under Kehinde's bedroom window and unbeknown to Chris, Maureen and Wale, he had opened his window slightly to listen in on what they were saying. All Kehinde had planned to do was eavesdrop on the latest gossip; little did he know that he would be the subject of their conversation.

Kehinde had listened intently to everything his parents and uncle Chris had said but hearing Josie's story had broken something inside him. He started to sob quietly; gradually his sobbing became uncontrollably loud and he quickly stepped away from his window so as not to attract attention. Then standing in front of his wardrobe mirror he took a look at himself; he hated what he saw, or rather what he had become.

At that very moment Kehinde decided that if only for the sake of his mother, he had to change his ways. He had pretended not to know what she was going through, but at unguarded moments he often heard her crying; he had noticed but was just too selfish to care.

Kehinde thought back to his time in the States and how he had dropped out of university; if only he could convince his father to enrol him at any of the universities in Nigeria, then maybe, just like Josie he too might be able to make something of himself. Now was the time to show his folks that though it might take a little longer, what Taiwo did, he could do also. It was not too late for him to surprise all of them and that is exactly what he intended to do.

If there was one thing Kehinde did not appreciate, it was being compared to his twin brother. He remembered while they were in in the States how Taiwo had warned him about the company he was keeping but he had dismissed them as rants from a dullard. The truth was Kehinde had always been envious of his brother because he was everything that he aspired to be but had not achieved.

His twin was the perfect son, he did everything right, listened to corrections and always sent his college reports home for mum and dad to see. He went to church and even joined the Scripture Union while at university. He had no time for girls especially American ones and had always maintained that when the time was right he would marry a Nigerian girl irrespective of her tribe citing his parents as an example.

The contrast between both of them couldn't have been any wider. Kehinde had fathered a child out of wedlock with a black American girl who he met in a bar while he was drunk; a one-night stand! He remembered how the girl had insisted that he marry her or else she would get her brother and his thugs to track him down. She told him explicitly that she wouldn't be responsible for whatever happened after they were done with him.

That was the beginning of his troubles. He fled that state for another, but her brother eventually found him. He remembered how her brother had held a gun to his head and told him that no one messed with his sister and got away with it, especially a dumb ass African boy. They forced him into being one of their carriers trafficking drugs between Mexico and the border states and threatened to kill him if he dared inform the authorities.

Standing in front of his mirror, he realised that he was actually a very lucky man. He had escaped from the hands of that gang and ran straight into the waiting hands of the state's law enforcement who had been monitoring the building where he was holed up with his captors. He cried as he told them the story of how he was forced into being a part of the drug ring, but his story fell on deaf ears.

No amount of explaining was enough to get him off the hook. To them, he was part of a drug ring that they wanted off the streets. He and the other gang members were locked up, but the girl's brother who was a notorious drug dealer, well known to the authorities, was still on the run.

Kehinde told the officer interrogating him that he had only just moved to that state because he was running away from the gang, but unfortunately, they had caught up with him. When asked if he had any family in the country he gave them Taiwo's number, who when contacted confirmed that he was his brother but that it had been a while since they last saw each other. The officer on the other end of the phone line then invited Taiwo to the station to be interviewed.

At the time, Taiwo was getting ready to present his final dissertation for his Master's degree and would have preferred not to, but he knew that if he did not attend the interview they would most likely come looking for him and ultimately find a way to link him to his brother's crimes.

Not wanting to go alone, Taiwo convinced a friend of his who was in the same university to accompany him to the station where his brother was being held. Before leaving, Taiwo had called his parents in Nigeria to inform them of what was going on. That was when his father told him to contact a friend of his who happened to be an attorney in the city where Kehinde was being held.

By the time Taiwo got to the police station, his father's lawyer friend was already there waiting. It turned out that he was a well-known criminal attorney who specialised in cases dealing with immigrants who were not aware of their rights.

When they walked into the building, they were ushered to the police lieutenant's office, who on seeing the attorney, asked why he was here and how he knew about this matter? Taiwo explained that he was their family lawyer and he wanted him to be present while they questioned him.

Having sorted out the necessary preambles, the lieutenant sent his deputy to get Kehinde. Taiwo was shocked at his brother's dishevelled appearance and noticed that he was walking with a limp. He concluded that either he sustained the injury at the hands of the police or the hands of the bad company he kept.

Kehinde remembered how his brother had looked at him with such scorn and loathing. If it were possible he was sure that Taiwo would have disowned him on the spot, and he didn't blame him; most likely he would have done the same if their roles were reversed. When he saw the attorney whom he later came to understand was his father's friend, he wondered if it was worth the bother because from all indications, he was headed for a long stint in jail. Now, as he looked back he knew that he had been a jerk because not once did he show any appreciation to his brother or his father for contacting the lawyer and for raising money for his bail.

During his wild days, one thing he never forgot to do was renew his passport, and knowing he had no plans of hanging around once he was bailed out, it came in very handy.

Listening to his parents and his godfather brought back all those nasty memories. He hadn't told anyone, not even his twin brother that he had fathered a child while he was living in the States. Now here he was in Nigeria causing his parents all kinds of grief.

Another mistake he had made was since returning to Nigeria he had not called his brother and now he had just heard that Taiwo would soon be coming home on holiday. How is he going to face his brother? He needed an ally, and not wanting to cause his ever-dependable mother any more heartache, he concluded it was going to have to be his godfather.

Kehinde was eager to grab his second chance with both hands and nothing was going to stop him. He had heard them talk about the English girl who his parents had helped and was now staying with the Archibongs; "I have to meet her and find out how she managed to accomplish so much in this foreign land despite going through so much heartache and pain," he whispered to himself.

Josie and Bosede's graduation day was now just a week away, and apart from picking up the customised outfits that they were going to wear on the day and their graduation gowns, they were good to go.

Josie had invited James Eastwood and his wife and they were only too happy to attend, while Bosede's parents had booked a double suite at one of the best hotels in Lagos between Victoria Island and Lekki to accommodate the Kimberleys who were scheduled to arrive two days before the graduation ceremony.

Kathleen had also received some good news about little Leah. She had been discharged from the hospital and was staying temporarily with Carol Pearce. She also heard that the new police Commissioner had not only reopened Josie's case, but was also investigating the sexual abuse of Annabel Leah. The police had concluded that they were looking at a case of a sexual predator who had over time become a paedophile and they were intent on putting him away for as long as they possibly could. No one had told Josie about any of this, but there would be plenty of time to do that after the family reunion.

Kathleen felt that on the whole Josie's sojourn had not been a wasted one. If anything, it had been rather fruitful and she believed that in the end everything would work out for Josie and her daughter.

While thinking about Josie tears began to roll down Kathleen's cheeks. They had all grown so fond and protective of Josie, who had become an integral part of their family, and to say that they were going to miss her was simply an understatement.

She remembered when they came back from church the other day, Kehinde was waiting for them and all he wanted to do was speak to Josie. At first, she was sceptical but then she reasoned that since he had come to their house he could not harm her in any way. However, she still made sure that she kept a close eye on them. It was later that Kathleen learnt that he had come to ask Josie how she had managed to survive and adapt to life in a place like Nigeria.

Josie had told Kehinde that apart from being determined and believing that it was actually possible to accomplish any goal you set for yourself, the love which the Archibongs had showered on her had enabled her to put her past behind her and focus on a brighter future. She had also decided to make the best of her stay in Nigeria and was determined not to return to the United Kingdom until she had achieved something significant that would make her family proud of her.

She inspired him in such a way that when he got back home Kehinde told his parents that he was willing to have another go at any university in the country that would accept him, even at the age of twenty-seven. He seemed to have matured overnight and was ready to make something of himself, even if it was just to prove to his family that he was a changed man.

Kehinde's parents were more than willing to accommodate what he had told them bearing in mind what Chris had said about giving their son another chance. However, the thought of the cult culture which was so predominant in most Nigerian universities, and whether their son would be able to resist the temptation of getting involved loomed at the back of their minds.

So, Wale and Maureen advised their son to give it some serious thought and if he still believed it was a journey he really wanted to embark on, then he should let them know.

"Dad, mum, I have thought this through and it isn't just something I want to do, it is something I need to do. I have to grab this chance now before I start throwing another pity party for myself. I have thrown so many years of my life away and like they say, time waits for no man."

"Okay Kehinde," his mother responded, "but you definitely will not be schooling here in Lagos. I will speak to my uncle who is one of the professors in F.U.T.O and hear what he has to say. Maybe he can help."

"F.U.T.O! What is that?"

"It is the Federal University of Technology, Owerri and it is in Imo State," his father answered.

Kehinde was grateful that his parents were willing to help and to their surprise he gave them both a big hug, something he hadn't done in quite a while. His mind went back to how they used to be a closely-knit family, that was until he messed up. He thought about his little sisters who were coming home from school this weekend. The last time he saw them was when he came to Nigeria, nine years ago; he was really looking forward to seeing them.

As he whistled back to his room to play his saxophone, the one thing he had brought back with him despite leaving America in a hurry, there was a bounce of satisfaction in his step. Somehow, he knew that his life was on the up and he planned to do all he could to make sure it stayed that way.

"So why did you say he was not going to study here in Lagos?" Wale asked his wife while they sat in the lounge later that afternoon.

"Lagos and all its distractions!" She exclaimed. "What do you think will happen when his old friends hear that he is back? They are going to want to invite him to all their social gatherings, and with his current state of mind I am not sure he will be able to resist."

"Are you saying there are no girls and bad boys in F.U.T.O?" Wale queried. "These cults are everywhere dear, but if Prof can help us get him admitted, why not. We just have to place it all in God's hands and hope he does not get himself into any more trouble."

"Remember we are helping him have a go at another chance. Let us not throw away the baby with the bath water. He is our son so we need to go the extra mile. He needs us now more than ever before."

"Don't tell me that you regret spoiling him so much?" Wale asked sarcastically. "You know, if you had agreed with me each time I tried to discipline him this would never have happened. You and your *Nna mu o*[8]. *Shebi*[9] that is the pet name you used to call him that always made the boy's head swell. You see now."

"Go ahead and blame it all on me again. After all, I did object to his going to America but you insisted that Taiwo would be lonely without him."

They were still engrossed in their tit for tat conversation when there was a sudden power cut. Wale got up to start the generator which gave Maureen a chance to start getting the house ready. With Taiwo and the girls coming in over the weekend it was going to be a full house.

Over at the Archibongs, frenetic arrangements were in top gear. Their guests from England were on their way and the girls had started the countdown to their graduation.

There was excitement in the air and it was contagious.

---

[8] *Endearment of a doting Igbo mother to her son*
[9] *"Isn't it true", in the Yoruba Nigerian dialect*

The Arrival

*I*t was Wednesday, Josie's last day at the British High Commission. She had finished work early so she could catch up with Bose. Both of them had planned to see the seamstress who was sewing the custom fitted outfits they were going to wear on their graduation day. Bose had purposely made sure that their appointment with the tailor coincided with when her parents were going to the airport to pick up Josie's family.

The plane arrived a few minutes after six that evening and Chris and Kathleen were waiting patiently in the arrivals hall watching as one by one the passengers walked by. They had been planning this moment for months but now that it was finally here the couple felt an air of uncertainty. Even though Kathleen had met Angela and Chris had spoken to John over the phone a few times, they still were not sure what it would be like when they eventually meet face to face.

They had been waiting in the arrivals hall for close to an hour when Kathleen spotted Angela, her husband and their three children looking around for a familiar face. She skipped excitedly towards them, Chris following closely behind her.

"Hello Angela," Kathleen gave her a warm hug.
"Hello Kathleen, so nice to see you again,"
"Nice to see you too. How was the trip, I hope it wasn't too tiring?"
"It was fine. I think I slept for most of the journey anyway," Angela smiled.
"Now you must be Daphne, and you must be Lois, right?"

Kathleen asked excitedly.

The girls nodded beaming from ear to ear.

"And you must be Bruce. Josie's told us so much about you."
"Nice to meet you, Mrs Archibong. I hope I pronounced
your name properly?" Bruce stuttered.
"Well, that was a good try," Kathleen giggled.

The two men stood back smiling, none of them uttered a word,
secretly sizing each other up. Finally, one of them decided to take
the plunge.

"So nice to finally meet you Angela," said Chris kissing her
on each cheek.
"It is nice to meet you too Mr Archibong," Angela smiled.
"And John, it's nice to finally be able to put a face to the
voice," both men smiled and shook hands.

The warm handshake did the trick. With the ice finally broken the
parents began to speak freely like long lost friends while Bruce and
the girls took in the warm Nigerian atmosphere. As they all walked
to the car park they ran into a familiar face.

Even though the thought had crossed their minds, both Kathleen
and Chris had forgotten to inform Mr Eastwood about the
Kimberleys' trip to Nigeria. So, imagine the surprise on every face
when they bumped into each other.

"Okay, now this is a surprise; a pleasant one I must say but it
would have been nice for someone to have told me that the
Kimberleys were coming to town," the disappointment was
evident in James' voice.
"That would be my fault," Kathleen admitted. "We were just
so tied up with making sure that Josie didn't find out that it

sort of slipped my mind. I really am sorry about that James."

"Ah, that's okay Kathleen." Then turning to the Kimberleys, "It really is a pleasure seeing you all once again. I hope you enjoy your stay here and if it is okay with Kathleen and Chris, maybe we can meet up for lunch or dinner before you leave."

"Of course, my friend," John Kimberley replied. "And I believe I also owe you an apology. It seems even I got so caught up in the excitement of surprising my daughter that I simply forgot to inform you of our travel arrangements. No hard feelings I hope?"

"Of course not!" James exclaimed. "I can only imagine the kind of emotions that you are all going through at the moment, and I just hope that the reunion will be everything that you have imagined it to be."

"Thank you so much James, for everything you have done for Josie over the last almost five years. We really do appreciate you," Angela responded with a heartwarming smile.

"It was nothing Angela. After all, what is a favour between friends," James winked.

Chris Archibong had been a spectator so far but now out of curiosity he had a question of his own.

"So, James I was just wondering, which special dignitary are you meeting at the airport today then?"

"Wouldn't you like to know," James replied with a smug smile. "Actually, I came to pick up my sister. She is spending two weeks with us before visiting some other African countries." James took a look at his watch. "Oops, I better get going. She will most likely be waiting for me in the arrivals hall right now."

They all waved goodbye to Mr Eastwood and finally arrived at the car park. The Archibongs had come in two seven-seater vehicles so that there would be enough space for their guests. Both the Archibong drivers, Fred and Mohammed, knew what to expect when it came to traffic bottlenecks, they also knew that the Maryland bypass was a no go. To avoid most of the traffic they took the Ikeja GRA route on to Ikorodu road which linked them up to the Gbagada expressway and finally on to the Third Mainland bridge.

They made it to the hotel in record time, avoiding all the shanty areas and slums that might put their first-time visitors off. Kathleen and Chris knew that the Kimberleys were tired and hungry, and understandably so considering they had been on the move for close to twelve hours. So, Chris got them checked into their rooms as quickly as possible and while they were settling in he asked what everyone would like to eat. The general consensus was Chinese food so Chris took the liberty of booking a few tables at the nearby Chinese restaurant which luckily was open until late.

The restaurant was teeming with diners which made sense as their food, especially the late-night buffet was highly recommended. They were ushered to their reserved seats and then, taking turns they got up and dished what they wanted to eat. Kathleen and Angela along with Daphne and Lois got their food first then the men went to get theirs. At first Bruce wanted to say that he was not hungry but when he saw the array of food, he suddenly realised how hungry he actually was; he heaped his plate so high that his father had to ask him where he planned to stuff all of it. Finally, when they had all dished their food Daphne asked the question that had been bugging her all day.

"Daddy, when are we going to see Josie?"
"That's true, how come she didn't come with you?" Lois asked looking at Kathleen. "Didn't she know we were..."
"Now girls," their mother butted in, "you both know that this trip is meant to be a big surprise for your sister. We are all going to see Josie on Friday at her graduation. Is that okay?"
"Okay mum," the girls chorused.

By the time they all finished eating it was almost midnight. The Kimberleys had finally run out of adrenaline and needed some well-deserved rest. Chris paid the bill, amidst John's objections and then they headed back to the hotel. After saying good night and promising to see them the next day, Chris and Kathleen took their leave.

It was James Eastwood who woke them up early the next morning.

"Good morning John, I apologise for waking you up so early but I was wondering if you and the family would like to join my wife and I for dinner later on this evening, that is if you do not have anything else scheduled?"
"Well, that sounds okay to me. Let me run it by Angela and the Archibongs and get back to you," John replied.

The Kimberleys had heard about the numerous tourist attractions in Lagos and were looking forward to exploring these themselves. So, after breakfast, they waited for Mr Archibong who, having taken time off work had promised to be their tour guide for the day.

This time around Chris drove himself so that there would be enough space in the car for everyone to sit comfortably. Luckily, he also knew the streets of Lagos like the back of his hand. So even if the roads were jammed he would find a way to ensure that his guests enjoyed their day out.

One attraction that the Kimberleys seemed to really enjoy was the Kuramo Waters. While crossing the waters by boat the girls got so excited that they asked if they could go for a swim. Just as Chris was about to respond he noticed that there were quite a few small boats and canoes on the waters. When he asked what was going on he was told that the locals had chosen that day to have a fishing competition.

The sight of the boats and the fishermen, with their self-made fishing rods was a beauty for the Kimberleys to behold and they immediately brought out their cameras and started taking pictures.

By the time they finally got to their destination, the sun was high and the weather was getting quite hot. They got out of the boat and walked over to the place where they saw some men cracking fresh coconuts and selling the water. The Kimberleys had never tasted fresh coconut water before and definitely wanted to try it; the girls wanted it chilled while everyone else wanted it fresh from the coconut. Considering that this was the first time they were drinking fresh coconut water, Chris was a bit concerned at the rate at which they were consuming it and warned that they take it easy as drinking too much could make them feel nauseated or even upset their tummies. But Mr Kimberley seemed to think that their host was worrying over nothing.

"Thank you for the warning but this coconut juice is too sweet and refreshing to pass up," John said while ordering another cup. Then noticing the concerned look in Mr Archibong's eyes he said, "Don't worry about us Chris, I am sure we will be fine."
"Do you think we can take some of this back home with us? Daphne asked.
"I think so, but it will have to be checked in because carrying liquids in your hand luggage is no longer allowed," Bruce replied.

They took their time as they strolled along the beach and after taking in all that coconut water, Daphne and Lois still wanted ice cream and hot dogs.

As much as Chris wanted them to enjoy their outing, he couldn't help but think his guests were overdoing things a little; first with the sun, then the coconut juice, and now with the ice cream and hot dogs, and it did not take long before he was proven right.

Walking in the scorching heat was beginning to take its toll. Initially Chris thought about taking them back to the hotel then decided to hire a couple of tents instead to shield them from the blazing sunshine.

"Is it always this hot in Lagos?" John asked as he lazed on the bamboo chaise longue inside the tent.

"No, not really. Just like England, we have different seasons. There is the rainy season, the harmattan season and what we call the August break," Chris replied. "We plant our crops during the rainy season, which is usually between March and May. We have a bit of a lull in August when it hardly rains at all, then the cold and dusty harmattan season kicks in between November and January."

"Wow, now that sounds interesting," Bruce said excitedly.

Bruce was already thinking ahead about how he could entice Peter Rowe and some other friends of his to come to Nigeria on a Safari-like holiday. So, he asked a pertinent question that would help him map out his strategy.

"Mr Archibong, I was on Google last night checking the wildlife in this area and I came across a place called the Obudu Cattle Ranch. Do you know where that is?"

"Yes, I believe I do. It is in Cross River state and incidentally the part of the country that I hail from. The state shares a border with Cameroon and is actually quite far from where we are right now so we most likely won't be going there," Chris smiled.

While this conversation was going on, Chris realised that Angela and the girls were rather quiet and when he turned to look he saw that they were fast asleep, and they were not the only ones. Both John and Bruce were also finding it difficult to keep their eyes open. The breezy atmosphere of the Kuramo Waters usually had that soothing effect on people.

Chris left his guests to rest while he read a newspaper. It was not until late in the afternoon that everyone finally woke up and after some stretching and yawning they all walked back to the hired boat. From afar Chris saw that the boat was empty and wondered where the two men at the helm of the boat were, but as they got closer he saw both of them preparing the boat for the trip back to the pier, which was near the hotel. It turned out that even though Chris had hired the boat for the day the men had made two trips ferrying other passengers to and fro while Mr Archibong and his guests were away. So, it was a good day's business for the boat owners.

The waters were calm and the fishing competition was long over, so the journey back was smooth and short. Once the boat was anchored, Chris tipped the two men as he and the Kimberleys alighted and made their way to the hotel foyer.

Before Chris Archibong left the Kimberleys, Josie's father remembered that he hadn't told him about James Eastwood's dinner invitation. So, while Angela, Bruce and the girls went to their rooms John asked Chris if he could have a quick word.

"Chris."
"Yes, John."
"There is something I forgot to tell you."
"What is that?"
"James invited us for dinner this evening. He called this morning and I told him that I would run it by you and get back to him. Will that be okay or should we reschedule for another day?"
"That is totally fine by me. Just wondering, do you want me to pick you up tomorrow or has Mr Eastwood got something arranged?"
"I guess I should be able to confirm after dinner. Do you mind if I call you later on tonight?

"That's fine," Chris smiled.

"Chris, I never really thanked you for all you have done for my Josie. My family and I are extremely grateful."

"The pleasure is all ours. Josie has become like family and I know that my youngest daughter Bose who orchestrated all this will feel her absence the most. But we are happy that Josie spent this time with us and I believe it has not been in vain. She is an intelligent and determined young lady and you should really be proud of her. Do you know that just like Bose, your daughter made a First Class in her chosen field? They both worked really hard to achieve this and trust me the University of Lagos is not the kind of university that dishes out awards without merit."

"I guess First class grades run through the family," John boasted flashing a proud smile. "I had a First Class during my time in Cambridge and Bruce also got a First two years ago from Warwick University."

"Well, it looks like the intelligence gene flows in the Kimberley family then," Chris smirked.

Both men shook hands, then John went upstairs to join his family while Chris walked to the car park.

As he drove home, Chris realised that none of them had spoken of how to break the news about little Leah to Josie. It was as if everyone wished the issue would melt away, but he knew that before the family left on Sunday, the issue had to be discussed. He decided that he would ask his wife how they should go about it; she was good at things like this.

As Chris entered the house the first person he saw was Josie. She was waltzing up and down with excitement.

"So, Josie, what is making you so excited," he asked.

"Uncle Chris, you did not tell me that I made a First Class!

Well, I just found out and you will never guess how?"

"You are right, I will never guess," Mr Archibong replied anxiously hoping that her family had not contacted her behind his back. "Are you going to tell me then?"

"Well, I got a congratulatory text from my friend Lily Ann. I am not entirely sure how she got to know but my thought maybe either auntie Kath or yourself told my mum, who told my brother who in turn told my friend. Not to worry, I am not upset with you for not telling me. Actually, I am very happy with myself. Thank You Lord."

"I am so sorry. It must have slipped my mind. I actually thought I had told you and Bose all about it. But on the other hand, it could have been a very pleasant surprise. Don't you like surprises?"

"Well, sometimes I do, but some surprises could give you a heart attack you know," Josie quipped.

Josie gave Mr Archibong a hug and ran to her room.

As she lay on her bed, it dawned on Josie that now that she had her degree there was nothing left to do but to go back home and make up with her family. She felt that if she needed to pursue a Master's degree, she could do that in any of the universities back home, and with her first-class degree from the University of Lagos, she just might be able to secure a place in a top one.

She had discussed the matter extensively with Mr Eastwood and he thought she needed to go back to England, not just for her family but more importantly for herself. He had been in touch with her father all through her stay in Nigeria so they all knew back home that she had finished her degree programme, and it went without saying that they all missed her and couldn't wait to see her again.

After living with the Archibongs for almost five years she knew she was really going to miss them. They had made her feel like part of the family and she definitely felt at home. She also wondered how life would be without Bose. They had always been there for each other so it was hard to see how they would cope apart.

All these thoughts brought back memories that she had brushed aside; memories of the attack and of her child who was taken away from her. It was then that she decided that when she got back to England she would try everything within her ability to get her daughter back. After all, nobody asked her before taking her little baby girl away from her.

Something else she was determined to do was pursue the case against Michael Doland even if it meant taking out a private prosecution against him. There was no way he was going to go free after what he did. He had to pay for violating her innocence, and this time around she would not entertain that rubbish story of how his grandfather had helped her grandparents after the Second World War. No one had the right to do to another person what he did to her. She made up her mind that she would no longer wait for three weeks before leaving Nigeria. Instead she planned to bring her journey forward and travel immediately after she submitted her thesis: 'EVERYONE DESERVES A SECOND CHANCE'.

Josie resolved to put her thoughts on hold until after the graduation. As she stood in front of the mirror she mused on her upcoming graduation ceremony and how wonderful it would have been if her parents could be there. In hindsight, maybe she should have asked the Archibongs if her family could come, but it was obviously too late for that now.

Anyway, tomorrow was going to be a happy day and she planned to enjoy every second of it. Josie had promised herself an early night so that she could wake up fresh and raring to go, but before going to bed she wanted to say goodnight to her friend.
Josie poked her head through Bose's door and was about to say goodnight when she saw her ironing her graduation attire. Josie had totally forgotten that her dress needed ironing. She dashed to

her room to get it.

Both of them chatted away as Bose helped with the ironing; Josie's plans for an early night had been thrown out of the window. After stacking the ironing board away, both girls knelt at the bottom of Bose's bed and prayed. They thanked God for everything He had done for them and committed the graduation ceremony into His hands. Then they prayed about Josie's trip back to England and for God to place His peace in her heart.

When they got up, they hugged each other and with tears in her eyes, Bose said, "I am really going to miss you, but I know that God has a plan for you and I pray that it will all work together for good. I will definitely come and see you whenever I come to the United Kingdom, either to see my uncle and grandmother in England or my sister and her husband in Aberdeen."

"I am really going to miss you too BA, but I think I will miss my fried plantain and beans dish a bit more," Josie said, her laughter lightening up the atmosphere.

"The last time I checked you could cook the dish better than me, and since the ingredients are readily available over there, I don't think that making your favourite dish will be that much of a problem. Also, from what I heard, my mum may have bought some ingredients for you to take along so I guess you can cook up as many beans and fried plantain and jollof rice and moin-moin dishes as you like. Who knows, at this rate you just might end up marrying a Nigerian guy," Bose teased.

"Yeah right! If no one has caught my fancy after being here for almost five years I very much doubt that tall, dark and handsome chap that's meant to sweep me off my feet is going to show up before I leave the country in a few weeks' time," Josie giggled.

They both screamed when they noticed the time; Josie and Bose had been talking for more than three hours and they hadn't realised. But how come no one had come to ask them if they wanted anything for dinner? That was strange. So, the following morning at breakfast when Bose enquired of the maid what time her mother and father ate dinner the day before, Gift said, "Oga and Madam comot and de no come back til late, so they no chop for house."

It turned out that Bose's parents had gone to see the Dadas. Chris and Kathleen had promised that they would pop in to see Taiwo and the girls who had arrived the weekend before. It was also another opportunity to see Kehinde, their godson. Since they had also taken both Eyo and Tope along with them, it meant that only Bose and Josie were left in the house.

James Eastwood had told Chris Archibong not to worry about transportation for the Kimberleys as he had made the necessary arrangements for a High Commission vehicle to pick them up from the hotel. He also assured Chris that they would all meet up before the start of the ceremony so that they could sit together.

Everything went according to plan; the Archibongs, the Kimberleys, the Dadas and the Eastwoods all sat together in seats that were placed in such a way that they would not miss any of the upcoming action.

After observing protocol by acknowledging the academic staff, government representatives, diplomatic corps members, business establishments and distinguished ladies and gentlemen, the University of Lagos' fifty-first convocation ceremony began. It was announced to all the guests and students that the university was going to honour all the students who had excelled by achieving First Class Honours in their various fields of study.

With both Professor Bode Davies and his deputy on the podium, the plan was for the Deputy Vice-Chancellor to announce the names of the individual students and for the Vice-Chancellor to hand over a Scroll of Accomplishment to each student as they stepped up to the platform. The actual certificates would be handed out later or sent to the student, their guardians or representatives by post.

The name of each graduating student was called out by the Deputy Vice-Chancellor and as each approached the stage the Vice-Chancellor presented them with a scroll. So, when it was the turn of the faculty of International Studies students, there was excitement in the air. This was Josie and Bose's faculty!

The faculty of International Studies students lined up in alphabetical order which meant that the first student called was Miss Abosede Archibong. Bose's family and friends rose to applaud her as she approached the stage with a big, wide smile. As she received her scroll from the Vice-Chancellor, she gave a slight curtsy and waved to her parents.

People clapped as one after the other the students walked onto the stage to accept their scrolls. Proud parents and friends were beaming with joy, and some were even sending text messages and pictures to loved ones who were unable to attend. This went on for a while until finally it was Josie's turn. As they were about to call her name she looked towards where Bose's family were sitting and for a moment thought she was seeing things. She rubbed her eyes and looked again; she saw the Archibongs, the Eastwoods and... "No, it can't be!" Josie thought.

The Deputy Vice-Chancellor called Josie's name and as she approached the rostrum she took another glimpse; "Is that Bruce?" she thought. At that same moment Josie missed her footing and would have fallen if not for the Vice-Chancellor who caught and steadied her just in time, most likely attributing her stumble to nerves considering she was one of only two Caucasian students graduating on the day.

Josie thanked the Vice-Chancellor, accepted her scroll and pointedly looked again towards the section where Bose's family were sitting. She wasn't dreaming! She spotted Daphne and Lois waving frantically, and there right beside them was Bruce smiling and waving too. She wanted to run and hug them all but had to abide by the rules for the programme. She skipped over to where Bose and some of her friends were and politely pulled her friend to one side.

"BA, I'm not dreaming, am I? Is that my family up there?"

"Yes Josie, it is your family," Bose smiled. "They came specifically for your graduation. I couldn't say a word about it because I was sworn to secrecy, but I hope it is a pleasant surprise."

"Definitely," Josie giggled excitedly. "I am so happy they are here and thank God I made a First Class. I am pretty sure my parents will be proud of their renegade daughter now," Josie gave Bose a big bear hug.

All the graduating students were excited as they looked forward to the party which the academic and non-academic staff were hosting for them after the ceremony. Everything was in place and extra security had been drafted in to thwart any chaos especially from outside the campus. As the graduation ceremony drew to a close, parents were asked to stay for the party if they wished.

Immediately after the ceremony both Bose and Josie scurried over to where their families were seated. Josie ran to her parents and hugged them, then she began to cry when her dad said he was so proud of her. She turned and saw Daphne and Lois jumping up and down. "Some things just never change," she thought as she smiled and hugged her sisters.

Josie marvelled at the difference five years had made. Daphne and

Lois had turned into such lovely girls; both had shot up in height and beauty, and the teeth braces were gone.

"Wow! Josie you have grown so tall," Lois said.
"And I really like your tan," said Daphne.
"Thanks girls," Josie replied, smiling as she struggled to control her emotions. "And look at you two. I barely recognised you beauties."

Tears still streaming down her face Josie turned to her big brother. She could see the forgiving look in his eyes as they embraced each other for what seemed like an eternity.

"I am so sorry Bruce," Josie whispered.
"It's alright Josie," Bruce whispered back.

Josie introduced her parents to the Dadas. She told them about the part Mr Dada had played in the events that led to her travelling to Nigeria; how he had helped her sort out her visa and, along with Mr Archibong, had played a major part in making sure she secured admission to the University of Lagos.

While they all stood there talking, the Vice-Chancellor Professor Bode Davies made his way over and after being introduced to Josie's family, he invited all of them to his own little after party. He told them how it was truly a privilege to be the Vice-Chancellor of the university at such a time as this, despite all the ups and downs. He praised the students for their faithful and disciplined nature which had helped with the success they achieved in their academics.

The party had a carnival feel to it. Music belched out from the gigantic speakers mounted all over the grounds and there were large screens displaying clips of the recently concluded graduation ceremony. The Archibongs, the Dadas, the Eastwoods and the Kimberleys then followed Professor Davies to the marquee that had been set up to entertain his guests.

While under the marquee, John remembered something that had been on his mind for the last forty-eight hours.

"Chris, I was wondering if it would be possible for Angela and I to make a donation towards research work carried out in the universities biochemistry department?"

"Well, I am quite certain that it is something that can be done. However, I am not too sure how one would go about it," Chris admitted. "What I can do is find out from Professor Davies what the modalities are."

"Thank you, Chris. I would really appreciate that."

It was a little after six o'clock in the evening and the party had started to fizzle out. Students and their guests had started leaving and those with vehicles gradually made their way to where their cars were parked.

Before the Kimberleys got into the High Commission's 7-seater SUV, Josie hugged and kissed her sisters, her brother, her mum and her dad one last time before she bade them good night. Understandably Daphne and Lois did not want to leave without their big sister, but after Josie promised to see them the next day, they smiled and reluctantly said goodnight. With that the Kimberleys got into the vehicle and drove off while Josie stood there waving, rooted to the spot, tears of joy flowing down her cheeks as the car disappeared into the distance.

Once they got back home, Chris and Kathleen were not sure what Josie's reaction would be, so they quickly called their daughter aside and asked her if Josie had said anything about the surprise appearance of her family.

"Erm, yeah! She totally loved the surprise. I thought that was pretty obvious," a confused look in her eyes as she replied her parents.

"Phew! Now that is music to my ears," Chris heaved a sigh of relief. "I just wanted to make sure that Josie was okay with it because yesterday she said something about surprises that could give one a heart attack. When she stumbled on her way to the rostrum, even my heart skipped a beat."

"Dad, Josie loved it," Bose flashed a reassuring smile.

Then Josie came into the lounge seemingly oblivious to everything around her, ran straight to Mrs Archibong and gave her a big hug, the tears still in her eyes.

"Auntie Kath, I am so happy. I am just so overwhelmed. They were the last people I expected to see and yet there they were. Do you know what my father said to me as I hugged him? He said he was very proud of me. Those were the words I wanted to hear from him, but never thought I would. Who says there is no God?" Josie sniffled. "Thank you so much for all you have done for me; for making me feel a part of the family. Just like one of your children you provided all my needs, and you even took me to Dubai for Margaret's wedding. Thank you for the many times you let me follow you to your majestic family mansion in Calabar, for all the times you went out of your way so that we could climb Olumo Rock and of course for sending Bose and myself to the Benin Republic so we could do the French course. Thank you; thank you so, so much. You are such a wonderful family and I pray that even though I have to go back to England to face my future, our paths will surely cross again."

Now, even Kathleen and Chris were getting teary-eyed.

"Come on Josie, you may be off to England but we will always be here for you whenever you need us. Think of here as your second home; whenever you need to get away from family and friends you can just come over. Besides, with my mother in law, my daughter and her husband and even my brother in law, all in the United Kingdom, I get the feeling you will be seeing more of us than you think," Chris winked.

The front door opened and Eyo walked into the lounge with Taiwo Dada. Her father was secretly pleased that things were going as he hoped between his daughter and his friend's son. He had chosen not to say a word to Kathleen until their relationship went beyond the 'holding hand' phase.

When Josie saw Eyo she went over to her and said, "Thank you." She thanked Eyo for always reminding her to hold her head up high and to refuse to be intimidated in any way. Josie reminded Eyo of the many times she had run into her room in the middle of the night to talk about her misgivings, and the wonderful counsel that Eyo had often given her, not to talk of those times she had helped her out with school assignments.

Everyone in the room, apart from Taiwo, was looking at Eyo as if she had dropped from another planet. Was Josie actually talking about the same Eyo they all knew? For the first time, Kathleen and Chris were seeing their daughter through someone else's eyes, and so was Bose. They realised that they had often dismissed her because of the way she behaved, and Bose definitely thought her sister was a snob. But after hearing what Josie had to say they began to wonder if there was something they had missed.

"Thank you, Josie. That's very kind of you," Eyo replied, blushing. "I will miss our midnight chats too, but I am sure we will keep in touch. I haven't told you this yet, but I am really proud of your achievements; against all the odds you overcame and made a First. Proud of you girl!"

While they all laughed, Taiwo was pondering what he had just heard, especially the compliments made by the young English lady.

"Maybe Eyo is the kind of girl I've been looking for," he thought to himself. Without realising it, it seemed like Josie had helped him make up his mind.

There was another lady in the picture who Taiwo had gotten to know through his cousin; she worked in one of the banks in the city. The girl had not been particularly keen on him until she learnt that he was living in America and since then his phone had not stopped ringing. Even though his cousin assured him that she was a wonderful girl, Taiwo wasn't really convinced. He believed that most Nigerian girls were the same, they were out for what they could get. He had been proven right time and time again and this girl's case seemed exactly the same.

But Eyo was different. Here was a girl who did not care what others thought about her, yet she had such an intelligent and beautiful mind that one couldn't help but listen to what she had to say. Taiwo's mind was made up. He was going to propose to Eyo before leaving for the States in a month's time, and even if she said that she had no plans of following him to America, he actually would not mind relocating to Nigeria just to be with her.

About an hour after arriving at the Archibong residence, Taiwo said his good nights and was escorted to his car by Mr Archibong himself.

"Good night, Uncle Chris and thank you for the advice you gave my brother. I have seen quite a few changes in him of late but there is still a lot to be done."
"Don't you worry about Kehinde, at least now he is back in Nigeria. I believe that with the right people around him he will be okay."

Taiwo wanted to tell Eyo's father what was on his mind regarding his daughter but refrained from saying a word in case it went pear-shaped. So, after waving goodbye, he drove back to his parents' place which, without traffic was a twelve-minute drive away.

It had been a long day in Archibong household and they were all tired. As Josie closed her bedroom door she wondered if she would get any sleep. She was so excited that she had to keep pinching herself to confirm that she was not dreaming. She was tempted to call her family but just about managed to resist the temptation by somehow convincing herself to wait until the next morning.

As Josie lay on her bed reminiscing she drifted off to sleep.

Restored

Saturday had always been a chill out day for the Archibongs. A day when everyone was free to have a late breakfast or even have breakfast in bed, but when at one fifteen in the afternoon there still was no sign of either Bose or Josie, Chris had to ask one of the maids to wake them up.

Both girls jumped out of bed, ran into the shower, quickly got dressed and by a few minutes past two, just as lunch was being served, they both sat down sheepishly at the dining table. While they were eating, Mr Archibong turned to Josie.

"Josie, I promised your parents that we will all come over to the hotel this afternoon. I hope that is okay?"

"Of course," Josie replied with a wide grin on her face. "You know, last night I did not want to sleep because I was afraid that I would wake up to find out that it was all one big dream."

"Well, let me assure you that it is not a dream, my dear. I'm just happy that we all succeeded in making it a complete surprise."

"Not just complete uncle Chris, but a pleasant one too!" Josie exclaimed. "And I believe it has all worked out perfectly for me. God is so good!"

Going by the way everyone was picking at lunch, it was obvious that no one was really hungry. Even Tope who normally licked his plate clean was only interested in talking about football. Rather than eat, he went on and on about how he was going out to play football with his mates and then asked his mum to find out what time she needed to pick him up.

"Mum, will you help me find out what time we're meant to finish so you can pick me up? I will be waiting for you," Tope said nonchalantly.

"Ah, ah! Why should I be the one to find out when you are supposed to finish. Don't you think it should be the other way around?" His mother asked.

"Actually, I don't have any credit left on my phone, and before you ask where all my credit has gone, I used it to call sister Margaret and uncle Emmanuel. You can ask them if you don't believe me," Tope replied.

"More like you were calling to ask if they could buy you one thing or the other, right?" Bose smirked.

"Well, it is none of your business if I ask my big sister to buy her kid brother a few quality items. Maybe you should come to my school and see what my mates are wearing; I am sure that you will pity your poor brother. Compared to them my poverty stinks to high heaven," Tope moaned.

"*Chei!*[10] This boy, *Ma Abasi*[11]," Tope's father began, "if you were not my son I would say you are very dangerous. But I don't blame you anyway; mama pikin!"

"I would have been surprised if I wasn't dragged into this conversation in one way or the other," Kathleen joked. "Tope, if I remember correctly there are still some new clothes that Margaret and I bought you from London that you haven't even touched yet. What is the purpose of accumulating all these new clothes if you are only going to wear the old stuff, and moreover were you not the one who told me that there were thieves in your school who specialised in stealing other people's clothes? Na wa for this boy sef!"

"Okay, I guess it is safe to say that everyone is done with lunch so let us get ready to go to the hotel. We don't want to keep the Kimberleys waiting," Chris Archibong said, and with that they all jumped up and left the dining table.

---

[10] *Commonly used by Nigerians to express disbelief or deep admiration tempered with a dose of disbelief*
[11] *"I swear by God", in the Nigerian Efik dialect*

Chris, Kathleen, Bose and Josie went up to the Kimberleys suite. Josie knocked on the door and as soon as it flew open, Daphne and Lois ran into her arms. When she was finally able to pull herself away, she hugged her mother and Bruce, while nestling her head on her father's shoulder.

"It wasn't a dream," she whispered to herself.

Chris, Kathleen and Bose all stood in the doorway, each of them taking in this emotional moment. Then Angela looked at them, tried to wipe the tears from her eyes and smiled.

"Where are my manners? I am so sorry. Please, do come in," Angela finally waved the Archibongs in.
"There is no need to apologise. We totally understand," Kathleen replied.

Chris and Kathleen sat down in the suite lounge while Bruce got them something to drink. Daphne and Lois, just like their cousins Rebecca and Lovette, were besotted with Bose.

"Girls, stop staring," Josie said tapping both her sisters on the shoulder.
"It's okay, I have this effect on young girls. Remember Becky and Lovette?" Bose giggled and winked at Josie. "So, I'm guessing you are Daphne, which means that you must be Lois.

Daphne and Lois didn't say a word. They just nodded; they were truly mesmerised.

Realising that the parents, Josie and Bruce might need some time to themselves, Bose who had already come prepared, offered to take the girls swimming in the hotel pool.

"Would you like that?" Bose asked smiling at both of them.

"Yes, yes, we would love to," Daphne and Lois chorused delightfully.

Josie closed the door behind Bose and the girls and as she turned she sensed an uneasy silence in the room. "What's going on?" she thought as she sat beside her brother. Bruce took her hand and gave it a gentle squeeze as if to prepare her for what she was about to hear. She looked at everyone in the room one by one trying to figure out what was going on in their minds.

Was it her mum? Was her illness terminal? Josie sat as still as stone. Then she stopped looking at everyone and fixed her gaze on the floor. Enough of this silence; she could take it no more.

"Is somebody going to tell me what is going on here?" Josie asked slowly in a voice a little above a whisper.
"Josie," her father cleared his throat, "your mum and I want to apologise for what happened to you a few years ago and the role we played, or didn't play, as your parents. At the time we took measures into our own hands and did what we thought was right. Now we know that all we did was push you away; we alienated you from your own family; we betrayed you. But please find it in your heart to forgive us."

The room was silent, so silent you could hear a pin drop. Finally, with her eyes still fixed on the floor, Josie found the courage to say what was in her heart.

"It's alright dad, but somehow I don't think that is what you really want to tell me. The truth is there is nothing to forgive. I have come to understand that everything that happened in the past has made me the better person I am today. I know that you and mum love me, and though it really hurt at the time, I believe you did what you did to protect me. Seeing all of you at my graduation only confirmed something I already knew: I love you and mum and Bruce and Daphne and Lois and I would not trade anyone of you for the world," Josie whimpered, her eyes glazed with unshed tears.

Once again Bruce encouraged his sister by gently squeezing her hand.

Angela could feel the pain that Josie had been through and decided that she was no longer going to hold anything back from her. It was time to tell Josie about little Leah; time to tell her about her daughter.

"Josie, there is something you need to know about your daughter."
"What is it mum? What is wrong with her?"
"Josie, please hear me out. A lot has happened to little Leah since we gave her to the Dolands."
"What! Are you saying that you are still in touch with that family?" Josie asked looking at her mother, then her father and finally Bruce.

Josie sensed that her mother was about to tell her something she was not ready to hear. She jumped up, snatching her hand out of Bruce's and sat down beside Bose's mum. Then she clutched Kathleen's hand as if to brace herself for what she was about to hear. Josie was still waiting for her mother to continue when she was taken aback by the sound of Mr Archibong's voice.

"Josie, over the last four and a half years I have watched you grow from a fragile, insecure girl into a strong, purpose-filled young lady. I need you to be strong right now because there is no easy way to say what you are about to hear; it is simply heartbreaking."

Chris paused for a brief second to compose himself then continued.

"What your mother was trying to tell you is that little Leah has been mistreated by Michael Doland and possibly his family. From what we know so far, there seems to be evidence that she has been sexually abused by that brute of a father. Recently Leah was made a ward of court and is staying with a lady called Mrs Carol Pearce, who just happens to be a good friend of your mother. Mrs Pearce was the one who called the police when she found Leah sleeping at a railway station, and she was also the one who Leah confided in about running away from home."

"Wait a minute, uncle Chris, for how long has this been going on?" Josie asked, her voice quivering.

This time around it was Kathleen who replied.

"We are not exactly sure how long it has been going on for but I learnt about it when Samantha and I went to England to look after our mother, by which time it was already a police case. Knowing that little Leah was safely in Carol's care, and your finals were around the corner we decided not to tell you until after your graduation."

Josie's shoulders slumped. She couldn't believe what she was hearing; she couldn't believe that it was happening all over again. She looked at Mrs Archibong, Josie was no longer holding her hand.

"I recall you telling me that you met my mother and her friend when you came back from your England trip, and I guess I understand why you didn't tell me about my baby girl at the time. But my question is: What exactly are the police doing about it? If it is the same corrupt policemen that handled my case, then you might as well forget all about it. From my experience, there is no way my Leah is going to get any justice in a corrupt system where the elite only take care of themselves. In a way it is no different to what happens here in Nigeria where the rich take it all and the poor and underprivileged are marginalised. I see it on the television every day; the rich rarely end up in jail and even if their cases are brought to court, they hardly ever get convicted."

Bruce looked confused. Since they arrived in Lagos he had been watching and listening to his sister closely; there was definitely something different about her.

"Josie, why are you being so cynical? Even though I may not entirely understand, I know that you have had unpleasant experiences at such a tender age, but this time around I want to assure you that Michael Doland will not get away with what he has done," Bruce declared vehemently.

"Oh, my dear brother Brucie, you sound so naive. Can't you see? The system rarely jails its own. They all belong to the same club. Don't be surprised if you hear that the judge presiding over my Leah's case is a good friend of Michael's father or his obnoxious mother, and that's even assuming her case makes it to court in the first place."

"Josie, we understand how you feel," John started, "but this time..."

"What do you mean by 'this time', daddy?" Josie cut her father short. "Was it or was it not you who surrendered your own granddaughter to those monsters? I have always suspected that the real reason behind your giving my baby away without putting up a fight was simply because you and mum were not willing to face the disgrace of your daughter having a child out of wedlock. Instead of protecting your own blood, you were more concerned about what others would say. If there is going to be any 'this time', I would prefer if you let me do it my way, after all I am now a grown lady with a university degree under my belt."

"That is enough, Josie," Mr Archibong called Josie to order. "Under no circumstances do you talk to your parents like that, especially not while I am here. Now, on the issue of little

Leah's case, I can assure you that it is not a lost cause. You see, myself and the new commissioner of Police in London, Mr Dominic Parkes met in Oxford while I was doing my Master's degree, and we have stayed in touch because of our affiliation with the OK Youth Club in Kilburn. I know what happened to his younger sister, and so I have no doubt about his passion for justice, especially when it comes to rape and sexual abuse cases."

Chris looked at John and Angela, as if to apologise for what he was about to say and continued.

"Your parents do not know this yet, but I have made a few enquiries myself and when I spoke to Dominic at the last Alumni meeting he assured me that if Leah's case was the last he was to handle before he retired, then so be it."
"Thank you so much, Chris," said John. "From what Mrs Pearce told us, the new Commissioner has also brought out Josie's cold case file and is investigating it along with Leah's."

Mrs Archibong made room on the couch as John and Angela both stood up and walked over to where their daughter was seated. Angela placed her arm around Josie's shoulders while John held his daughter's hand with a firm, protective grip.

"My dear Josie, your mother and I made an unforgivable mistake the last time but trust me, we will not make the same mistake again. This time around we will see this through to the end, together."
"I am so sorry for my rude outburst, daddy," Josie cried.

Angela, John, Josie and Bruce all huddled together. Once again united; the past forgiven, the future hopeful.

"Dad, mum, when are you going back home?" Josie sniffled.
"We fly out tomorrow night, and I take it you won't be coming

with us?" John asked, looking at Chris for clarification.

"Well, I had planned to stay until September, but with this news about my Leah I will be making alternative arrangements. There are a few things I need to do like submit my final thesis and visit the Vice Chancellor and his family, they have been so good to me. Also, I want to thank the Eastwoods before I leave for their care and advice, and for always looking out for me even when I didn't listen to what they had to say," Josie smiled. "Then of course I will have to sort out my ticket and hopefully, by God's grace, I should be able to fly home in a week's time."

"I will have a word with James this evening to see if he can pull a few strings with British Airways or Virgin Atlantic. I am sure I have enough air miles to get you a Business class seat on any of these two airlines," John smiled, raised his eyebrow and flashed his daughter a wink.

"Thank you, daddy!" Josie exclaimed, then she turned to her mother. "I appreciate everything you have done too, mum. Once again, I want to say sorry for running away from home and for all the confusion and grief I put you through."

Josie paused as she seemed to remember something.

"I still have unfinished business in Scotland," Josie continued. "My behaviour towards aunt Jacqui and her family was disrespectful and rude; it was totally out of order. I owe them a face to face apology."

"Well, you do what you need to do, Josie," her mother replied, "but your auntie now knows all about what happened and what you were going through at the time. In fact, before we left England, I called to let Jacqueline know that we were travelling to Nigeria to see you, and she told me to let you know that she is so proud of what you have made of yourself. Her only request was that you hurry home because they, especially Becky and Lovette really do miss you. Your cousins were heartbroken when you left without saying goodbye."

"That wasn't the plan," Josie shook her head regretfully.

Then Mr Archibong's phone rang. Chris excused himself to take the call. It was the hotel's restaurant confirming his reservation for fifteen people at seven o'clock. Chris thanked the lady on the other end of the line, hung up and turned with a child-like smile on his face.

"I have reserved a table for all of us for seven this evening," Chris said excitedly. "I also took the liberty of inviting the Dadas and the Eastwoods, and asked James to bring his sister along as she is also leaving for Kenya on her Safari trip tomorrow. I hope you don't mind?"

The dark cloud had finally lifted and the sun was shining once again. There were smiles all over. There was a knock on the door, then it flew wide open. Daphne and Lois ran into the room, with Bose following a few steps behind. Angela told her daughters to quickly get ready for dinner and both of them happily obliged.

At ten to seven they all made their way to the first floor where the hotel's restaurant was situated. As they walked towards the entrance they saw the Eastwoods, and lo and behold following not too far behind were Taiwo and Eyo. Both of them were holding hands and never stopped flashing smiles and glimpses at each other; it was as if they were in a world of their own. Chris looked at both of them and smiled, "It looks like these two were always meant to be," he thought to himself.

James apologised to Chris and Kathleen on behalf of his sister who could not make it due to a prior engagement. Taiwo also found himself in the same shoes as he had to tell his godparents that his parents had been caught up in a minor emergency.

"I hope it is nothing too serious?" Mr Archibong asked, a concerned look in his eyes.

"I don't think so but dad said he will call and explain later on," Taiwo replied.

They were shown to their table by the maître d'hôtel Bibi Farang, who was Lebanese but was a naturalised Nigerian. He spoke the three main languages of the major Nigerian tribes quite fluently and was also learning how to speak the Efik language with the help of his good friend, Chris Archibong.

As they all sat at the table, Chris entertained them with his life history of being the perfect Nigerian citizen; born in the east in Enugu, raised in the north, in Kano and married and settled in Lagos, the south-west. He also guided his captivated audience with their choice of wine and food, which he assured them would be prepared to the satisfaction of their taste buds.

By the time the food they ordered was placed in front of them they all knew that their eyes had been greedier than their stomachs; it was way too much!

John and Angela looked on in awe.

"I guess you are wondering how much this would cost if we were sitting in a restaurant in Central London right?" Chris smiled looking at John and Angela.

"Well Chris, you just read my mind," John replied.

"The truth is, my wife Kathleen, Bibi, the gentleman who ushered us to the table and I actually own the restaurant," Chris flashed that child-like grin again.

"That's great!" Angela exclaimed. "I guess you and Kathleen are great cooks then?"

"I wouldn't go that far," Kathleen giggled. "I am not too bad and Chris is useless, but Bibi is the connoisseur of good food. All we do is take care of the financial side of things."

Chris went on to explain how the previous owners had abused the staff, and that customers had rated the quality of the food as very poor; some customers even went as far as to accuse them of serving leftovers. In the end it was closed down.

Three years afterwards, Chris had negotiated with the hotel's management to reopen the restaurant. He had assured them that with Bibi Farang handling the kitchen, and he and Kathleen looking after the books, it would be a partnership that the management would never regret. Since that day almost four years ago he, Kathleen and Bibi had never looked back and over the years their restaurant had become the talk of Victoria Island.

Though he appeared very genial, Chris Archibong was an astute businessman; he did not suffer fools gladly when it came to business. One day he hoped his son Tope would acquire the relevant business acumen and take over from him, but he had his doubts.

By the time they finished their three-course meal everyone was ready for bed. However, John Kimberley still had something he needed to ask James.

"James, are you able to secure a seat for Josie for next Saturday on either British Airways or Virgin Atlantic?"
"I didn't know that Josie was travelling back so soon. Were you planning on leaving without telling us?" James gazed at Josie through squinted eyes.
"Of course not! How could I leave without saying thank you? That would be a crime," Josie smiled. "I was planning on coming to see you next week; it is one of the reasons why I am not travelling back with the rest of the family tomorrow."
"I knew you wouldn't," James replied. "I have gotten to

know you quite a bit over the last few years and I have to say that you truly are a smart and respectful lady, and it has been a pleasure knowing you."

Josie was blushing. She did not know what to say. For some reason she had not expected such kind words from Mr Eastwood, especially considering the rocky relationship they had shared.

James continued the flight arrangement discussion with Josie's father.

"Alright John, I'll see what I can do. How do you plan to pay for the ticket?"
"I will use my air miles for that. I am sure I have more than enough to secure a business class seat for Josie on either of these airlines. However, I would prefer if you book her on a direct flight to London Heathrow Airport, no stopovers. We can't take anything for granted nowadays; these are dangerous times."
"Daddy, I have managed my life for five years without anything going wrong so any airline is fine by me."
The men exchanged glances. Unknown to them this was observed by their wives who shook their heads as if to say, "These men and their bloated egos."

As agreed after dinner the night before, the Kimberleys checked out of the hotel early on Sunday morning and were picked up by the vehicle and driver assigned to them by James Eastwood courtesy of the British High Commission. They were driven to the Archibong residence for breakfast, and as the Archibongs were not attending their normal morning church service they all decided to have a brief time of Thanksgiving with songs and prayers thanking God for all he had done.
After breakfast, they took time out to relax a little talking about

various topics. Even though it was not planned Chris and John found themselves talking mostly about football and cricket. As this was not exactly to the ladies' taste, both Kathleen and Angela discussed the latest dress designs and eulogised Josie and Bose for their achievements. Angela also used the opportunity to thank Kathleen once again and made her promise to get in touch the next time she was in England.

While the parents had their tête-à-tête, Tope was getting to know a bit more about Bruce. He particularly liked Bruce because he seemed to know a lot about rugby and football, the two ball sports that happened to be Tope's passion, even though his father did not approve. Anyone who had any knowledge of these two games could be a friend of his any day.

"Who knows, my dad just might allow me to study in England" Tope said to Bruce, winking at his dad.
"That would be wonderful!" John exclaimed. "And what would you want to study?"
"Well, my first option would be Sports Science or Sports Media. However, my dad wants me to take up Business Administration and Accountancy. The truth is that, apart from not wanting to do it, I really don't think I have the brains for it. I wouldn't mind being a pilot either, but my parents think it is too dangerous. Please, can you try and convince them," Tope lamented with pleading eyes.

Josie's father was not sure how such an intervention on his part could be construed in the African culture, so he just looked at Tope's dad, shrugged his shoulders and smiled.

Mr Archibong realised that his son had put him in a bit of a tight spot and told his guests that Tope was yet to meet the requirements for his course, so in a sense it was not up to him to deny or accede his son's request. Chris went on to explain the system that prospective undergraduates had to go through to gain admission into a Nigerian University. It was called the Joint Admissions and Matriculation Board (JAMB), similar to the Universities and Colleges Admissions Service (UCAS) in the United Kingdom. He assured the Kimberleys that if he deemed it necessary for Tope to study abroad, he would not hesitate to send him over there under the watchful eye of his daughter and son in law. Chris stood up laughing and patted his son on the back which indicated the end of that discussion, but Tope knew that his father would bring it up again once the Kimberleys had gone.

It was true, Chris knew his son wanted to be involved in sports or end up being a pilot, but he had managed to cajole him into selecting a degree in Business Management and Accountancy instead. However, now he was beginning to regret it.

The boy's admission into university to do the course Chris wanted him to study was already in doubt as his JAMB examination result was below the cut off mark, and Chris had no plans of pulling any strings to get him in. He could not understand why his son seemed to be interested in piloting imaginary aeroplanes and playing football. First of all, being a pilot was way too dangerous, and then how was playing football going to earn him a proper living? Chris just could not get his head around it.

Everyone had been so engrossed in conversation that they did not realise the time had gone by so quickly. The night before, Mr Eastwood had offered to give the Kimberleys a brief tour of the British High Commission grounds before leaving for the airport, so they knew that James would be waiting.

The Kimberleys jumped into the waiting vehicle and were driven to the British High Commission office while the Archibongs followed close behind.

Just like they thought, James Eastwood was waiting to take them on tour around the High Commission grounds. Since it was a Sunday there was hardly anyone on the premises except the Marine guards who manned the gates, and those who worked in the Information Systems department, the one department that never went on holiday in case there was an emergency.

31

Homebound

While Mr Eastwood showed his visitors around the premises, he received an emergency phone call from the Intelligence Room. Before excusing himself, James escorted his guests to the High Commission's cafeteria and told them to help themselves to a variety of juices, tea, coffee and whatever else they desired.

James was gone for about fifteen minutes and when he came back, he handed John an envelope; it had "Confidential" written on it. John took the envelope and placed it in his jacket pocket. The tour lasted for about two hours and once they were done, the Kimberleys and the Archibongs said goodbye to James Eastwood and made their way to the airport.

Even though it was a Sunday, the drive to the airport still took almost two hours thanks to the perennial traffic along the Murtala Mohammed International Airport Road. Finally, they pulled into the airport drop-off lane. The driver jumped out to help with the luggage while everyone else casually alighted from their vehicles. It was after they were safely standing on the pavement and the suitcases loaded on the trolleys that John Kimberley remembered the confidential envelope that James had given him earlier on. He pulled it out of his pocket, opened it and read the contents. "Interesting," he thought. Without saying a word or giving anything away, John handed the letter to Chris; his reaction was exactly the same as John's.

As the families entered the Terminal 1 departure hall, both John and Chris excused themselves. They walked towards a less crowded area and started to discuss the contents of the confidential letter written by Dominic Parkes and addressed to the Deputy High Commissioner, James Eastwood.

The Metropolitan Police had finally arrested the main suspect in the Annabel Leah sexual abuse case: Michael Doland! Michael's wife, had also been invited to the station and after hours of grilling which saw her break down in tears, she was released. She was however advised by the investigating officer not to leave town as they would most likely need to talk to her again sometime soon.

Both men were buoyed by the turn of events as it finally seemed like justice would be served. From the confidential note they also learnt that they would have to persuade Josie to return to England as soon as possible as the police needed her to give evidence against Michael Doland in the upcoming case.

After they had all checked in, Josie hugged her parents and siblings, Bose gave Daphne and Lois some hand-made Nigerian souvenirs, Angela and Kathleen hugged each other and promised to keep in touch while John and Chris simply shook hands and smiled. They all said their final goodbyes and waved as the Kimberleys were escorted to the First-Class Lounge by a British High Commission Liaison Officer.

It wasn't until past ten that night when the Archibongs and Josie finally left the airport, and because the traffic was considerably lighter they were home in a little over an hour.

The next day, Bose's parents told Josie about the contents of the letter which Mr Parkes had given to Mr Eastwood.

"Well, thank God for that. Do we know when the trial is

going to begin?" Josie asked.

"Interestingly, that just might be dependent on you. Going by Mr Parkes' letter, the police want to hear your side of the story rather than go by what was documented at the time of the incident. Taking everything into consideration, I believe that Michael Doland's arrest could not have come at a better time, or what do you think?" Mr Archibong asked.

"I totally agree, and I know it is definitely not a coincidence. I see it as God doing things in His own time," Josie replied.

"Just to let you know, Mohammed will be on hand to drive you around this week. So, just let him know what you plan to do each day and he will do all he can to help."

"Thank you, uncle Chris and auntie Kath. You guys are simply the best and I just love you both so much," Josie declared shyly.

"I think we are blessed to have met someone like you. Throughout your stay with us you have carried yourself with dignity; you did not throw a pity party and you did not take your frustration out on anyone. We are so proud of you," Kathleen replied.

"Oops! I almost forgot," Chris jumped in excitedly. "James called me this morning with some good news. He was able to get you a seat on Friday's British Airways flight. Unfortunately, Saturday's flight was fully booked. Is that okay?"

"That is fine," Josie replied. "That should give me ample time to complete and hand in my thesis, visit Professor Davies and sort out the remaining bits and bobs. I was thinking of resting on Friday anyway so it's perfect."

Later that day, Josie went to the British High Commission to thank Mr Eastwood and her former work colleagues. She gave Mr Eastwood a set of carvings that she bought when she last visited Calabar.

"Thank you very much Josie, but you know you didn't have to?"

"I know Mr Eastwood, but I want you to know that I appreciate you and Mrs Eastwood, and all the advice you have given me over the years."

James smiled and asked Josie to make herself comfortable. After asking his secretary to make her a cup of tea he went on to ask Josie what she planned to do on her return to the United Kingdom. He also repeated the latest developments in the Annabel Leah sexual assault case; about Michael's arrest and the need for her to testify against him.

"So, what do you think, Josie? Are you ready to take the stand?" Mr Eastwood asked.

"I am more than ready to testify against that brute," Josie replied without hesitating. "And I can assure you that I will not be intimidated in any way by the Doland family."

James was very impressed with Josie's response and was once again reminded of how much this once timid looking girl had matured over the last few years.

After their discussion, Mr Eastwood asked if she didn't mind waiting a little so he could take her out for lunch. Considering she hardly had any breakfast, she did not mind one bit.

While seated in a restaurant near the High Commission, Mr Eastwood told her that he had managed to reserve a seat for her on Friday night's British Airways flight.

"Yes, I know. Uncle Chris told me this morning. He said that all the seats on the Saturday flight were taken, but Friday suits me just fine. Thank you, Mr Eastwood. By the way, have you spoken to my father about it?"

"I called to let him know that the airline had a few seats

available in First Class and he said that he would use his air miles to buy the ticket online and send the booking reference to either Chris or me."

"That's great. Most of my stuff, especially the books, paintings and carvings that I have acquired over the years, were taken home by my family so most likely I will be travelling light," said Josie.

"Well, that is brilliant! Anyway, your flight is at night so you can still indulge in some shopping if you so desire," Mr Eastwood winked.

By the time they finished lunch, it was almost three in the afternoon. James escorted Josie to where her driver was waiting and wished her the very best. He also promised to check on her and the rest of the family when next he was in England.

Between Monday and Thursday Josie managed to accomplish everything she set out to do; she handed in her completed thesis and she also paid the Vice Chancellor and his family a visit. Josie's visit to Professor Bode Davies' house was one that she thoroughly enjoyed. She had bought gifts for the lovely couple; a set of 24-carat gold cufflinks for Professor Davies and a set of 24-carat gold earrings with a complementary bangle set for his wife; gifts that Josie purchased in Dubai when she went for Margaret's wedding.

Apart from being a God-fearing family, Professor Davies and his lovely wife happened to have a cool sense of humour. The Vice Chancellor's wife was also an amazing cook; her food was so delicious that Josie was tempted to ask if she could take some home with her. Then, as if she could read Josie's mind, she offered to pack some food for her. Josie was overjoyed!

Before leaving the Vice Chancellor's house, Josie told him that she would never forget how he had helped with her admission and also with her settling into the university. She also thanked Professor

Davies for being a source of encouragement from the first day she stepped on campus, especially in the early stages when she found the teaching methods quite difficult to grasp.

"Josie, I can assure you that you deserved the grades you achieved in your exams because I know how hard you worked for them. I watched as you faced those daunting challenges head on and I saw you overcome each challenge. I am very proud of you Josie and I honestly wish the university had more students like you," Professor Davies remarked.

"Thank you very much sir. That means a lot coming from you," Josie replied. "I will be travelling back to England this weekend and I believe my time here in Nigeria has helped prepare me for the future that lies ahead."

Josie turned to the Professor's wife.

"And thank you ma for treating me to all these delightful, tasty dishes. I will definitely miss the Nigerian hospitality, it is truly second to none."

"You are welcome my dear. Remember, our doors are always open to a visit from you. By the way, have you considered getting involved with the London branch of the University's Alumni Association? It will definitely help you keep abreast of what is going on over here," she advised.

"I haven't thought of that actually," Josie replied. "I guess that is something I need to look into."

As Josie got up to leave Professor Davies wished her all the best in her future endeavours.

As Mohammed drove Josie back home, it dawned on her afresh how much she was going to miss the Archibongs, especially her friend, Bose. The thought of this once again brought tears to her eyes, tears which she tried to hide when she got home by running straight to her room and locking the door.

In Bose, Josie had found not just a loyal friend but more importantly someone who she shared a sisterly bond with. Now, barely twenty-four hours before her flight she was pondering how to say goodbye to her. It wasn't going to be easy and she knew it.

The following morning Bose woke up early and prepared a sumptuous breakfast. As usual she and Josie sat beside each other and tucked into their food. While they were all eating Bose turned to Josie and dropped a bombshell.

"Josie, after giving it a lot of thought I don't think I'll be able to see you off today. I thought I could, but I can't. You know I'm really going to miss you and even though I have told you this before I want you to know that I am truly grateful to God for causing our paths to cross. Make sure you take good care of yourself and see you again soon."

Josie and Bose smiled and gave each other a long, warm hug.

Though this caught everyone by surprise, no one said a word as they watched the two friends cry on each other's shoulders.

Unsurprisingly, breakfast was relatively quiet. Everyone knew that one day Josie would have to go home, but no one had imagined that it would affect Bose this much.

Later that afternoon, the Dadas came over to say goodbye to Josie and brought along some gifts for her and her family. There were caftans for John and Bruce, Nigerian tie and dye fabric for Angela, and crocheted handbags crafted with precious stones for Daphne and Lois. Josie went ecstatic at the sight of the gifts. She hugged uncle Wale, auntie Maureen and Kehinde, who had accompanied his parents, to express her appreciation.

Unknown to Josie, while Eyo was helping her pack earlier on, she had also secretly placed some gifts for Josie's parents and her siblings inside Josie's suitcase. It wasn't until she went upstairs to put the other gifts in her suitcase that she saw the wrapped items that Eyo had hidden in her case. She decided that she would unwrap the gifts later; before she left for the airport.

While she was getting ready for her journey to the airport, Josie suddenly remembered that she hadn't had a proper look at the gifts that the Archibongs had given her. She unzipped her suitcase, and as she unwrapped each gift she was left amazed. Josie once again counted herself lucky to have met such a kind and generous family. Without a shadow of a doubt she would be going back to England with fond memories.

As she walked down the stairs, where the Archibongs and the Dadas had assembled to wish her a safe journey, Josie smiled. They all said a prayer of thanksgiving before the hugs and kisses took over. Once they had all said their goodbyes, Josie walked through the front door, tears flowing down her cheeks, without looking back at anyone, especially Bose and Eyo who were already sobbing quietly.

Mrs Archibong and Josie sat in the car while Mr Archibong made sure that Josie's luggage was arranged properly in the boot. Then finally he took his seat behind the wheel. Mr and Mrs Dada, along with their son Kehinde had also decided to see Josie off.

Kehinde was going to miss his talks with Josie. She always spurred him on and told him not to let anyone or anything come between him and his aspirations. Even though the temptation had been great, Kehinde had not touched alcohol or smoked a cigarette since the last time they spoke; such was the effect Josie's life had on him.

He had long concluded that Josie possessed wisdom way beyond her years and even if it was for the last time, he needed to see her again. He wanted to tell Josie he appreciated all she had done for him and that he would try his very best not to let her down.

So, at the airport, after Josie had checked in, Kehinde took her hand and squeezed it gently as he promised to stay in touch and keep her updated on his progress. In return, Josie wished him the best and told him she would be praying for him.

As she walked towards the departure gate, Josie struggled to keep her tears at bay. Even though her life as she knew it would never be the same again, she looked forward to what was ahead because she had an assurance that her life was in God's hands.

The London bound British Airways flight BA74 took off at three minutes to eleven in the evening and soared into the starry, dark blue sky. As Josie looked out of the window to catch one last view of the beautiful city of Lagos, she thought about the opportunity she now had to finally put Michael Doland behind bars, and the joy of being reunited with the daughter who had been snatched away from her at birth.

Then Josie shuddered.

All this while she had blamed her parents for taking her baby away and handing her over to the Doland's, but Annabel knew nothing about that. For the first time it dawned on Josie that once little Leah found out that her birth mother was actually alive and well, she would blame her for all the pain and abuse she had suffered. Was Josie ready for that? The simple answer was, "No". The painful truth would have to be revealed before true healing could begin; it was a bridge she would sadly have to cross.

The daunting task that awaited her once she arrived in England sent shivers down her spine. It was not going to be a walk in the park, but Josie was determined to fight for justice; justice for herself and more importantly for her daughter, Annabel Leah.

Thank You

Fulfilling my long-held dream of writing a book has been such an amazing experience, only made possible by the grace of God and the love and support I have received from my family and friends.

Embarking on this project was like journeying into the unknown; like opening the window of my soul to the whole world, not knowing what to expect, but I have truly been overwhelmed by all the good wishes and prayers. They have kept me going and given me the impetus to write "Restored", the second book in the Atonement series.

So, to everyone who has bought my book, prayed for me, and encouraged me in one way or another; I would like to say a big "Thank you". I appreciate you so much, and I hope this book will set you up nicely for "Justified", the last book of the Atonement series.

Also, as a little token of my appreciation I will be giving three signed copies of "Justified" to the first three people who identify three distinctive characteristics hidden within the pages of "Restored". The answers will be posted on my blog on the 31st January 2019. *(Anyone associated with the author, editor or publisher in any way is not allowed to take part in this competition)*

With all my heart I hope you enjoy reading this book as much as I have enjoyed writing it, and remember it is never too late to follow your dream.

*~ **Stella Jackson** ~*
www.stellajackson.uk

"**JUSTFIED**", the final chapter of the Atonement trilogy, promises to keep you on the edge of your seat as Josie returns to England for a head-on battle with the Dolands; a fight for justice for her family, herself and more importantly her daughter, Annabel Leah.

Lightning Source UK Ltd.
Milton Keynes UK
UKHW040914021118
331646UK00001B/8/P